THE OVERSEER

A THRILLER

CONLAN BROWN

REALMS
A STRANG COMPANY

Most STRANG COMMUNICATIONS BOOK GROUP products are available at special quantity discounts for bulk purchase for sales promotions, premiums, fund-raising, and educational needs. For details, write Strang Communications Book Group, 600 Rinehart Road, Lake Mary, Florida 32746, or telephone (407) 333-0600.

THE OVERSEER by Conlan Brown
Published by Realms
A Strang Company
600 Rinehart Road
Lake Mary, Florida 32746
www.strangbookgroup.com

Cover design by Justin Evans
Design Director: Bill Johnson

Library of Congress Cataloging-in-Publication Data:

Brown, Conlan, 1984-
The overseer / by Conlan Brown. -- 1st ed.
p. cm.
ISBN 978-1-59979-955-1
1. Supernatural--Fiction. I. Title.
PS3602.R689O94 2010
813'.6--dc22

2010002171

First Edition

10 11 12 13 14 — 9 8 7 6 5 4 3 2 1
Printed in the United States of America

For Mom and Dad:
I am truly blessed

Chapter 1

SCREAMS RANG OUT from the rain-soaked street.

Feeling the horror rise, Hannah fell to her knees in the pounding deluge, hands touching the ragged edges of the craterlike pothole.

The impact of the car splashing into the pothole.

Thunder. Lightning. Rain.

A trunk opening.

Three teens. Terrified, screaming, kicking.

Eyes begging for help.

Hands slapping, punching bloodied mouths.

Frightened girls torn from the car—thrown to the wet street.

A needle—

Bodies going limp.

Thrown into another car.

Tires shrieking into the stormy night.

One man remaining in the street.

The tattoo—a dragon.

Thunder cracked as the images disappeared with the flash. Lifting her head, she looked around, the thick spring storm churning around her.

The screams.

Already gone from the world—but the street remembered—and Hannah could still hear them calling out from the past. She was their only hope now—the one person who realized that these girls had been conned and taken. The only person who could follow a trail snaking backward through the past—a trail that had gone cold to the negligent, rain-drenched world.

Hannah Rice looked to her right and saw the liquor store. That was where he had gone—the man with the dragon tattoo.

Just through those doors. Hannah breathed in with resolve and walked toward the lights of the liquor store—

—toward the dragon.

Hannah pushed the soaked hood of her sweatshirt off her head and looked around.

She had never been in a liquor store before. The floor was white like a supermarket—but none of the same sweet, homey smells were here. No bread or fruit. Simply rows of metal racks, stocked with a forest of bottles. The sounds of clinking glass and cooler doors opening and closing filled her ears. An older man in a plaid shirt and a wiry blond beard approached the door, looking her up and down out of the corner of his eye.

For being in a seedy part of New Jersey, the store was big and fairly clean. Hannah looked around, waiting for someone to realize that she was only twenty and have her sent from the premises in handcuffs and a swirl of red and blue lights. The only looks she received were lecherous at best. She pulled her jean jacket close, pressing the metal buttons into place with little pops that seemed to echo through the cavernous room.

"Can I help you find something?" a jockish-looking guy in his midtwenties asked from behind the counter.

She shook her head, embarrassed. "No, thank you." She moved to the far end of the store, looking down the aisles as she walked.

No one realized she was too young to be here, or else no one cared. She watched the aisles change as she moved along, shifting from colorful bottles of flavored rum with shirtless cabana boys adorning their labels to the dark glass of the wines.

Hannah wasn't unfamiliar with alcohol. Half the reason she'd left college was because of her roommate's drunken binges in which she had brought so many of her friends over to party. It reminded Hannah of all the nights she had spent in the dorm lounge, studying subjects she didn't understand, sleeping on couches she resented being on. It was the next day's cleanup, inevitably left to Hannah, that had taught her to recognize various forms of alcohol bottles and the hazards of a hungover roommate.

Her grandfather had left her enough money to get whatever degree she wanted, wherever she wanted it, but she had chosen a medium-sized state college to start out. The idea had been simple: get her core classes out of the way, and buy herself some time to figure out what she wanted to be when she grew up. After she gave up on college, she moved to New Jersey to be near the Firstborn and enrolled in an online program. Distance learning at her own pace better suited the lifestyle she had grown to accept: following dark trails through back alleys. The ongoing searches for—

—the dragon.

It was always jarring to see her visions in the flesh. She was a Prima—gifted with hindsight, the ability to see the past. And the past tended to have the good sense to stay in the past and fade away to the naked eye and the observing world. But there he stood in the middle of the aisle—fifteen feet away—comparing labels on vodka bottles. His arms bare, short black hair wet. A blue short-sleeved T-shirt and green cargo pants. The tattoo curled up his arm, its tail resting against the back of his hand, its scaly body coiling around the man's arm like an anaconda, the dragon's head poised to strike like a hooded cobra, a forked tongue lashing out from beneath a spray of flame.

The man looked up from the bottles, turning his head—toward her...

Hannah dropped back around the corner. A sting of panic nipped at her heart. She waited a moment—her pulse and breath slowing as she pulled herself together. She looked back.

Gone.

She moved down the aisle to where the man had been and

passed, heading to the end of the aisle. She stopped and turned her head, looking for him.

Nowhere.

Hannah moved fast, looking down the aisles once again, coming to the end of the rows. She must have lost him somewhere in the—

She saw him at the front of the store, at the cash register, the boy behind the counter stuffing a bottle of vodka into a perfectly sized brown paper sack. The man with the tattoo reached into his pocket, pulled out a thick roll of bills, and slid one from beneath the tight hold of the rubber band that encircled them. The boy hit a button on the cash register, and the man with the tattoo turned, walking toward the door.

"Hey, Dominik," the boy called after him, "do you want your change?"

Dominik simply waved a dismissive hand and pushed through the front door, back into the rain.

Pushing the glass door open, Hannah followed, plunging into the downpour. Her eyes scanned the cars in front of her parked diagonally to the storefront. A set of lights flashed on toward the far right end of the row—a black luxury sedan—the engine humming, the wipers swishing away a wide swath of pooling water as the man in the driver's seat lifted his eyes—

Dominik.

His dragon-clad shoulder moved, putting the car into drive. The vehicle slid backward out of its space, through the veil of rain, past the unnatural glow of the liquor store's neon lights, and then slipped into darkness.

Her one lead.

The one trail.

The only chance to find the girls.

And he was getting away.

For a split second Hannah did none of her own thinking. Her

feet took off, rushing into the night, as the car pulled parallel to the street. The brake lights lit up. The backup lights dimmed. The car began to drive away.

Her first thought was to chase after, screaming, shouting, demanding he stop. Her next thought was to memorize his license plate number. Hannah's eyes squinted into the darkness, but the lights surrounding the license plate were all burnt out. Nothing to see but darkness.

The red taillights, glowing like the eyes of the dragon on Dominik's arm, glared at her through the onslaught of falling droplets. Turning the corner, leaving her in the street—alone.

"Lord," she stammered to herself. She could feel her panic rise at not knowing what to do. But now was not the time to focus on problems or obstacles. Now was not the time to *feel* or *do*. Now was the time to clear her mind. To *be*. To *be* what she had been called to—

Hannah turned her attention to the end of the block, where she had parked her car. That was where she needed to get. To think *past* the problem and to move effortlessly with the solution.

Wet and cold, she thrust her hand into her pocket, reaching for her car keys. Suddenly she was at the car door, her hand holding the key, the key in the door. The old door to the station wagon groaned as she pulled it open and climbed in. She turned the key, and the engine sputtered.

"Not *now*," she whimpered, pushing down on the pedal, feeding the engine gas. A moment of whirring, then—

Click.

The engine went dead. She'd flooded it. The old jalopy did it all the time, but this was the worst possible—

Hannah stopped. Gathered herself. She had to get past the moment. She had to find her strength—a strength that could only come from God.

She took a long, deliberate draw of air, letting it fill her lungs in a cool cloud that expanded inside her chest. Somewhere in the distant reaches of her mind she felt her body act, working with the world around her—neither rushed nor distracted—to bring the car to life.

She turned the key again. The engine growling, she fed it gas.

Hannah's foot came down in a steady push, feeding the car, and she took off into the night—

—chasing after *him*.

Her car sped to the end of the block—a stop sign ahead.

Her attention snapped to the right—the direction Dominik had gone.

Nothing.

Hannah rolled into the street, peering through the rain—and then she felt where he had been. She was on the trail again.

The wipers sloshed, thumping beads of water away from the glass.

Dominik yawned. It was getting late, and he was getting tired of work. He'd stayed sober as long as the new girls were at the storage house, but now that they were being moved, he was ready to drink again.

He eyed the jostling bottle of vodka in the passenger seat, ready for the familiar burn of alcohol in his chest. Dominik missed Russian vodka—the stuff that had been cheaper than water during the cold war. He was hardly a connoisseur, but he knew that American vodka tasted different to him. He was told that good vodka had neither taste nor smell. But who cared? Just so long as it kept him warm—a lesson he had learned in prison twenty years ago.

He thought about the girls and how much money they would bring. Altogether, maybe three thousand dollars in Ukraine. Here? More. But it wasn't enough. Dominik wanted a line of cocaine—the stuff he'd gotten used to as a teenager when the iron curtain fell. But for now, vodka would have to do.

Dominik reached out, steering with his forearm. He held the neck of the bottle in one hand and twisted the cap with the other.

He took a slug. The same amount would have sent most Americans into a hacking fit. Dominik didn't flinch as the stinging liquid seared his throat, filling him with a glowing sense of well-being. He felt good. Safe. But not overly safe. He looked in the rearview mirror, double-checking for cops.

A single set of lights behind him, moving in quickly. Much too quickly. He screwed the cap back on the bottle, stuffing it in the armrest.

Thoughts of a cop watching him throw back a mouthful of hard liquor as he passed by filled Dominik's head. Was he being followed?

There was an alley ahead. He signaled left. The car behind him signaled a left-hand turn as well. Dominik cranked the wheel hard right, and a spray of filthy water splashed up against the windows of his car as he hit the accelerator and raced down an alleyway. His eyes shot upward, toward the rearview mirror. The car behind him screeched past the turn, then slammed its brakes, laying rubber and a wake of erupting rainwater. The car pulled into reverse, pulling perpendicular to the alley for a moment, its silhouette fully revealed.

A beige station wagon?

The following car's front end nosed toward the alley. The headlights, which had been shrinking with distance, stabilized in size, then began to grow.

Dominik didn't signal; he simply grabbed the wheel and yanked to the left. Water crashed against the passenger window as the car fishtailed, his foot pressing hard into the gas—jetting down a dark street.

He nearly spun in his seat to look back. This was insane. His heart was racing. His face red and sweaty. Who was this person following him? In a station wagon? Not the police. Someone trying to steal their latest shipment? It simply didn't make sense. But whoever they were, they weren't trained in following people with subtlety. And in the rain, he'd lost them for sure.

Dominik took another turn, just to be safe. Then another.

He took a deep breath and relaxed, pulling onto a familiar street. Whoever they were, he'd lost them.

His eyes lifted again, just out of paranoia, certain he wouldn't see anything except...

A beige station wagon?

This had to be dealt with.

Hannah watched Dominik's car through the swishing of wiper blades as his sedan took a slow, ambling turn to the right, pulling into another alleyway. She followed him into the darkness of the alley. The front end of her car slammed down hard then rebounded from the chasm-like pothole her front tire had dropped into.

She couldn't see a thing in this darkness except the red taillights up ahead and—

Brake lights.

Dominik's car stopped suddenly fifty yards ahead. The driver's side door flew open, and a burly figure dashed away from the car—the door hanging open. Hannah stopped her car, leaving the distance unfilled.

What was he doing? She sat in her car. Waiting.

It was like the stories of road rage she heard, where one driver would get out to confront another—only to have someone get shot in the middle of the street.

Hannah peered into the darkness, gripping her steering wheel. She closed her eyes, trying to reach out—

There was nothing to feel. Not here anyway.

She bit her lip, considered for a moment, then turned off her car, taking her keys. She wanted her keys—that was certain.

Fear would have been the natural response, but envy filled her mind. Envy for the Domani and the Ora, people like Devin Bathurst and John Temple, who could see the present and the future. Others had told her not to envy the other orders and their gifts, that she had been given exactly what she was meant to have and that she had to make the best of it. But she missed the proactive way that John and Devin could use to approach the uncertainty of the world. The Prima were a stabilizing force—a means of keeping everyone grounded and remembering the truths that proactive working so often forgot. But none of that changed the fact that she was in the moment now, groping in the blind spots of her gift.

Hannah opened the car door and stepped into the rain, looking around. He wasn't anywhere to be seen. Hannah walked toward the car ahead, the interior lights illuminating the leather interior.

She stopped, listening for any sound she could hear—only the thumping rain. Another set of steps closer. She stared into the vacant interior, looking for a person who simply wasn't there, and her eyes wandered to the center partition, hanging slightly ajar. It had been where he'd stored his—

Vodka.

A thick, heavy bottle, pulled from its cubby.

Gripped by the neck like a club.

Dominik, slipping into the darkness, waiting for his moment to…

Hannah spun as Dominik ejected himself from his hiding place in the dark, bottle in hand, raised over his head.

She thought fast, throwing herself into the car's open door. The bottle came down on the roof of the car and blasted apart in a shower of shards and cascading liquor. She threw herself at the passenger's door, scrambling for the handle. She looked back.

He was behind her, hurling his body through the same open

door she had come through, grasping the steering wheel with his left hand for support, clutching the razor-sharp remains of a pungent vodka bottle in his right.

The survival instinct kicked in; the self-defense classes triggered her response.

She lashed out with her leg like a battering ram, her heel smashing into Dominik's clavicle, just below the throat. He made a pinched hacking sound as his body hurled to the side, slamming into the dashboard. A hiking boot would have been ideal, but a kick of any kind could be fatal, even in her tennis shoes, if she meant it, held nothing back, and lashed out with the vicious intention to cause serious trauma.

She kicked again and again—his head snapped back like a melon as her foot connected with his face. Her hands searched frantically for the door handle she'd lost track of in the furious exchange—fingertips catching on the outline, hand grasping. Dominik was recovering. Covering his face with his left hand, he reached out with the razorlike bottle with the other, like a shield.

Hannah flung her body into the door as she pulled the handle. She felt her body tumble to the hard, wet pavement beyond. She looked back in time to see Dominik coming down at her, bottle in hand. She kicked his descending arm away, and the bottle exploded against the ground. Dominik reached for her body, trying to hold her down. She felt the car keys, still in her hand, clutched them like a dagger, and came down hard on Dominik's arm. He winced, recoiling. She lashed out for his face, searching for his neck.

He threw himself back against the car, evading Hannah's swinging attack, then stood.

Hannah pushed herself away, trying to keep her distance.

And then he ran.

Dominik rushed toward the end of the alley, water spattering against his face and arms.

Who was this woman? This *girl*? She'd followed him. Knew where he was going and what he was doing. She had to know about his business. She wasn't FBI. Police? Maybe.

No. That wasn't likely. She was too young for either. She was obviously trained in following people—but not with subtlety. Her mistakes were too glaring—too inexperienced.

Surveillance for someone else was his only thought. Someone who wanted to rip off their shipment. It happened all the time with drug trafficking. Why not in this business too?

Dominik made a sharp right, ducking into a trashy, overgrown backyard, shoving past a metal trash can. He had to fix this or it was going to cost him his head.

Hannah tore after Dominik.

Her one lead. Her only chance of finding these girls. She couldn't let him get away.

She turned the corner fast, running through someone's backyard, chasing after as fast as she could, Dominik's form merely a dark blotch against the impossible conditions of night and drizzle.

He was ahead, crossing another yard, leaping a short chain-link fence. Hannah pushed herself, gaining slightly. She approached the fence, hands stinging as the cold, rain-soaked metal ripped at her bare hands. She hurtled the fence and continued her pursuit.

Dominik rushed across the street, dodging between parked cars, knocking over a boxy plastic trash can, sending garbage spilling. Hannah dodged to the left, losing time from the circuitous route, but it was less than she would have lost from fighting the obstacle she'd been presented with.

Her feet splashed through puddles as she forced herself forward, chasing as fast as she could. From yard to yard, across another street, low-hanging branches snapping at her face. A tall wooden fence, knotted and old. Dominik clambered over the fence. Hannah followed, charging toward the obstacle, hands digging in as she made her way to the top—throwing her body over the other side. Her feet connected with something she didn't expect—a trash can—and she lost her balance, hitting the grassy lawn with a painful lurch.

She looked up. Dominik was already making his way over the far fence at the other end of the yard. Hannah leapt to her feet.

The back door to the home opened, and a young boy—maybe ten—watched her rush at the fence.

"Mom! There's someone in the backyard!"

Hannah ignored the boy, throwing herself at the next fence, pulling herself into place with her arms, tossing a leg over the fence, hitting the ground with a splash on the other side. She pushed herself up from the muddy puddle, covered in dirt, and gave chase once more as Dominik turned a corner. She came to the gate in the fence. Locked. Hannah slammed her shoulder into the gate, sending it flying open, propelling her into the front yard.

Rain covered her face, and she wiped the thick drops from her eyes. Her head turned hurriedly, side to side. He was nowhere to be seen.

What had happened? How had she lost him? He must have taken a different turn.

She walked into the street, looking around in all directions.

This couldn't be happening. She couldn't let this happen. The girls were too young—thirteen at most. She couldn't let this happen to them. She couldn't let them disappear into the night.

Hannah pushed her hands through her soaked hair, trying to think. She needed to know where he had gone.

A set of headlights rolled toward her, a sharp honk on the horn, and she stepped out of the car's way, the vehicle rolling lazily past.

The world was going on as usual. She was failing her charge, and the world didn't even know enough to care.

She needed to pick up the trail again. She needed to see the past. A vision of where he had gone. She needed a magic wand to wave, to bring her the sight she needed.

But it didn't work like that.

Hannah looked up at the rainy sky. "God?" she beseeched. "I can't do this. I can't find them. I need You and Your sovereign power and…"

No. She scolded herself. It's like people to go to God, thinking they had something to say—yammering to an almighty God who formed the world from the palm of His hand. How like her to think that florid prayers somehow pleased God.

No, it was not her place to talk. It was her place as a creation of God to do something else…

"Listen," she whispered to herself.

She closed her eyes and listened to the rain, her thoughts filled with her calling and mission.

No. She scolded herself again. Listening wasn't done only with the ears but also with the mind and the heart.

She cleared her mind. Focused on her breathing. Focused on God.

The rain thundered in her ears, every droplet exploding against every surface of metal, asphalt, and grass. Each sound blurred into the other in a cacophony of white noise.

Listen, she said to herself in her mind.

The drops faded toward the background, only a thumping rhythm of a select few drops tapping out an erratic beat. Bit by bit the rhythm thinned, only a few proud beats pounding out a pedantic march.

Listen, she said to herself again, her body relaxing.

A single droplet of rain made a tiny plinking impact.

Then silence. The world without time. Where she wasn't hurried or forced into action.

Listen, she thought again. And then she heard.

Dominik's shoes thudding against the path…

Leading away…

His ragged breath wheezing—

Removing him from the scene.

The cries of the girls reverberating in his mind—

Remembering the thud of blows.

The ringing slaps to tender faces—

The sobs pounding into his brain.

The house that he had been working from.

Creaking from the strain.

The place he was returning to.

Thunder rocked the air as Hannah's eyes opened, lifting to the house in front of her. A sigh of anguish escaped her lips.

There.

Hannah quietly grasped the doorknob and felt the door swing lazily inward, left ajar by someone before her. Stepping into the house as quietly as possible, she paused. If he was in the house still, she didn't want him to know. Not yet. There would be a moment soon, when she had something to report, that she would need to call the police to finish this. But visions of the past weren't evidence enough. She needed to find the girls. To know for certain they were here before she did something that might spook Dominik.

She moved into the living room. Shoddy furniture bulleted with holes. An ashtray on the coffee table filled to the brim with dark ash and cigarette butts. The whole place reeked of stale smoke. Magazines littered the remaining surface of the coffee table—like a doctor's waiting room.

Men, sitting in the living room—each waiting their turn.

A quick thump reverberated through her chest. These had been different girls, before the ones Hannah was looking for. Older—Russian? It wasn't any easier to consider.

Her stomach churned, and she stepped into the next room—the kitchen. No signs of cooking or supplies. No one lived here. At least no one ate here.

Hannah looked at the table—a sprawling forest of vials, needles, alcohol, and soda bottles. She picked up a container of medicine, reading the label.

Flunitrazepam. Whatever that was.

There was a smacking sound, and Hannah turned. The back door hung open, the screen door slapping loudly in the rainy wind.

Dominik exiting out the back.

She thought about following him—but this was what she was looking for. This was where they'd brought the girls—she could feel it. If she was going to find the girls, she was going to have to do it here.

There was a set of stairs near the hallway, leading up. It felt right, like this was the way they had taken the girls.

The girls, Hannah thought. She didn't even know their names. But that wasn't how this worked. She wasn't called out of personal obligation. She was called to help them because it was her purpose.

Hannah reached the top of the stairs, looking around. There was a set of three bedrooms lining the hallway. She stepped toward one with the door ajar. The door pushed aside easily, revealing a virtually empty room.

An old mattress lay in the middle of the room, filthy blankets thrown across it in twisting heaps.

And suddenly Hannah saw the horrible truth of what had been happening here.

Dominik kicked open the door to the shed, scowling into the darkness as the spring rain shower assaulted the tin roof in a reverberating frenzy. He shoved the lawn mower to the side, ripping a canvas tarp away from a stack of tools. The cold canvas twisted with a kind of whiplash as its soggy corners tried to double over onto the shell of hard cloth that had molded itself to the stack of tools.

A toolbox scattered with a rough toss, and it hit the floor somewhere to the right with a raucous clatter. He kicked a bag of screws out of the way, and the contents went spilling in a deluge of tinkling barbs.

There.

Dominik grabbed the gas can by the handle and gave it a forceful jiggle. Half a can's worth of gasoline sloshed inside the container, undulating on a swishing axis that caused the whole can to swing in a wide arc.

It was enough to do the job. To get rid of as much evidence as he could before whoever that girl was could find her way back here. Dominik hated the place anyway, all the time he'd spent there minding the shop while the others stayed in the big house across town. He wouldn't miss it.

It would be obvious that it was arson. The investigators might even find some of the things they had been hiding, but with luck they'd be out of the state by the time anything was found—and the merchandise would be out of the country by then. And it wouldn't be traced back to them. They'd made sure the lease wasn't in any of their names.

Dominik reached into his pocket, found the metal object,

removed it from his pocket, and flicked the cap open. His thumb spun on the back of the lighter, checking to see if there was enough fuel.

A tiny flame leapt upward, then was dashed out by the snapping of the cap back over it. He walked back toward the house in the rain.

Hannah backed away from the bedroom door, stumbled into the wall, and slid to the floor. Her body shook as she ran her hands over her head, trying to blot it all out of her head. So many girls had been brought through here. So much pain. And suffering. And hopelessness. So many monsters lurking in the shadows.

The walls remembered what had happened here—and they were closing in.

"O God," she stammered in agonized prayer, mind freewheeling with the torment of it all.

And she felt something else: another calling—

She looked up at the ceiling and saw the wide hatch leading to the attic. A padlock dangled open at the end of a swinging latch that had been left undone.

She reached upward, and the trapdoor snapped downward as she grabbed at the string, tugging, the ladder sliding downward with a gentle pull. Hannah stepped onto the bottom rung and moved upward, compelled by purpose but delayed by dread.

She lifted her head into the attic. The floor was covered in brown carpet; drenched in dust that made her cough. Hannah lifted herself into the darkness. Tiny fingers of light glowed through the slits between the boards covering the one tiny window at the far end. The hatch below her swung gently upward, pulled back into position by creaking springs.

Her hands groped for a moment as she stood, hunched in the low space. A dangling string brushed her fingertips, and she tugged. The lightbulb snapped on from an overhead fixture, and she looked around.

She thought she might never start breathing again.

Both sides of the attic were lined with bunk beds, chicken wire surrounding them in tightly fastened grids that filled in the gaps between small metal struts. Hinged doors with padlocks locked every set of beds, making each its own tiny prison.

Lurid underwear hung from hooks and littered the floor. Dirty clothes were piled in the corner.

Hannah walked to one of the beds, its door hanging open, and looked in. Sitting on yellowed sheets was a ratty stuffed bear with one eye missing. She picked up the bear and looked it over as a hot tear ran down Hannah's face as she saw the face of the girl who had clung to this bear—

Maybe fourteen years old.

The bear fell from her hands and hit the floor.

Whoever these people were—she would stop them.

Wherever the girls were that they had taken—she would find them.

Then she heard something.

Petroleum-scented splashes of gasoline washed across the walls and tables as Dominik slung the can in all directions. He set the can down for a moment and rummaged under the sink for a trash bag. Quickly he swept the drugs off the table into the plastic and pulled the tethers shut with a swift yank. He set the bag near the door, stuffed his cell phone between his shoulder and ear, and reached for the gas can again.

"Hello?" a female voice said in Dominik's native language.

"Do you know who she is?" Dominik replied in the same language as he soaked the curtains in gasoline.

"Who?"

"The girl that followed me. She knew where I was and where I was going."

"What are you talking about?"

Dominik sloshed more gasoline onto the living room carpet, sending a splash across the back of a ratty recliner. "Some girl—midtwenties maybe. She found me in the liquor store. She followed me. Chased me back to the house."

"You ran away from a girl?"

"Shut up, Misha." He grunted. "She came out of nowhere. She knew where I was and where I was going. She must have been watching us for days." He moved up the stairs, spilling a trail of gas.

"What are you going to do about it?"

Dominik let the last drops trickle from the can, dousing a pile of sheets in the bedroom, then tossed the can into the corner. "I'm closing down the storefront."

"Use the gas can in the shed. Burn it down."

"I've already started."

"Good. Get going, and get out of there." There was a click, and the line went dead.

Dominik felt the lighter in his pocket as he moved toward the stairs, then stopped. A creaking in the ceiling from the attic above. He looked at the trapdoor in the ceiling, slightly ajar. Another creak and the distinct sound of footsteps overhead.

He eyed the padlock dangling from the hatch—an overt violation of fire code if he wasn't mistaken—but the reasons for that seemed more useful than ever.

Hannah took another step back.

Someone was in the house.

They were down there, but there was no way to know for certain if they'd heard her. She wanted to get away from the hatch—away from the center of the noise she'd heard. There had been the sound of someone talking. It wasn't English. Russian maybe.

She herself had been kidnapped just over a year before. Nothing as hideous as this—but it had still left its mark on her—a lingering fear, almost a dread, hung over her like a cloud. She'd chosen to face it head-on, to walk straight into the blackness alone. Now she feared it would engulf her.

There was a clattering sound near the far wall and a funny smell.

She took another step back.

Footsteps moved toward the hatch—then stopped just below. What were they doing down there?

Hannah turned, looking at the boarded window. Was it a way out? Maybe she could tear the boards away. The hinges on the hatch squeaked with a minute adjustment.

Were they coming up here? To grab her? To kill her?

Hannah forced herself to stop it. To let go of the questions. To silence her mind. Her life really could be in danger, but this time she could choose to do something. To take control. She was not tied up or caged, and she would not let fear paralyze her. She could act.

Then she heard it.

A click.

She thought of the window. A moment of quiet, then footfalls moving down the stairs. They were leaving.

Hannah moved to the hatch, putting a hand on the thick wood. It didn't budge. She shoved. It wouldn't move. She stomped.

She was trapped.

Dominik heard a loud thump strike the attic entrance. They'd figured out that it was locked. There was another thump. They'd specifically reinforced the hatch to keep the girls from knocking it open if they ever had the guts to try. The padlock would hold, and the thick bolts would stay in place.

He kicked the back door open and stood in the threshold.

The lighter came open with a snap.

His thumb rolled across the wheel, and a thin blade of flame conjured itself up from the metal casing. He shielded the tiny flame for a moment, then tossed it into a puddle of gasoline.

There was a split second where nothing happened—Dominik froze, worried that the puddle had drowned the fire. Then it spread in a violent blossom, devouring the surrounding air with an audible howl. The house caught ablaze in a matter of seconds, fire consuming up the stairs.

Dominik pulled on a jacket he'd taken from one of the closets and zipped it as he walked away.

Hannah knew something wasn't right.

She couldn't have explained how, but something had changed. The smell—the pungent aroma that had been rising from below—suddenly seemed to vanish, replaced by something else.

Then she recognized the smell that had been. And her eyes went wide as she realized what the new smell was that had replaced it.

Greenish smoke slithered up from the cracks around the attic hatch. The smell was foreign—not like campfire smoke with its earthen richness, but the putrid scent of melting plastic and burning synthetics.

Then the floor started to get warm.

Fire travels up, she thought. Heat rises. Smoke rises. There was nowhere further up to go. She was at the tip of the spear.

She turned to the window, tugging at the boards that covered it—the rain smacking down just beyond.

The amount of smoke doubled in seconds, filling the attic with an acrid cloud. No fire yet. Just smoke. Her eyes stung, pinpricks stabbing at her tear ducts. Hot tears slid involuntarily down her warming face. It was all happening so fast. It reminded her of the fire safety videos she'd seen in elementary school, depicting how a cigarette in a trash can could send a house into an unrecoverable blaze in less than two minutes.

Arson could work so much faster.

She hacked and coughed, fingers digging into the boards, pulling at the wood. She lifted her foot, giving a solid kick that split the boards, crushing the glass beyond. Hannah grabbed the loose pieces and pulled them free, revealing the window.

Street light poured in through the rapidly thickening smoke. Rain tapped at the spiderwebbed glass. The whole window was little more than a slit. Less than six inches. She would never fit. It had been boarded up purely to keep light out.

Her lungs seized, fighting to keep out the dark haze. Her body convulsed with a violent cough. Heat permeated her.

Hannah coughed once more, then lifted her leg, jamming her heel into the tiny window, sending beads of glass splashing outward. It wasn't big enough for her to get out, but it was big enough to let a little air in.

She shoved her face to the opening and pulled in a lungful of the chilled air beyond. Then she pulled the jacket off her back and put it to her mouth. She crouched down, moved back into the prisonlike room, and searched for the trapdoor. Found it. Her hands worked at the latch, pulled. Nothing. There had to be some way to get out.

The blurring of her vision worsened, tears and smoke clawing at her eyes.

She coughed. Her body felt heavy and unwieldy. She tried to adjust her body with her right arm, but all the strength seemed to be slipping out of her. Fighting hurt so much. Moving sapped her energy. The searing floor suddenly seemed welcoming. Her body started to relax, curling into a ball. The unrelenting stinging in her eyes suddenly seemed unbearable.

Her eyelids shut.

The attic suddenly seemed far away. Her mind slipped into

silence. The kind of silence she could try so hard to cultivate in times of trouble now seemed so easy. Everything that seemed to worry faded, and rather than doing she was simply…

Being.

She could feel the past again.

Before it had been such a horrible place. When others had lived here. When family pictures and Christmas ornaments had been stored here in cardboard boxes. And then the old occupants moved out and others moved in—the ones who had perverted this place to be something else. Rolling carpet over the plywood, not bothering to nail it to the rafters.

Hannah's eyes snapped open, and she stumbled toward the window for a life-saving breath of cool air. Then she dropped to the floor and grasped at the carpet, pulling the shaggy covering loose. She reached for the floor, pulling at the boards, only to realize that she was standing on the edge.

Hannah moved and gave another pull—the heat was overwhelming. The plywood pulled away, clattering to the side as she tossed it.

Rafters—a few feet apart—partitioned themselves between sections of pink insulation. It looked like cotton candy, she thought.

Her hesitation lasted only a second, and then she jumped, feet first toward insulation.

The world seemed to freeze.

Then her body crashed through the billowy pink insulation, smashing through the thin layer of sheet rock, and she felt herself hurtling through the gray smoke toward the carpet one floor below.

She landed with a thud, losing her balance as her body slammed into the wall.

The heat enveloped her, blasting at her like a furnace, smoke stabbing at her eyes. Hannah looked up and saw the window at the far end of the hall. She pulled her jacket tight against her face and rushed forward, trying to stay low. Moments later she was at the window, the glass fogged over with a greasy black smear from the heat and smoke. Then she saw the gas can, tossed at the floor below it, fire clinging to the outside wall where gas dribbled down.

A kick could break the glass—but glass shards would slice her leg to unrecognizable ribbons if she tried. She took a smoky breath and reached for the can with her jacket, grabbing the handle. Her body swung, then released the metal container.

The smoke-fogged glass exploded outward and skittered across the sloping roof that covered the back porch.

She threw herself through the window—arms and legs catching on the fragile teeth of glass that remained, her body landing on glass shards that pricked her skin. She rolled uncontrollably down the roof, then slammed into the soggy grass below.

Hannah looked up at the blazing house—bleeding, burned, and weak.

Her eyes fluttered shut, only to open again after several minutes, and she found herself on the other end of the yard, farther from the flames. She was looking up at a man with long dark hair, in a black coat. Rain rolled off him as he said something to her. His lips moved, but she didn't hear anything.

And then the world faded to black.

Chapter 2

Monday morning. Holding a latte, John Temple stared out the window, looking down across the city of Manhattan.

Somewhere just below were the famed Fifth Avenue and West Thirty-fourth Street. John wondered what the people on the street were doing. Thinking. Saying. He wondered how long it would take him to get down to street level and find a bench where he could sit and watch the world passing in its busy flurry. Mothers, fathers, businesspeople, small children in strollers, drivers honking and yelling. A glorious mess of humanity.

"What are your thoughts, Mr. Temple? John?"

He turned his head back to the conference table, looking at the people in business suits staring at him. Half a dozen of them. The members of the Domani in their sharp suits and streamlined appearance, the members of the Ora with their brightly colored and textured ties, and Jerry Kirkland, the only member of the Prima in attendance, wearing earth tones. It was hard not to stereotype orders that were so distinctly different. Often they wore their lapel pins when they were feeling more obvious about their affiliations—blue triquetras for the past-seeing Prima, gold for the present-seeing Ora, and red for the future-seeing Domani, for whom Domani Financial was named and operated by.

"Uh..." John tried to think of a way to cover. "I'm sorry; I missed your question. What were you saying?"

They stared at him for a moment, knowing full well he had been daydreaming again.

He adjusted his suede jacket worn over a blue T-shirt. There had been discussion about his ideas of professional dress, and this was the best he could bring himself to do—even if he was underdressed compared to the dozen or so suits in the room.

John had spent his adult life trotting the globe doing part-time missions and relief work. He wasn't used to office life. He was used to digging wells and building sheds, planting churches in foreign countries. But that life was over now. Part of his work now put him in charge of Domani Financial—venture capital and investment. Putting people with money with people with needs. John's longtime friend Vince Sobel—dark suit, perfectly sculpted hair, bright red tie—spoke up. "We're in trouble, John."

"The economy's bad." John shrugged. "Everybody's in trouble."

Vince cleared his throat, looking side to side, almost apologetic to his colleagues. "Did you hear what I said about the SEC?"

John rolled his eyes. "Sure. I heard that. They're like the FCC or something, right?"

Shoulders seemed to sag across the conference room as trained professionals finally let their disgust with John show through. "No," Vince explained. "The Securities and Exchange Commission."

John covered up his ignorance with a sip of latte. "What about them?"

"We're being investigated by them."

"So?" John rebuffed, casual as ever. "We have nothing to hide."

Vince seemed to wince under the pressure of a reply he obviously didn't respect. "Do you remember when that telecommunications giant went bankrupt last month?"

"Sure," John agreed. "You guys said they were going under, so I had you pull all the stock before we lost everything."

"Do you remember that we advised against pulling all of it?" Vince asked.

"Yeah." John blinked. "But with all these companies going broke we've got to save our money somehow. We'd have lost a *lot* of money if I hadn't told you to yank everything."

"In the short run," Vince conceded. "And do you remember

the automotive manufacturer that tanked?"

"Sure." He nodded. "I had you pull everything out of that investment."

"And do you remember us advising against that one as well?" Vince asked, prodding as if John were a child.

"Yeah, but I saved a lot of money for us that time too." John smiled. It pleased him to think that he was finally getting past his dislike of people being focused on making money.

"And then there was the investment firm earlier this week."

"I know," John acknowledged. "You guys said not to pull everything because it might look bad, but you remember how much money we saved." John looked at one of the accountants across the table. "It was somewhere in the millions, wasn't it?"

The accountant nodded.

"See?" John said in his own defense. "I knew that keeping us financially afloat so that we could continue to fund missions was the best thing for everyone—so as Overseer I gave the order."

"Yes." Vince accepted his explanation with a forced smile. "Devin Bathurst did appoint you as Overseer. And we've obeyed your position of authority as Overseer. But it's more complicated than that."

John looked up. "How so?"

"We found out those investments were going under because members of the Ora and Domani were able to predict what was going on with those companies before they tanked."

"And?"

"And..." Vince cleared his throat. "As a result of receiving that information by means of *visions from God*, we have no documentation regarding *why* we dumped those stocks."

John sat back, bored with all the financial mumbo jumbo. So what if they had some problems with record keeping? Why would the Securities Executive Council, or whatever they were called, have a problem with that? "Seriously, I don't see the problem, guys," John replied.

"It looks like insider trading," someone said from across the room, firm and unapologetic.

John blinked. His body froze. The term was scary to say the least. He remembered something about Martha Stewart and jail time. "But it's not insider trading," he replied slowly. "They can't prove that it is."

Vince closed his eyes slowly in a decidedly defeated look. "We can't prove that it's not. Intuition is the only way to explain those investments away. What are we going to tell them? That *God* told us a telecommunications giant was going under?"

"People get lucky," John suggested. "Intuition can be a crazy thing."

"Once?" Vince replied sternly. "Maybe. Twice? Probably not. By number three, there's a distinct pattern—and our competition in the investment world has noticed."

"Noticed what?"

"That every time they lost their shirts on an investment, we miraculously—literally *miraculously*—got out of those investments unscathed. They're jealous, they're angry, and they've contacted the SEC and the IRS."

"Then it's just angry competition making unfounded accusations," John replied, trying to blow it all off. "Right?"

Vince tapped his fingers anxiously on the boardroom table. "We got a call this morning from the *Wall Street Journal*. They're doing a piece on the investigation. By this time tomorrow the entire financial community will know we're being investigated for serious white-collar crimes. From Internet chatter alone we've already had several major investors pull their money—and good luck attracting new investors once this hits the presses."

John looked at the table and let out a long breath. This was more serious than he had previously realized. "So, it's a PR problem? We can deal with this. We'll just have to pull together a team to—"

"There's also the IRS," Vince interrupted.

"Why are they involved?" John asked, confused by all the business concepts being thrown in his direction.

"The SEC and the IRS are often a package deal, and the IRS is very interested in our charitable contributions."

"The missions money?" John asked. "That's tax exempt. Why would the IRS care about that?"

"Because," Vince explained, obviously trying not to lose his temper, "we have millions of dollars in deductions from 'charitable giving' that's going to members of the Firstborn. People we have relationships with."

John shook his head. "I don't understand."

"The money is tax exempt and going right back into our own community. It looks like we're hiding and laundering assets."

A frown formed on John's face. "But we aren't hiding money. The money is all accounted for."

"True," Vince said with a nod. "But the IRS has contacted us and said that they are considering auditing us and that they may freeze our assets while they do so."

"But the money is still ours, right?" John asked. "We'll get it back when they're done, won't we?"

Vince was silent for a moment, rubbing his temples with the thumb and forefinger of his right hand. "That could take a very long time, and as long as they've frozen our money, it's as good as gone. We can't pay the rent for this office, the staff that runs it, or even the active missions you've got going." A choked sigh came from Vince. "We're as good as bankrupt until they're done. And if they find *anything*, we're looking at fines, penalties, and fees. Combined with the blow to our reputation, we are faced with the very real possibility of actually going bankrupt."

John sank back into his seat. He let his gaze wander to

the right—toward the window, into the city beyond. His eyes closed, and he heaved a sigh, trying to breathe slowly as his heart weighed down under the news. "How did this happen?"

Vince waited a moment before speaking. "You didn't listen to us. We tried to warn you that this was going to happen. We tried; we really did. But you gave orders as Overseer, and we did what you said."

The room was silent for a moment more.

The phone in the middle of the table rang. John waved to someone, and they hit the button, turning on the speakerphone.

"Mr. Temple?" a receptionist said from the other end of the line.

"Yes?"

"There's a call for you regarding Hannah Rice. They say it's an emergency."

Chapter 3

THE WORLD WAS a globular white, shifting in focus from thick blobs of impenetrable haze to a thin membrane, veiling a crisscrossing grid beyond.

A deep sleep, not wanting to let go, wrapped its fingers around her, cradling her in a warm embrace. It was as if she had been pulled beneath the surface of reality, her barely aware consciousness bobbing on the surface like a rubber duck on a storm-tossed ocean—a moment of dizzying lucidity followed by a sudden plunge back into the depths.

Her world was nothing for a moment—then she bobbed to the surface of reality again, reminded that somewhere in it all she was real.

It might have been ten minutes or maybe several hours—possibly a day—but the warm cradle of unconsciousness seemed to vomit her from its cozy depths, spitting her—exhausted—onto the shores of waking life.

Hannah stared at the ceiling, lying on her back—wherever *here* was.

The grid of the ceiling came into focus—the metal separators between porous ceiling tiles. An involuntary groan bubbled up from somewhere in her chest. Her eyelids—which felt more like lead than flesh—exerted themselves against their own weight to open, and her body shifted a fraction to the side. The surface beneath her crinkled—the sound of shifting plastic.

Her eyes, the only part of her that seemed to move without a concentrated effort, listed to the side. There was a window to her left—the sun glowing against the white curtains that were pulled shut. Her eyes continued their journey to the left, and she knew where she was.

A bag filled with clear fluid hung from a metal rod. An IV,

with a twisting tube that hung lazily, moving from the clear liquid to the back of her left hand.

She was suddenly aware of her body. Not so much her limbs, but the sensations of aching pain that seemed to cleave to her like a glove, giving definition to her physical form in the same way a vacuum-packed bag gives definition to its contents.

Hannah lay on her back for several more minutes, suddenly feeling very warm.

Then, just as she had been ejected from the unreal world of sleep, exhaustion seemed to evaporate.

"Hello," an elusive voice said.

Hannah turned her head to see the speaker—a man sitting in the corner, dressed all in black, dark curling hair dangling unceremoniously around his face. Despite the light in the room he seemed to melt into the only sliver of shadow in the room. She didn't reply; instead, she looked around the room to see if there was any chance he was addressing someone else. There was another bed to the right—but it was empty. The door, leading out toward a nurses' station, was half shut.

The man in the corner lifted his head, looking her squarely in the eyes, as if to remove all doubt about his intentions. "Good morning, Hannah Rice," he said with a certain gentleness.

Hannah opened her mouth to speak, then suddenly didn't.

"You don't know me," the man said, eyes intense despite his otherwise casual demeanor.

She felt the past:

The burning house. Smashing out of the window. Rolling off the outcropping of roof. Consciousness flitting in and out—the man who found her in the rain, lifting her from the ground.

—him.

She squinted through her still-blurred vision. "Who are you?"

"My name is Angelo."

She touched a throbbing temple. "Do you know me?"

"You are Hannah Marie Rice," he said without leaning forward. "When you were a small girl, you found a dead bee. You dumped a tiny box of matches and put its body inside. You buried the bee under the porch."

Hannah shook her head, confused. She had completely forgotten about that.

"Later that year you were stung by dozens of them in a nest you discovered at your birthday party. You wondered sometimes if the bee you buried was one of them and if they stung you because they blamed you."

Hannah opened her mouth—she remembered the bees and the fleeting thoughts of a little girl, trying to make sense of it all. Thoughts she had never shared. Could he see…?

The man named Angelo continued. "Yes," he replied, "I can see your past. I can see where you've been."

She shook her head. "I just thought that?"

He nodded. "And you're going to ask me about the girls."

Hannah frowned—what was he talking about? "Do you mean the girls that I was looking for?"

He didn't shift at all, remaining perfectly still. "You were right about your fear—they are being sold. They are going to be taken to an auction and sold to foreign buyers. Once they are gone, you will never find them again. They will be gone forever."

Hannah was suddenly awake. "What do you know about the girls?"

Something that could have been a smile appeared on Angelo's face. "I told you you were going to ask about the girls."

She stared. "You're one of the Firstborn?"

His eyes dipped then lifted. A subtle gesture that for any other person would have had no meaning at all—yet from this person, it had all the subtlety of a blast furnace—a look that said yes, he was indeed one of the Firstborn.

She sifted quickly through the conversation they had just

had—the past, the present, the future—he seemed to see them all. "Do you belong to one of the orders?"

He shook his head.

She bit her lip for a moment, then spoke. "You have all three gifts, don't you?"

His eyes lowered again, then lifted—*yes.*

Hannah peered into the dark recesses of the corner. "Who are you?"

"I'm here," he said quietly, "to bring you a warning."

She shook her head. "What warning?"

"That it has begun."

"What?" she asked, mind churning in the confusion. "What has begun?"

"The Firstborn—those gifted at the time of Christ's death with the eyes to see the past, present, and future—have begun to come together. After years of division, you have been instrumental in their attempts to unify. It has begun."

"I don't understand," she said again. "What has begun?"

"A unified Firstborn is a threat to machinations of evil—the Thresher will be unleashed to destroy the Firstborn."

Hannah thought for a brief moment. "Why are you telling me this?"

"Because," Angelo said softly, "the downfall of the Firstborn is the deficit between the power to see and the wisdom it demands."

She studied what she could see of his face, trying to see past the trancelike expression that he spoke through.

"As the Firstborn draw together, the Thresher will be unleashed. The same spiritual realm that your sight allows you to tap into has dark reaches that are turning on you and the Firstborn. The Thresher will not stand for a unified Firstborn—and the Thresher will destroy the Firstborn."

Hannah shook her head again. "Why me?"

Angelo stood. "I was only given the sight to see you, not the wisdom to know why. You only need to know that the struggles have begun." He turned toward the door, starting to walk away.

"What about the girls?"

Angelo stopped, looking back at her. His shoddy clothes seemed to swish, his long, curly hair moving from his face. "Their names are Tori, Nikki, and Kimberly. All three girls are under the age of eighteen. They snuck out at night. They fell in with the wrong people. They were kidnapped, and they are being taken across state lines. They will be beaten, drugged, and sold into slavery—their bodies to be used to fulfill the appetites of paying clients. You can still help them—but you must hurry or they will disappear forever."

Hannah nearly leapt from the bed as he moved closer to the door. "How do I find them?"

He shook his head. "I left a note by your bed; it's the address for Kimberly's home. You'll find her parents there. It may be a place to start. Beyond that I don't have the power to see. But be careful. The Thresher is coming."

Then he left.

John Temple passed through the parting glass doors, moving toward the hospital's front desk.

Burns. Smoke inhalation. Dehydration. Lacerations. That was what he'd been told on the phone—that Hannah Rice was hurt but being taken care of at Jersey City Medical Center. He never did get the man's name. The conversation had been brief. But Hannah was one of the Firstborn—one of his flock, as he sometimes thought of them—and she was a friend.

He stepped up to the desk, leaning against it with a sense of urgency. "I need the room for a Miss Hannah Rice."

The woman behind the desk tapped the name into the

computer and gave the room number. "It looks like she's going to be released later today."

John let his mind skim through the situation, trying to think of everything a good leader would take care of. "Medical bills," he said suddenly. "When will we get her medical bills?"

The woman continued typing. "Let me see."

Perhaps the Firstborn were having financial troubles, but certainly they would be able to afford the medical bills of a friend who had been hurt fulfilling her purpose.

"Actually," the woman said, putting a fingertip to the screen to follow her reading, "it looks like her bills have already been taken care of. Someone already paid."

John frowned. "Who?"

"I'm afraid I can't give you that information, but I can assure you that the costs of her care have already been paid in full."

John stepped away from the front desk. "Thank you," he said as an afterthought, then moved to the bank of elevators.

A few minutes later he was at the door of her room. Hannah stood, leaning against the hospital bed, fully clothed. Her face was yellowed with bruises—yet rosy and burned. White bandages covered obvious cuts on her face and neck. She trembled as she tried to pull her jean jacket on.

"Hannah," John said, stepping forward to help her with the jacket, "are you OK?"

"I'm fine." She buttoned up her jacket. "A little sore, and my nose keeps bleeding, but I'm OK."

"What happened?"

She shook her head as if it were nothing. "I was in a house that burned down."

John took a step back. "A house that burned down? What were you doing there?"

"I was led there," she said with a sniffle, running a finger under her nose to check if it was bleeding again. "On a mission."

John frowned. "How many times do I have to tell you I don't want you chasing off into dark alleys on your own? You could have been killed."

"They were kidnapped. Like I was, John. Three girls kidnapped—teenagers." She turned her face to him. "They're going to be sold, John."

He blinked. "What? Sold to who? For what?"

She shook her head. "Human trafficking. I have to find them before they're gone forever."

John looked thoughtful. "It's a worthy mission, but I don't want you operating on your own. I'll get someone to back you up, and funding too. Vince won't like it, but I'll just tell him that we saved money on the hospital bills."

"What?" Hannah asked.

John shrugged. "All your medical bills were taken care of. Any idea how that happened?"

She looked up, considered for a moment, then gave a knowing nod. "It must have been Angelo."

"Who?"

"Angelo." She shook her head out of confusion. "I have no idea who he is, but he appears to be a special kind of Firstborn. One that can see past, present, *and* future."

John frowned. "He can see everything?"

"Yes." She nodded. "That's what he says."

"Like D'Angelo himself?"

She nodded again.

His frown stayed, a sense of anxiety filling him. "That's unusual. And a little concerning."

"He's the one who found me and brought me to the hospital." She looked at the floor for a moment. "He saved my life."

"He did more than that," John said in agreement—then stopped a moment to think. "Was he rich?"

Hannah shook her head. "No. He was dressed kind of like a bum—with stringy dark hair."

"You talked to him?" John asked, intensely interested.

"Yes," she replied. "He told me that I could save the girls—if I acted quickly enough. He also told me that the Thresher had been unleashed."

John's heart stopped for a beat, his hands flashing with cold.

Hannah pondered for a moment. "What do you suppose he meant by that?"

John stared at her for a moment, having trouble summoning the words. "Vince told me about Thresher when I first got started with the Ora. One of the last prophecies made by Alessandro D'Angelo foretold how any time the orders became too successful, Thresher—a force of evil—would be let loose to divide the First-born before hunting them down and destroying them."

A small gasp left Hannah's lips. "So, what does that mean for us?"

"It means things are about to get very, very bad."

Chapter 4

HE'D SLUGGED THE man in the face and stripped him of the handgun before the man had a chance to fire.

Swift. Accurate. Correct. Approach the problem with the solution in mind—the only way to solve a problem in Devin Bathurst's opinion. He dropped the man off at the correct institution and got back in the car. Mission accomplished. Back to the office in time for lunch.

Over the last year he'd grown to resent the missions and errands John Temple sent him on. At least this last one was in Central Park, as opposed to the others he had been sent to deal with all over the country—and even one in the Cayman Islands. But he'd made John Overseer—a decision he felt more mixed about every day.

He sat in the stop-and-go lunchtime traffic of Manhattan. The midday light crisscrossed in yellow stripes through spaces between the buildings.

The construction worker three hundred yards ahead waved the last motorist through then turned his sign back to the "Stop" side. The lumbering herd of automobiles returned to its standard, docile halt. A car horn announced someone's malcontent with angry fanfare. Something inside of Devin wanted to lay on his own horn. Honk back. Roll down the window to make rude remarks and gestures. He declined the impulse and maintained his composure as a courteous motorist. Back straight. Hands on the wheel—ten o'clock and two o'clock positions. He let his eyes close for a moment.

The Lord's Prayer—just the way his grandmother had taught him so many years ago.

"Our Father, who art in heaven..." The words rolled from his lips—perfectly rehearsed, flawlessly articulated. He glanced at traffic to see if it had moved, then closed his eyes again.

"...hallowed be Thy name. Thy kingdom come, Thy will be done—on Earth as it is in heaven—"

His car. The street. The seething city filled with noise and anger. All of it seemed to melt into the distance as he let his words take shape. "Give us this day our daily bread, and forgive us our trespasses as we forgive those who trespass against us."

The Manhattan skyline no longer existed outside the window. The city folded into itself and was gone.

"And lead us not into temptation"—the words surrounded him like a blanket—"but deliver us from evil..."

A rush of images. Incomprehensible.

Devin's eyes snapped open, staring forward.

He waited.

Nothing happened.

He waited another moment, then let his eyes resume their closed position. "For Thine is the kingdom, and the power, and the glory..." He let the words settle around him for a moment. "*Forever.*"

He opened his eyes and unclasped his hands. "Amen."

Devin thought for a moment, considering whatever it was that had washed over him just a few moments before. What was its purpose? Why had it happened, and how did it inform his actions? He let his mind dissect the sensations for several moments more, executing a thorough sweep of all the possibilities he could conceive.

Nothing.

He shook his head and began to stand—

Images. In an onslaught. The future—

Ski masks. Automatic rifles. Shotguns.

Bullets breaking glass.

Screaming and fleeing.

Dozens wounded.

A well-known politician dead—

—assassination.

Devin reached into his jacket for his phone—his mission was clear.

John stepped off the elevator onto his floor, cell phone pressed to his ear.

"Hello?" the other end answered.

John moved down the hall. "Vince, it's John. We need to talk."

"What happened with Hannah Rice?"

John shifted the phone as he approached the door to his office, reading the plaque: *John Temple: Overseer.* He hated the sign. It seemed pretentious, but it seemed like the only way he could remember which office door was his. "Hannah was in a house fire."

"A house fire?"

"She was tracking some girls who are going to be trafficked. Something went wrong. One of the people she was following spotted her or something."

John opened the door to his office and stared.

Devin Bathurst—striking dark skin in a crisp suit—turned from his place at the window and looked at John.

Vince continued on the other end of the line. "Is she OK?"

"She's fine. Some guy named Angelo—" He paused. "Hey," John interrupted himself, eyes focused on Devin, "it looks like Devin needs to talk to me. Can I call you back later?"

"If you need to, John," Vince said firmly. "But keep me updated on Hannah."

John nodded. "I understand." He said good-bye and closed his phone.

"You didn't need to get off the phone for me," Devin said in his typical commanding tone, eyes unblinking as ever.

John waved a dismissing hand as he moved to the other side

of his desk and took a seat. "Boring conversation anyway. So, how did things go with the suicide?"

Devin took a seat across from John. He cleared his throat before speaking with very deliberate words. "I dealt with it."

Concern tugged John to inquire, "What do you mean by you 'dealt with it'?"

"The man didn't complete his suicide attempt, and he's now at an institution where he can recover and rehabilitate."

John nodded. "So, how did you talk him down?"

"I told him that I was there to help and that life was worth living."

"And?" John motioned for Devin to continue.

"He denied it at first until I told him I knew about the gun and that he planned to take his own life right there in Central Park."

"And he just *gave* you the gun?" John asked.

"No. He said that his wife had left him after he lost everything in the crash. He said that he just couldn't take the loneliness anymore and that he was helping the world as a whole. The man told me that he'd come to that place three other times before but had never had the courage to do it until that day."

"Wow," John said with genuine interest. "What did you say to him?"

Devin coughed awkwardly into his fist. "I told him that he was trolling for sympathy and that if he really wanted to die that he would have done it already."

"*What?*" John exclaimed.

"I told him to suck it up. That loneliness was part of life. That we're all born alone and that we all die alone and that he'd better get used to it."

"Devin," John stammered in disbelief. "That's exactly the *wrong* way to talk to someone threatening suicide!"

"He was trolling for sympathy," Devin repeated. "He'd meant

to do it three times before. Three times. He wasn't serious about doing it."

"You can't say that," John groaned, rubbing his palm into his forehead. "Just because a person makes a series of *false* suicide threats doesn't mean that *this time* they aren't serious. A person only has to mean it once—and the vision said that this time was going to be it!"

"Whose vision was it anyway?" Devin grumbled.

"Gina Holst."

"From accounting?" Devin shook his head. "I told you not to send me on this one."

"It was important," John argued, still trying to come to terms with what he was hearing. "I needed someone who I knew I could trust to get it done."

"And I dealt with it," Devin retorted calmly.

"But..." John scanned his desktop with big eyes, trying to think of what to say. "How? How did you talk that guy down after *that*?"

"I took the gun."

"Took it?" John asked, eyebrow raised. "How?"

"He went to use the firearm on himself, so I delivered a swift jab to his face and stripped the firearm, like I would with anyone making threatening motions with a firearm."

"You punched the man in the face?" John choked.

"Then," Devin continued, "I took him to a reputable institution where he can get the help he needs from people who have better...*people skills*. I'll be paying his expenses personally."

John closed his eyes, still recovering from the shock. "At least he's safe now." John sighed. "First it's Hannah, then you—"

Devin snapped to attention. "What about Hannah?"

"I just visited her in the hospital. She was caught in a house fire while on a mission."

Devin's eyes glared into his. "Was she hurt?"

"Yes—I mean, no. Not badly anyway," he stammered. "She's already been discharged."

"Did you send her on that mission alone?"

"No! You know I don't like her operating on her own. She just felt…called. It involved a kidnapping—of young girls. You can guess that would get her attention."

Devin processed the information. Literal input, literal output. "She's overcompensating. The trauma of her own kidnapping is causing her to project onto these girls. Perhaps it's an attempt to cope, but she's not being wise."

John nodded, glad they were on the same page on this one. "I told her she could continue work on it—but not alone. She needs backup. I know I've had you working on other people's stuff that I shouldn't, but is there any chance I could get you to help her?"

Something passed through his eyes—a flicker—but before John could identify the emotion, it was gone. "I'll do it."

"Another thing." John looked away. "This is weird, but Hannah was rescued by someone named Angelo. Claims to be a Firstborn, but get this—he can see past, present, *and* future. And he made a warning about Thresher."

Devin waved away the concern. "The Thresher is an intellectual bogeyman. There have been a lot of false scares over the years."

"You don't view it as a threat?"

Devin stared him down. "We have nothing to fear but fear itself. Our real focus should be on achieving what God put us here to do. Now, let me show you what I've got. It may even have a connection to Hannah's mission."

Devin reached for his briefcase. He snapped it open on his lap and lifted a few items before tossing a newspaper on the desk between them.

"Senator Foster to Visit Nevada to Investigate Sex Trafficking," John read from the page, looking at the picture of an African American politician—American flag pinned to his lapel. "So?"

Devin set down his briefcase and sat up straight. "He's going to be assassinated in Las Vegas. I think it's going to be racially motivated."

"Really?" John shook his head. "That stuff still happens?"

"We have an African American president now," Devin stated. "The illusion that America is a purely white nation is evaporating. Some people don't like that—and the death knell is going to be loud."

John looked at the picture again, studying the image. "I don't buy it. It sounds like something from the fifties or sixties. Not today." John shook his head, still having trouble with the idea. "And why Foster? There are other African American politicians—including the president himself."

"He made some very unflattering comments about the white supremacy movement," Devin said, brushing something from the sleeve of his perfectly pressed tan sport coat. "He's even made allusions to the idea that the FBI should declare war on those groups again like Hoover did decades ago."

John shook his head. "They'd really kill him over that?"

Devin shrugged. "I don't know the details. You know how vague our visions can be."

John held the paper in his hands for several seconds, looking it over, feeling the thin pages on his fingers. He looked up at Devin—the difference in their skin tones suddenly painfully apparent—a fact that John worked very hard not to acknowledge and even harder still not to think about.

"I need funding," Devin said in his usual businesslike manner, handing John a piece of paper. "This is a cost breakdown. I need the money to get people and equipment to Nevada, a place to keep them, and funds to support them at the time. We need to stake out the area and be prepared to stop the assassination before it begins."

John looked at Devin's skin, moving to the eyes that were

housed in it. He couldn't say no. Not to this. Could he? He picked up the sheet of paper, the numbers blurring on the page as they washed together.

"Look," John started, "there's something I should probably tell you."

"Yes?" Devin said without blinking.

"Well," John replied, hesitant. "It looks like we *may* have drawn the attention of the SEC."

Devin's ire was somehow crystal clear, despite his placid features. "What?"

"And the IRS."

"The IRS? You're joking."

"No," John chuckled nervously. "I really wish I were. It looks like they may even freeze our assets."

"On what grounds?"

"We've been accused of insider trading," John offered as calmly as he could.

Devin didn't flinch. "You dumped that stock, didn't you?"

John nodded.

"I told you it only takes once."

"Three times actually." John shrugged, trying to make light of it.

"Three times?" Devin shook his head. "I told you not to take me off of financial duty. But instead you've had me running all over the continental United States for the last year chasing visions had by people in HR and accounting."

"I'm doing the best I know how." John felt himself get defensive. "I still think you should have kept the Overseer job when they gave it to you instead of handing it over to me. Just the other day I had one of the Domani Financial staff tell me that God appointed you as Overseer, and you were therefore unable to step down, making *you* the rightful Overseer."

"I'm the wrong man," Devin insisted.

"What makes you say that?"

"Because the job of a leader is to get people to do things, and there are only two ways to make that happen—you can either make people want to do things, or you make them afraid not to. And I'm not above using fear to push people."

John heaved a sigh. "But at least you'd be pushing people in the right direction."

"No," Devin retorted. "Bullying people into doing good is just as despicable as charming people into doing evil." Devin stood, picking up his briefcase. "This is your job, whether you like it or not."

John followed him out the door.

"The Firstborn are going to need a strong and worthwhile leader through this," Devin said. "Listen to counsel, but lead with your conscience." Then he turned and walked away.

John nodded. "I'll keep that in—"

She was standing in the hall, typing something into her cellular telephone. Blonde hair. Business attire—black and red. Her features—every one of them—sculpted and beautiful. Her eyes lifted, as if she could sense that she was being looked at.

"John," she said with enigmatic shock.

The syllables fell out of John's mouth without heed: "Trista."

Devin nodded at her. "Miss Brightling."

Trista's eyes snapped away from John. "Devin, just who I was looking for. I was told to see you to get up to speed on the financial situation." Her eyes darted back to John for a split second as she approached Devin.

"Yes," Devin said, "I can have you up to speed in very little time. I'm headed back to the office; I can brief you on the way."

"Excellent," she replied with a nod.

"Trista," John said again, just trying to get her attention in some way now. She looked at him, face neutral. "How are you?"

"I'm good," she said, eyes only making contact with John's

for a moment, then looking away.

"Last I heard you were in Belize."

She nodded, looking at him again. "It was good."

Devin cleared his throat. "I'll be in the lobby."

Trista smiled, nodding at Devin. "I'll be right with you."

Devin turned away, walked down the hall, and disappeared around the corner.

"So," John asked, feeling a bit unsteady, "how was it?"

"What?" she asked, expression stoic.

"Belize."

"Oh," she replied, snapping back to the conversation. "It was..." She paused for a moment, thinking. "It was good."

"I'm glad to hear it," he said, nodding, as if the movement would shake the feeling of awkwardness from him.

The hall was quiet for a moment as they simply looked each other over.

"So," John began again, heart rate a little quicker than before, "any chance we could catch up?"

"Sure." Her eyes searched his face. "It has been...awhile."

"A year," John agreed, stuffing his hands in his pockets. He looked to the sides, realizing they were alone in the hall. "So, are you free tonight?"

"Uh," she said with a lilting smile, "I think so."

"Dinner?"

"Sure, I guess we could do dinner."

"Good." He cleared his throat. "I'll give you a call. Does that sound good?"

"Do you have the number for my new phone?"

"No, I..."

"I'll call you," she said, walking the same way Devin had gone, looking back.

"Does eight work?" John called after.

"That should be fine," she nodded, waved, then turned and walked away.

John watched her disappear around the corner. Trista was back. And his world had turned upside down.

Devin Bathurst stood in the lobby, waiting for Trista.

His cell phone buzzed in his chest pocket, and he reached into his jacket to retrieve it. "This is Bathurst."

"It's a trap," the voice announced in a hushed tone.

Devin looked around the lobby, trying to see if someone was watching him. "I'm afraid I don't follow."

"Do not help the senator—it's a trap. The Thresher will be unleashed."

Devin continued turning in his slow circle, eyes open for someone with a cell phone who might be watching him. "I'm afraid I didn't get your name. Who did you say you were?"

"That doesn't matter now. The Thresher will be unleashed—the Firstborn will turn against each other."

"I've seen that happen before. It can be survived."

"No," the voice warned, "the Firstborn won't survive this. They'll be marched to destruction if you do this."

Devin shook his head. "I'm going to need evidence if you want me to listen to you."

"You have to trust me."

"I don't make a habit of trusting anonymous callers," Devin stated. "Do you have any evidence?"

"I've seen what happens if you move forward."

"And I've seen what happens if I don't," Devin rebutted.

"You have to listen to me!" the voice said again, emphatic.

"I would be more than willing to sit and talk," Devin said, watching Trista approach, "but until you're willing to meet me in person, I'm afraid we have nothing to talk about."

"I won't do that, Mr. Bathurst. You have to understand that—"

"I do understand," Devin replied.

"You aren't listening to—"

Devin snapped his phone shut.

Trista approached. "Who was that?"

Devin returned his phone to its pocket. "Wrong number."

The man named Crest sat in his office playing Solitaire on his desktop computer. It had been a slow morning, and he had a few minutes to kill. Government work wasn't always as secure as people liked to think it was, but it was enough so that playing digital cards every now and again wasn't the end of the world. The position of government desk driver was only his cover anyway, and as far as he could tell, showing too much of a work ethic might draw unwanted attention.

The phone rang, and Crest gave it a moment, adjusting his glasses and clicking a few cards with his mouse before he lifted the receiver. "Yes?"

"Mr. Crest," the assistant, a guy named Jim, said on the other end of the line. "You have a call. They wouldn't give a name but said it was about someone or something called *Angelo*? He said that you'd know what he was talking about."

Crest sat up, clicking out of his card game. He thought his heart might have stopped for a moment. "Put him through," Crest ordered without hesitation.

"OK," the confused assistant said, transferring the call with a click. He waited for a moment.

"Mr. Crest," the contact said from the other end of the line, an unrecognized voice. Probably some low-level person who had been given the task of passing on information. "The asset known as Angelo may have appeared on the grid again."

"Where?" Crest asked, glancing at the door to make sure it was closed and firmly latched.

"A hospital in New Jersey. One of the cards he was issued by the Agency three years ago was used to pay a hospital bill for what appears to be a random patient."

"Who was the patient?" Crest asked, eyes fixed on the door, glancing at the windows, trying to make sure he kept his voice low in case someone was standing too close outside his office. Not the ideal talk space for this kind of discussion.

"Uh..." whoever the contact was searched through files, "Hannah Rice. Sound familiar?"

Crest frowned. Rice? That did sound familiar for some reason. Something having to do with the Pennsylvania incident the previous year? "Nothing solid," Crest replied. It didn't matter. Keeping track of the names of the so-called Firstborn wasn't his job anyway. There were other people for that. "Has the OGA changed Angelo's status?"

"Not yet," the contact replied, "The Agency still considers him MIA—missing in action. The use of a credit card is certainly a breach, but it doesn't guarantee Angelo is alive."

"Do the..." Crest paused, reminding himself he was on an open line. "Do the *analysts* have any guesses as to what he might be trying to do?"

"No word from them, but management thinks that if he's still alive, he might know about your current operation regarding the senator."

Crest cleared his throat with discomfort, knowing that these phone lines were relatively secure but not so much so that he wanted the senator mentioned in any way. "Assuming that Angelo *is* alive, do they have any reason to believe that he ever recovered from the..." Crest tried to think of a word that might serve as a mutually understood euphemism for things they had done to Angelo, things like psychotropic experimentation, mind-altering drugs, or draconian cold war–era research.

"The work he did with the OGA?"

"Yeah," Crest agreed, considering the idea of pumping a human being full of LSD and how that might be considered "work." "Between the effects of that work," Crest continued, "and the fact that he was confirmed as having all three 'skill sets,' I thought he wasn't capable of trade craft or even civilian life."

"The analysts think if he is alive that he may be recovering," the contact said with a certainty that frightened Crest. "Regardless," the contact continued, "they doubt that he'll attempt to make contact with anyone from the OGA—even on the outside chance he is still alive."

"Then why did they want me to know?"

"I wasn't briefed about the specifics," the contact conceded. "All I was told was that Angelo may be alive—and active. Regardless, this is the kind of information that can change everything."

Crest nodded to himself, slumped back in his office chair. "This changes everything."

Chapter 5

JOHN WALKED THROUGH the largely vacant offices adjoining Domani Financial. These offices had been set aside for the Prima to use, but they had shown little interest in having representatives at the Manhattan office. There were calendars on the walls of several offices where members of the Prima had set up shop for a few days at a time, but they were all set to October of the previous year. A fact that lay in stark contrast to the sunny spring weather they had been having all week.

Of course Hannah Rice came to the offices sometimes, but never for long. She'd moved to New Jersey, just across the river, so she could be closer to the central office that Manhattan had become, but it was still far enough that she didn't drop by often. Even when she did, it was mostly just to use the phone or to talk to one of the other Firstborn there. Usually Devin or himself. But it had been nearly six weeks since the last time she had done that. Hoping to keep a friendly eye on her, John had invited her to work full-time in the empty Prima offices, but so far she'd put him off. Something about not being ready for office politics.

John came to the door of the one occupied office and tapped on the frame with his middle knuckle. He waited for Jerry Kirkland to notice him. Jerry, who had been hunched over his computer, shot upward and turned toward the door.

"Hello, Mr. Temple." He reached out with a chubby hand to shake. Jerry was bald with virtually no distinguishable neck between his tiny ears and the collar of his brown polo shirt. He was the official historian of the Firstborn—a position John had created about nine months ago after becoming Overseer. It had been meant as an olive branch to the Prima, and indeed they gave their full blessing for Jerry Kirkland to work from the

Manhattan office, but he was still the only actual representative they had sent.

"Come in, Mr. Temple," Jerry said, beckoning with a hand. "Have a seat." He lifted a pile of documents the size of two phone books off the seat of the nearest chair. To the casual eye, Jerry's office looked like a mess, but he always assured people everything was in exactly the right place. The floor was filled with boxes, and the windowless walls were covered in charts with strings attached to pushpins.

Jerry moved the thick stack of documents on top of another thick stack of documents, evening up the edges as best he could before taking his own seat at his desk. Jerry swiveled his chair toward John and smiled. "Would you like a Diet Coke?"

John couldn't help but let his smile show. "Diet Coke?"

"I love the stuff." Jerry reached into a drawer and pulled out an empty can, crushing it in his hand before throwing it into a green recycle bin, where the can clanked as it landed among its fallen comrades.

"No, thanks," John said.

"Do you mind terribly if I have one?" Jerry pointed at a mini fridge at the opposite end of his desk.

"Knock yourself out."

"Thank you." Jerry removed a diet soda. He cracked the seal with a spray of minute vapor and took a swig. "So, how can I help you today, Mr. Temple?"

"I'm interested in the Thresher," John said with a bit of a shrug. "What do you have compiled on that?"

Jerry whistled, pointing to the corner. "See that filing cabinet? That's all Thresher stuff."

"Wow," John said, slightly stunned. "I didn't know there was that much stuff. I mean, Vincent Sobel and I used to stay up late in college, and he'd tell me stuff about the Thresher he'd learned from others. But it was mostly just 'friend of a friend' kinds of things. More ghost stories than anything."

Jerry nodded jovially. "And I've got a filing cabinet filled with ghost stories. You know how it all started, right, with Alessandro D'Angelo?"

"Sure," John replied. "Italian monk in the Dark Ages. Founded the Firstborn. Right?"

"Actually," Jerry corrected hesitantly, "he would be considered late medieval, early Renaissance. Especially since he was Italian, and the Renaissance started in Italy first around 1250 or so, depending on who you—"

"Jerry," John said as a friendly nudge to get him back on topic.

"Right." Jerry gave another of his noises, a swishing sound this time. "D'Angelo—who had all three gifts—was betrayed and stabbed on Ash Wednesday 1441, but he didn't die until Easter, six weeks later."

John nodded, trying to hurry things along. "And it was during those six weeks that he made his biggest prophecies."

"Right," Jerry agreed. "He died very slowly, so nobody really knows how many prophecies he made in that time." Jerry pointed to a place on his rotund side. "As far as I can gather, he was stabbed right about here. His friends were able to stop the bleeding, but I'm pretty sure it got infected. Maybe gangrene or something like that got into the wound and caused him to slowly—"

"Thresher." John interrupted gently, nudging Jerry back to the topic at hand.

"Right." Jerry raised his hands apologetically. "He started making prophecies about Thresher while he was dying—that the Thresher would eventually destroy the Firstborn."

"But?" John asked in anticipation.

"But we don't have most of those prophecies. The vast majority of them went underground with D'Angelo's friends when the Inquisition against them heated up." Jerry morbidly laughed to himself. "No pun intended."

John was confused. "What?"

"They burned them at the stake. Get it? When things 'heated up' for them?"

John didn't laugh.

"Anyway"—Jerry waved off his failed joke—"when D'Angelo's most trusted people decided to go into hiding, they took that stuff with them. Some of it has surfaced. But we still have only maybe an *eighth* of what they wrote down. So we really probably don't have a full picture on the whole Thresher thing." He shook his head as if it were all too bad. "A classic example of history being lost to the sands of time."

"So, the only thing you have are the ghost stories," John offered, trying to bait him back into conversation.

Jerry shrugged. "Not *only*, but that's a lot of it. Oral tradition. Something a friend passed on to a friend of a friend about something that happened to a long-lost uncle."

"Do you think the Thresher is real?" John asked candidly.

Jerry took a long draw of Diet Coke. "Yes," he said with some hesitation. "But we have to be careful. There have been some major Thresher scares over the last thousand years. There are some examples from the European side that I might buy, simply because the Firstborn are all but extinct over there, but here in the United States it's open to a bit more interpretation."

"Like?" John prodded.

"Well, in Europe there was a major scare that the Thresher had come to destroy the Firstborn during the Protestant Reformation. Of course, that was less than a century after D'Angelo died, so the Firstborn were still hiding in chapter houses across Europe at that point."

"Chapter houses?"

"Like office branches. Firstborn monasteries in Britain and

France and Italy and so on." Jerry shrugged. "They were pretty much underground at that point. A lot of the new generation had been raised in fear because the previous generation had been hunted the same way the church hunted the Cathars."

"Cathars?"

"A gnostic sect," Jerry clarified, then continued. "After the English Civil War is when most of the European Firstborn 'crossed the pond' and came to the American colonies. That was a Thresher scare—but they survived. There were a few others. The Salem Witch Trials were a biggie; I don't have any specific accounts of Firstborn dying in that, but they were hunted because of their gifts." Jerry took another sip of his drink. "And I don't have to tell you how bad things got during the American Civil War."

John frowned. "The Firstborn fought in the Civil War?"

"Oh, yeah. It was a big deal."

"I've never heard of that."

"Probably not," Jerry offered. "Because the Ora had all gone to California to make an instant fortune when the gold rush hit in 1848. Of course, on the East Coast the Prima condemned slavery but were in support of states rights—so they joined the Confederacy and stationed their militia out of Atlanta, Georgia."

"I don't understand how that's possible," John argued. "If they didn't support slavery, why did they join the Confederacy?"

"Many of the Confederacy's strongest supporters, including General Robert E. Lee, were not slave owners, or were deeply opposed to the idea. Almost none of the foot soldiers owned slaves or could even afford them if they wanted to. For Prima, like much of the Confederate South, it was a war of independence. No different than the American Revolution. They had no interest in invading the North and felt that they were fighting for their personal freedom."

"At the cost of someone else's freedom." John shook his head. "I guess I just don't understand their logic."

"Neither did the Domani," Jerry said with a shrug, "who enthusiastically supported and took part in Sherman's wildly destructive March to the Sea, burning a three-hundred-mile swath toward Atlanta."

"Which was burned to the ground," John said with a nod, remembering his high school history classes.

"Correct. And a Domani regiment personally saw to the destruction of the Prima headquarters in Atlanta. So, the embittered Prima settled in Colorado, the Ora stayed in California, and the Domani sought out positions of power in New York City. A major geographical division—but that didn't keep them from bumping into each other. There were serious attempts to recover D'Angelo's last prophecies in those days, and so the three orders came into a lot more contact with each other than you'd expect. Much of the Prima sought revenge over old Civil War wounds, much of the Domani sought to demilitarize the Prima, and in the middle of it all the Ora played both sides against each other in the hopes of keeping the attention off of themselves—which didn't work. A lot of Firstborn died."

John thought for a moment. "So, was that the Thresher?"

"Who knows," Jerry said, taking a noisy slurp of Diet Coke. "A lot of that violence started with the thinking that Domani had *become* the Thresher."

"So…" John frowned, thinking through the fog of facts. "The Thresher is a group?"

An accepting nod. "That's one theory. There's an oral tradition that one of the orders of the Firstborn will be corrupted and *become* the Thresher. Blake Jackson was a big proponent of that idea."

John shook his head. "A real shame about Blake Jackson and the things he did because of that belief."

"Others," Jerry continued, "believe the Thresher is a spirit.

Like a spirit of contention. A general propensity toward the sin of division."

"Or a demonic spirit," John offered.

"That's also a popular theory. Or the devil himself." Jerry shrugged, making another noise. "Who knows?"

John nodded to himself for a few more seconds, digesting it all. "Vincent always talked of the Thresher as some sort of invisible monster that stalked the Firstborn, hunting them into extinction. But that doesn't sound like it's the most widely accepted version."

"Well..." Jerry finished his Diet Coke, crushing and disposing of it the same way as the last. "It's not a popular belief among the Prima, so I'm unique in saying this, but when everyone agrees on something, they usually aren't doing their own thinking. And people who don't come to their own conclusions don't do anything of value."

"Why do you say that?"

"Because," Jerry said, reaching for his mini fridge again. "If a person believes the truth because they were told so, it doesn't make them wise. It just means they're a little gullible and a lot lucky. Even if you landed on the truth by accident, it's only a matter of time until someone tells you something that isn't the truth. And if you believe *that*, like everything else you're told—then you're stuck like Chuck."

John smirked at Jerry's pithy comments. "And the alternative is?"

"Do your own thinking as a solitary person."

"Isn't that lonely?" John inquired.

"Well..." Jerry shrugged. "Real truth isn't determined by a popularity contest."

"But," John fumbled, "if that's true, then how does one person make a worthwhile difference?"

"They don't very often," Jerry conceded. "It takes a group committed to the marketplace of ideas, where people, thinking individually, even disagreeing, can work together in the pursuit of a common goal—that's when powerful stuff happens."

They were quiet for a few seconds as John thought about it. "And that's precisely when the Thresher raises its head."

Jerry smiled coyly. "Most of the time people who are free to do as they please simply do as they're told. Because it's easier to have one person doing all the thinking and everyone else following that vision—whether it's right or not. Which is why we now have the position of Overseer." He raised a set of open palms. "No offense to you, of course."

"None taken," John assured, taking a moment to think. "So, what do *you* think the Thresher is?" John asked pointedly.

"Me?" Jerry asked, a set of chubby fingers pointing at his own chest. "Probably something demonic. Maybe it's a kind of battle plan, or a specific position a demon takes on—like Overseer for us." Jerry cracked open his new can, taking a swift sip. "But I do believe that the Thresher—whatever it is—is real. And its tools are fear and pride and a love of power."

Chapter 6

Hannah sat in the coffee shop by the window. Manhattan foot traffic passed her by in a silent parade just beyond the glass.

She took a sip of her coffee. House blend. Nothing too fancy or expensive. She had a budget to keep, after all.

Her fingers worked with the pencil, making tight strokes across the pad of paper she had pressed to the tabletop. A jawline. Eyes—young but soulful. Hair—curly and brown. They took shape, one by one, constructing the face of a girl. Whichever girl she was. Nikki? Tori? Kimberly? She was out there—

—somewhere.

And her time was running out.

Hannah looked at the other sketches she had made, all on small pages of lined paper. Ragged shreds across the top where they had been torn from the tiny rings that had held them. Each picture another piece of the bigger story:

The girls. The house. Abstract sketches of pain and suffering. A tattoo—*a dragon.*

She took the last sip from her cardboard cup and pushed it aside, eyes dipping. She would be on a plane now. She would be following after them now—but where was the right place to start?

Her eyes wandered to the window, slipping out of focus, watching the crush of humanity move silently past.

"Penny for your thoughts," someone said from across the table.

She looked up to see a tall coffee cup placed in front of her as the man sat down.

"Mr. Bathurst," she said with a polite nod. "What's this?"

"Hazelnut latte," he said, pointing to the fresh cup in front of her. "I come here myself sometimes. The hazelnut latte is a personal favorite of mine."

She nodded and took a sip. "Thank you."

"How are you feeling?" he asked. "You did just get out of the hospital, after all."

A hesitant smile to show she was fine. "Luckily the flames were mostly on the bottom floor. Some smoke inhalation, minor burns." She shrugged. "I'm OK."

Devin sat back—tan suit, strong features—crossed his legs, and took a sip from his own coffee as he lifted one of her sketches. "These are very good. I didn't know that you were an artist."

Hannah shrugged. "I've dabbled in it for years. I signed up for an art class a few months ago to help me with stuff like this."

Devin picked up another sketch, comparing the two side by side. "You must be getting As."

"Actually," she said with wry irony, taking an embarrassed sip, "I'm failing."

Devin frowned. "I don't understand."

"Too many absences."

"What happened?"

"An elderly couple were swindled out of their life savings and put in a home. I spent most of the semester tracking down their money in the hopes of returning it to them."

Devin set down the sketches. "And did you?"

Hannah shook her head. "I found some of it. But they still lost their house and most of their possessions."

"But I thought you were studying online?"

Hannah gave a thumbs-down gesture. "That's not working out very well either. It's just hard to get excited about studying when I could be doing something more...useful, more immediate. You know, helping people."

Devin shook his head. "Your grandfather was worried that you would neglect your schooling once you discovered your gift. Don't let that happen. Although it might seem like a waste of time now, education prepares you for the big stuff. You can't just fly on visions alone. And I'm worried about you operating by yourself. Why didn't you ask for help?"

Hannah shrugged. "I didn't want to pull anyone else off important things, like John has with you."

"Hannah, you nearly got yourself killed."

"So, what else is new?" she scoffed. "Besides, it's not like if something happened to me I'd be leaving behind an orphan or something. It's just me. My life."

Devin pinned her with his gaze. "That's no reason to go on suicide missions. You have to follow your callings, but you also have to prepare for your future. And take care of yourself."

"Like you do?" Hannah challenged, gesturing at him with a raised latte.

Devin shrugged. "I'm a workaholic; I'm probably not the best example to follow. But don't let your calling isolate you and overwhelm you. It *is* OK to ask for help and advice."

Hannah sniffed disbelievingly.

Devin pulled his chair closer to the table. "For instance, I'm interested in getting your help with my current calling."

Hannah shook her head as she picked up one of her sketches. "I can't. I'm already working on something."

"The girls?" Devin asked.

She nodded.

"I think they may be connected." He handed her a newspaper. "This is Senator Warren Foster."

"I heard something about him," she said, looking at the picture. "Embezzlement accusation from his former business career, right?"

"Yes," Devin said, looking around the room to see if anyone was listening, then leaned closer. "And there's an organized effort to kill him."

Her eyes lazed across the story title. "He's investigating human trafficking on American soil?"

"Yes." Devin nodded. "Saving him could help shut down the entire trafficking business here."

Hannah looked at the picture in her hand—a teenage girl who was out there somewhere. "I have my calling. I have to find these girls. That's the most important thing right now."

Devin took a final sip of his coffee and stood. "The assassination takes place in Las Vegas. Foster won't be there for a few days yet. That still gives you time to work on yours. I'd be willing to help you with your calling if you promise to join me in Las Vegas to prevent the assassination."

Hannah considered, taking a draw of hazelnut latte.

"The key to dealing with one of these may well lie in dealing with the other," he said as he buttoned his sport coat.

"You're right," Hannah said with a nod. "The hazelnut latte is good."

Devin straightened his cuffs. "Take some time to think it over. Pray about it. Let me know if I can count on you."

Hannah set down the paper. "I'll think about it."

"Good," Devin replied. He nodded at her as he left the coffee shop.

Hannah looked at the newspaper again. She already knew she would help.

John stirred pasta into the bubbling froth, adding a pinch of salt and moving back to the book that gave him the instructions he needed. He wasn't the world's greatest cook, he'd decided, but he was capable of more than simply microwaving a can of soup.

He checked the stove clock. Only five minutes until she was supposed to arrive. Like usual, he was running behind schedule. Like getting to meetings and work, punctuality was something that he had never gotten the hang of.

With Trista he'd imagined that he could at least start dinner on time. But this wasn't proving to be true with her either.

He caught sight of his hand, wondering if he'd seen it shake. His heart rate was faster than usual. Excitement did that to him sometimes—and tonight?

It had been a year since she'd left the country. Funny—last time he was the one who bolted. Now he had an inkling of how she'd felt when he'd abandoned her. Why did they keep running from each other every time they seemed to get close?

The doorbell rang.

John froze. The last thing he needed was an uninvited guest at this moment. He walked to the door of his apartment and looked through the peephole—

Blonde hair pulled up onto her head. Faded blue jeans and a red sweater. She always looked so good in red.

"Trista," he said as he opened the door, "come in."

She stepped across the threshold, looking around. The Firstborn had insisted that he have an apartment befitting his status as Overseer, so they'd found one already furnished with spare, modern pieces. He'd managed to cover the walls in art from around the world, giving the place some hint of personality. He gestured toward the kitchen, and Trista settled onto a bar stool at the counter and scrutinized the shiny new appliances.

"This is a very nice apartment," she said with an approving nod.

"Yeah," John agreed. "Vince Sobel got me put up here when I started working as Overseer."

"It's sure a change from the huts and tents you're used to sleeping in."

John shrugged as he moved back into the kitchen. He picked up a spoon and began to stir the pasta. "This is a nice place, but"—he tapped the spoon on the edge of the pot—"sometimes I miss the backwoods of Kenya."

They looked at one another for several moments.

"Tea?" he asked.

"Um"—she shrugged—"sure."

John reached into a cabinet. "Have you ever had tea in the Middle East?"

"I've never been to the Middle East," she replied, "even though I keep meaning to go."

"I forget that," he muttered, pulling ingredients from the nearly empty cabinet. "Anyway, the tea they make there—they call it chai—is amazing, and I've been working on finding out what they do that makes it so good."

"And?" she asked.

"Cardamom," he replied, holding up a container labeled as such.

"Cardamom?"

"Makes all the difference in the world." He turned on another burner, reaching for the teakettle. John set the water to boil and turned back to Trista. "So," he asked awkwardly, "how are you?"

She was quiet for a moment. "I'm good," she said after a few seconds.

"So," he asked excitedly, "how was Belize? I haven't been there in—"

"I met someone." She interrupted flatly.

John stopped. The only sound in the kitchen for several seconds was the sound of water boiling. His body felt cold, as if all the blood in his veins had evaporated in an instant. Something seemed to catch in his throat.

"Trista, I—"

"I was having trouble dealing with the loss of my uncle Morris and everything else that led up to it. He was there for me."

John's mind raced, a feeling of nausea overcoming him. He thought he might vomit right there on the kitchen floor. He shook his head, confused. "But before you left, I thought we kind of"—he shrugged helplessly—"reconnected."

She wrapped her arms around herself. "I needed someone, and he was there."

"So, it's over?" John asked.

"He asked me to marry him," she said.

"Oh," John replied, trying to sift through it all. "What did you say?"

She looked away for a moment. "I told him that I needed to get a few things in order before I could say yes."

"And that's why you're back in New York."

She nodded.

There was a small whine from the teakettle as the water began to boil. "Why didn't you tell me sooner?" John asked.

Trista didn't make eye contact. "This morning didn't seem to be the right time," she said. "And I wanted to tell you in person."

"Like this?" John rebutted, voice raising, the tea starting to whistle.

"I didn't want you to learn like this. I was going to—"

"What?" John demanded. "You were going to send me an invitation to the reception in Belize and hope I understood?"

"Please don't react like this, John."

"Like what?" he demanded, exasperated. The teakettle screamed. John crossed his arms. "You left the country with little more than twelve hours' notice, didn't keep in contact, and then you drop *this* on me." He picked up the kettle and dropped it loudly on a vacant burner. "How am I supposed to react? How am I supposed to feel?"

He turned off the burners with a snap and braced himself against the stovetop, head hung. Trista didn't say anything. The boil of pasta began to slow, evening out to a placid calm.

"What's his name?" John looked at her, waiting for a response.

Trista fidgeted for a moment. "Holden."

"What's his first name?"

"That is his first name."

Standing up straight, John shook his head. "So," he started, looking down at his hand, "what does... *Holden* do for a living?"

"He's a banker."

"Oh." John bobbed his head sarcastically. "A banker." His heart rate quickened with every breath. "So, that's what it takes to get a woman's attention? A banker? If I were a banker would you have stayed in the country?"

"It wasn't like that, John. I left because I didn't think that it was going to be safe for me."

John clenched his fists, leaning against the counter. "I was Overseer. I could have made it safe!"

"That wasn't the only reason I left," she argued.

"Then what? What was it that made it so stinking important for you to leave the *hemisphere*?"

Her cheeks got rosy. "It was *you*, John. I had to leave because I was falling for you again—and I couldn't let that happen."

He threw his hands up, letting out a furious sigh. "Oh, but of course—because falling for me is the *worst* thing that could happen, and escaping as far away from me as possible is the only solution."

"John!" she shouted. "What was going to happen? We'd already tried it before—"

"And it was the most meaningful thing I've ever experienced," he growled.

"Really?" she demanded. "Was that before or *after* you ran away to Thailand for a year, leaving me alone, humiliated, and heartbroken?"

"That was different!"

"How?" She snarled. "How was that different?"

"I came back for you!"

"Only after I had endured all the public shame and humiliation I could stand."

John shook his head with vigor. "And when I came back—eating crow by the mouthful—you fed me to the dogs!"

"Always the martyr," Trista spat. "Can't you just once think about the consequences of what you've done?"

John folded his arms, looking away. "This is ridiculous."

Trista was quiet for a moment. "I'm not going to take this, John," she said, reaching for her purse. "You want to know why I couldn't stay around you? Because you're an unstable, show-boating, lazy child!"

"And Holden is a real man?" John spat.

"Yes," she said, walking toward the door. "He's everything you aren't—and that's why I'm not marrying someone like you!"

The door slammed as she left.

John seethed. Kicked the refrigerator. Screamed to himself, then slid down the wall, sitting on the floor.

His head tipped back, resting against the kitchen cabinets.

It was all falling apart. His life. Everything.

He was failing as Overseer. In every way that he could fail he had, including a horrifying audit by the IRS. He couldn't get the Prima to send hardly anyone to represent them or join in the unification process, and he couldn't get the Ora to come out of their offices and deal with their Domani hosts, who in turn hardly spoke to John except to nod when he told them to do something. He had failed to protect Hannah—who had almost died in that house fire. He had failed Devin—deploying him in areas where he didn't belong and wasn't called. And he was failing Trista—who just wanted a real man.

John thought he might cry for a moment, but didn't. Not because he held it back—it was just too much work. Too much trouble to go to. The whole world of the Firstborn seemed to be crashing down in a hideous mess around him. And it was his fault; he knew it.

Outside tiny snaps of rainwater started to click against the windows—the only sound in the entire apartment.

John sat on the floor of his kitchen.

Alone.

Chapter 7

DEVIN BATHURST SAT in his office. There was work to do. An assassination to study, anticipate, and prevent—and a day job to keep his commitment to. The result was late hours. Alone in the office. The only alternative was to go home, but that wasn't really—

There was a loud, solitary crack of thunder. It was fast and unexpected—he nearly missed the flash, it was so quick.

Rain rapped at the windows that covered the wall to his right. The droplets hammered away as if they wanted to get into the dark office where he worked—a single lamp glowing on his desk.

He turned back to his computer. No one was surviving the economy well, and that had seriously hurt their investing opportunities. It was a fact of life that the market had its ups and downs, but John's attempts to save them from the market crash had only incurred the wrath of the federal government. And Devin had been so busy chasing after every wild goose people in other departments didn't want to deal with that he hadn't caught the problems in time. What a mess. Devin adjusted his tie, tempted for a moment to loosen it, but he still felt compelled to remain in his business attire as long as he was in the office. He returned to his work.

He was only too aware of how everyone in the office, how all of Domani Financial, looked to him to see what was coming next—to tell them where to put the money and what to sell the investors on. But that would all be irrelevant if the IRS froze their assets. The money would be as good as gone, and business would screech to a halt. And business was a living organism, a bit like a shark. If it stopped moving forward, it would die. Who knew how long an investigation would take? Devin had always prided himself that Domani Financial had six months' worth of assets to fall back on in case of a downturn, but with the economy going bad, those funds had dwindled. And they would ultimately be irrelevant if everything was frozen.

There was a sound across the desk from him, at the door.

Devin looked up.

A grungy-looking man in dark clothes and a long coat. Lightning flashed, revealing a detailed view of stubble and stringy hair. The man said nothing.

Devin closed his laptop computer and stood. "May I help you?"

The man stepped forward, through the darkness. "My name is Angelo."

"Like Alessandro D'Angelo?"

"Founder of the original Firstborn orders," Angelo responded. "We share a name."

"Angelo," Devin said with a nod.

"It means angel," Angelo continued, moving forward slowly. "A messenger."

Devin buttoned his gray sport coat, smoothing the front. "You have a message?"

Angelo stopped just in front of the desk. "You're walking into a trap."

"You called me on my phone," Devin said. "You told me the same thing then, and I'll tell you the same thing now."

"The Thresher will be unleashed," Angelo said, eyes unblinking. "If you do this thing, greater evil will result than any temporary good you might do."

"I can't help that," Devin said unapologetically.

"You don't understand!" Angelo shouted suddenly. "None of you understand!"

"I'm not entirely certain *you* understand what you're saying." Devin leaned forward, bracing himself against his desk. "But I'll be certain to take your concerns under advisement."

Angelo seemed to crumple, hands twitching in some kind

of repetitive tick as he pulled at his long hair. "I see it coming," he said frantically, not looking at Devin. "I've felt it happening. I've watched it happen."

Devin stood, reaching for his phone. "Do you require assistance, sir?"

Angelo shrieked to himself.

"Do you require a doctor?"

"You can't do it," Angelo said again, continuing to pull at his hair, delivering a blow to his own forehead.

"Do you want me to walk you to the elevator?" Devin asked, patience getting thin.

Angelo began muttering to himself under his breath, none of the words audible or coherent.

Devin looked the man over. He was crazy. Completely insane. A raving lunatic.

He snapped his phone open and walked toward Angelo. "You need help, Mr. Angelo. I'm going to make a phone call to an institution I think can help you."

Devin approached, setting a hand on Angelo's elbow—the only legal place to touch a person in an unsolicited manner—and moved to lead him toward the door.

Angelo stopped muttering and twitching. He stood up straight, facing Devin, looking him in the eye—noses mere inches apart. "I know you feel an obligation to help, Mr. Bathurst," he said with a calm voice, suddenly and eerily lucid. "But I simply cannot allow that."

Devin Bathurst looked the man back in the eye, neither blinking. They seemed to size each other up for a moment, then Devin spoke. "I'm sorry, sir, but I'm afraid that I can't let this go."

Angelo's eyes remained fixed on Devin. Hawkish and predatory. Steady and calm. "Mr. Bathurst," he said again, "I cannot allow that to happen. And Hannah cannot be allowed to help."

Devin studied the other man for a moment. "I think that it's time for you to go."

Angelo's hand was on Devin's chest, as if by magic. A rough shove, and Devin felt the small of his back hit his desk, his body tipping backward.

"I cannot allow you to continue with your plan!" Angelo barked.

"Take your hand off me," Devin replied, unflappably.

Angelo shoved again, slamming Devin's shoulder blades into the desktop. "*I cannot allow it!*" Angelo shouted, ravenous. The man's hands moved to Devin's collar, grabbing fistfuls of shirt. "Do you hear me?"

Devin took a deep breath, looked Angelo in the eye, then jammed his fingertips into Angelo's side—watching as he backed from the desk, sucking for air. Devin stood, facing Angelo, and then saw a shift in the other man's demeanor.

Angelo came at him—fast and ruthless.

They slammed into the desk—papers scattering, a cup of pens clattering. Grappled, spun, hit the bookshelf—a loud thud. Their bodies clawed at one another as they hit the shelf again and again—books raining down in an avalanche.

Angelo—attacking with savage blows, arms swinging wide. Devin holding his arms close, trying to protect his sides from the onslaught.

Devin took a punch to the face. He saw stars. Took a blow to the stomach—suddenly nauseous, pain running up his sides like a zipper.

They spun again as Devin grabbed a fistful of long hair, tugging hard—swinging for Angelo's throat.

Angelo blocked, knocking away a series of perfectly executed moves—saw an opening—kicked Devin in the back of the knee.

Devin hit the floor, landing on his knee. Felt an arm reach

across his chest and grabbed on—performing an expert throw, sending Angelo tumbling onto his back.

Vicious blows traded from one to another as Devin came in fast. Punches turning to grappling as they tumbled across the office floor, grabbing for throat, gouging at eyes, delivering elbows and punches.

They hit the side of the desk. Papers falling. A picture toppling—glass cracking as the frame hit the floor.

Devin lost control—not certain what had happened in that moment. Both sitting—sides pressed against the desk. Angelo was behind him—arm around Devin's throat, squeezing tight. Vision blurring. A blood choke.

Devin coughed. Losing strength. Punching over his shoulder directly into Angelo's face, causing him to flinch. Devin capitalized, lifting to his feet—Angelo on his back—flung his back into the tall windows.

Lightning. Glass crashing.

Angelo shoved off the glass, pushing forward, trying to send Devin face-first into the floor.

Devin captured the momentum—spinning all the way around—Angelo slamming into the glass again.

Glass flexing in expanding cracked circles.

Devin broke free—pressing the advantage—throwing punches. Shoved back with precision—slamming into the desk. Back hitting the desktop. Breaking free of Angelo. Rolling away—off the other side.

A moment of hope—looking for a way to make the most of—

Angelo was charging him—shoulder slamming hard—ramming Devin into the bookshelf again. More volumes tumbling—hitting the floor in a flapping mess.

A blow to the side. Devin sucked air, unable to breathe.

Angelo reached for the desktop—grabbed the lamp. Devin saw it coming in full swing—raising his arm to protect the side of his head—pain shooting through his forearm in a slicing pulse—the lamp striking hard. Devin hit the floor—arm trying to block the incoming swings.

The lamp hit him—over and over again.

Pain—in waves.

He kicked at Angelo's leg—fighting his way to his feet—vision going blurry. Another impact.

Devin grabbed at Angelo—trying to hold his arms.

They hit the bookshelf again—books dumping out by shelffulls—the shelf tipping forward. Angelo pulling away. Devin tried to run.

Too late.

The falling case came slamming down.

Devin's world went dark.

Hannah stepped into her apartment on the first floor, moving out of the rain. Light glowed between the drapes, and thunder rumbled outside.

She walked to a lamp, firmly ensconced on the wall, and clicked it on. The room filled with light.

She hugged her arms and tried not to feel cold as she looked around the room. Her things were still here—her books on the coffee table. Textbooks. History. Science. English. None of them had been opened. She was two weeks behind on most of her work, and there was no way to explain it to her professors. Not really. There was no way to explain that she had been given a vision—by *God*—of teenage girls being lured into…

Hannah shook from head to toe, trying not to think about it.

Life was too complicated for any one person these days—at least hers was. She had her college fund for her education, but the majority of her grandfather's estate was tied up in the ranch—property she didn't dare sell until the real estate market recovered. And that meant she had next to nothing to live off of.

The TV came on with a fuzzy snap, and she scanned through the channels. She really should have been studying—she knew that—but didn't feel like it. Not after the day she'd had.

There must have been three dozen channels, but they were all music videos from bands she'd never heard of, or infomercials. She stopped on a movie. A romantic comedy with some guy standing in the rain, declaring his love in the most adorably awkward way possible. Hannah watched for a moment, letting a hungry feeling fill her as she watched the romance unfold.

Hannah snapped the television off. Devin Bathurst had warned her about what would happen to her life. Isolation. Overwork. She had thought she could avoid it—maybe. But the needs were so great. How could she not respond?

She sat on the arm of the sofa for a moment, then moved to the bathroom. A shower was calling to her—a chance to wash the day away and feel like a real person again.

Devin existed out of space and time for a moment—the world blurry. He blinked. Focused. Let his mind work through where it was.

He let his body feel itself and was once again aware of his physicality.

His body was on the floor. He hurt.

Serious physical trauma? No. But he had been knocked unconscious. A dangerous occurrence that worried him. Devin looked around.

He was on the floor of his office—rain falling just beyond the glass window—the sound chopping loudly through an empty section the shape of California that had broken free from the spider-webbed glass. There was water on the floor. Books everywhere. A lamp with a broken lightbulb nearby.

He was alone in the dim room.

Something pinched the lower half of Devin's body, and he

looked. The bookshelf pinned his legs to the floor.

He strained for a moment, pushed against the heavy case, pulled his body free. Devin stood, touching his head—blood.

Angelo had beaten him hard. What was it that he had wanted anyway? To keep from protecting the senator? To not help Hannah?

Devin felt sudden concern.

—Hannah—

The faucet came on with a twist, and hot, steaming water tumbled down the drain. There was a sound from the next room, and she paused, straining to hear. She turned off the faucet and listened.

The room was silent for a moment—then her phone rang.

She stepped into the room—and stopped.

Angelo stood in the middle of the room. "I need to talk to you," he said with a strange intensity.

The phone, tossed on the sofa, rang again. Hannah turned her eyes to the phone. "I should answer that," she said timidly.

Angelo nodded.

Hannah reached out, just past Angelo, and picked up the phone. "Hello?"

"Miss Rice."

The voice was unmistakable—*Devin Bathurst*. "Yes?"

"I was just attacked by the man named Angelo. He came to the office demanding that I not pursue my calling."

Hannah eyed Angelo, his face eerily stoic. "What happened?"

"He subdued me." There was a momentary pause. "He beat me unconscious."

Hannah's heart raced. Devin was the most physically powerful and skilled man she had ever known. If Angelo had subdued him...

"You need to be careful. I think he may come for you too."

Angelo continued to watch her.

"I'm sorry," Hannah said, watching Angelo watch her, eyes never breaking, "now isn't a good time to talk. Someone is here."

There was a crackle of static across the phone line.

"Angelo? Is Angelo there?"

Hannah blinked. "Yes."

"Hang on, Hannah. I'm already on my way."

The car smashed through the curtain of splashing water, wiper blades swinging madly.

Devin steered the car with one hand, dialing his cell phone with the other. It rang a moment, then connected.

"Hello?"

"John Temple, this is Bathurst."

"Devin, I—"

"What do you know about Angelo?"

"Nothing, really. He helped Hannah after—"

"He came to my office," Devin reported quickly. "Demanded that I not pursue the Warren Foster issue. There was an altercation, and I was subdued temporarily."

"Angelo?"

"Yes," Devin continued, spouting rapid-fire facts. "He was violent and nearly incoherent at moments, followed by bouts of undeniable lucidity."

"He attacked you?" John asked.

"Yes."

"Where is he now?"

"He's with Hannah in her apartment," Devin announced, shifting sharply as he cornered at a rainy intersection. "I need you to get to there ASAP! I'm on my way now, but I'm going to need help."

"Devin, I—"

"He's dangerous, John. Very dangerous. We have to stop him now."

Devin closed his phone.

Hannah stood in front of Angelo, waiting for him to talk.

"How did you get in here?" she asked, surprised that her curiosity was so much more overpowering than her fear.

"I'm quiet," Angelo said emotionlessly, and left it at that.

"What did you need to talk about?" Hannah asked.

He blinked, then took a step forward. "I understand that you and Devin Bathurst plan to prevent the assassination of Senator Warren Foster."

Hannah considered her options. The only thing she could think of was to keep him talking. "We had discussed it," she stalled, "but there is something I need to do also."

"Don't do it," he insisted, tone almost violent.

"But they aren't the same—"

"He'll listen to you," he said, face intense, taking another step. "And he's walking into a trap, Hannah Rice, a trap set by the Thresher. It's a trap that you cannot allow Devin Bathurst and the Firstborn to fall into."

Hannah nodded slowly. It was like petting a rabid dog. Scruffy, greasy, and scary. With sympathetic eyes and bared teeth. In need of tenderness, but only a moment away from biting you. "We should talk," she said with a nurturing tone. She sat on the couch slowly. "I'm afraid that I don't understand, and I need you to explain it to me. Can you tell me more about the Thresher?"

Angelo remained standing, dark stringy hair hanging across the sides of his face like drawing curtains—features in shadow. "For every good that exists," he began, voice low, "there will arise an evil to crush it, to corrupt it, and to turn it into its own form of evil. In the case of the Firstborn, there is the Thresher."

Hannah nodded, letting him know that she heard him. "And the Thresher is a demon?"

"A simple term," he replied without hesitation. "A rancid, festering uncleanliness that will separate the Firstborn one from another—and from the source of their sight."

"God?" she asked. "The Thresher will separate the Firstborn from God?"

"Simple terms, still." His head bowed. "The Thresher will destroy the Firstborn—and they will no longer be a restrainer."

Hannah shook her head in confusion. "I still don't understand," she said softly, patting a place on the couch next to her. "You need to help me understand. What do the Firstborn restrain?"

Something changed. Angelo no longer seemed present—his hands began to wring, then run through his hair. "There aren't words to say what I've seen—the things I've seen. There aren't..." He stopped and made a strange, pained noise. "Do you know what evil looks like and feels like? What it does to the world?"

"Angelo, I need you to go back—start from the beginning."

"It smells like rotting flesh and sounds like screaming children—and it's rising." He got on his knees in front of her, eyes frantic. "Don't let it in. You can't let it in."

"OK," she said with a nod, looking into his pained expression.

"Don't save them. Any of them. It's a trap. The jaws are open, and they're waiting for you."

Hannah searched his face—his genuine fear reaching out at her. He grabbed her hands.

"Do you see?"

Hannah felt his touch, his hands leathery and rough. And then she felt it.

Angelo in the rain—lying on church steps. Looking up at the sky—lightning flashing across his soaked body.

He shook his head. "I remember the steps. I remember the rain."

"Angelo," she asked, "who are you?"

He bowed his head. "I don't know. All I see are visions. I don't exist anymore."

Hannah watched him, her heart breaking. She put a hand on his head, running her hand across it tenderly, wondering how long it would be before Devin arrived to—

His head snapped up, eyes looking deep into her own—suddenly lucid. "You're trying to trap me."

"No, Angelo," she said, sympathetically. "I—"

He stood fast, looming over her. "You're trying to keep me here so that Devin Bathurst can arrive."

"Angelo, listen to—"

"No!" He shoved away from her. "You haven't heard a thing I've said. I tried to warn you, but you still plan to do it. You are going to destroy it all!"

Hannah began to rise. "Angelo, you have to listen to what I'm—"

He planted a palm on her shoulder, shoving her back. "No." He snarled, once again feral and wild. "You tried to trick me. You lied to me. You tried to trap me!"

She tried to struggle, but he shoved her back onto the sofa. "*No!*" he screamed, face inhuman with anger and ferocity. "I tried to warn you, but you're going to do it anyway. You're going to destroy us all!"

"Angelo!" she pleaded, shoving a hand in his face, trying to break free.

"You didn't listen. You didn't listen, and now—"

The door to the apartment came crashing open. They looked in unison—Devin, holding a pistol, stance wide, gun lifted, rain tumbling down in the background.

"Let her go," Devin demanded unflinchingly.

Angelo stopped where he was, face turning slowly back to

Hannah. He looked her over for a moment. She studied his face, then looked back at Devin.

Angelo's move was sudden and unexpected. He ripped her violently to her feet, spinning her fast, using her as a human shield between himself and Devin. "Leave," Angelo insisted, as if it were a perfectly reasonable request. "Turn around and leave—now."

Devin straightened his arm—eye, gun barrel, and trigger finger in a perfectly stacked group, the weapon outstretched. "I will kill you if I have to," Devin replied with equal calm and normalcy.

Hannah felt her instincts start to take over—the urge to panic. To let her nerves and her fears overtake her—to stifle her. To *forget* the importance. Her body shuddered, threatening to let out a scream or an outburst of tears.

She breathed.

Remember, she thought, trying to remind herself of everything she had learned—that others were counting on her.

Devin—harsh-eyed and determined—stood in the threshold, unmoving.

Rain pummeled the ground just past the door.

She felt Angelo's body relax, hands still holding firm. He addressed Devin. "Do you believe that I can kill her with my hands?" he asked.

Devin remained stationary for a moment—then lowered the pistol. "I understand what you are capable of," Devin said with little more than a blink.

Hannah caught Angelo's nod from the corner of her eye. "Good," Angelo said. "Put the gun on the table."

Devin stepped forward.

"Slowly," Angelo added.

Devin set the gun on the table and backed away, hands held high.

Despite herself, Hannah began to panic.

Angelo watched as Devin put down the firearm—and the world began to slow like it sometimes did. There was no past or present or future. The world seemed strangely silent. Strangely distant. Ethereal. As if it were all happening to someone else.

There was that look in his eyes—the man with black skin. What was his name again? The one who had had the gun. He had that look he had before—the look people gave him before they told him he was being irrational.

They were the irrational ones—the way they would watch him and talk with him like a reasonable human being, and then suddenly get confused and scared.

It was as if they had all slowed down—stopped thinking or speaking or living. The world was so far away, and no matter what he said or thought or tried, they would never respond.

Hair brushed aside.

Whose hair?

The girl in his arms. How had she gotten…?

Oh, yes. Her. She was important. So very important.

Devin—was that his name?—seemed to disappear as a physical form until he was just eyes. Dark, intense eyes that stared.

Angelo had to leave. Had to go.

He was at the doorway. How had he gotten there?

In the rain—cold and wet. Looking out at a car pulling up.

A man stepped from the vehicle. The man who had the power to prevent evil. Blondish hair—a raggedy and impetuous man.

The Overseer.

A man named John Temple.

Would this man listen to reason? Would this be the man who would stop the girl and the black man—to tell them to let go of their endeavors—to hold back the evil?

He looked John Temple in the eyes. Even at this distance he

could see it. The resolve—to save the lives of a few at the cost of so much more.

Angelo didn't know what happened next. The girl was no longer in his arms. He was running.

John lifted his hand, holding some kind of device. It discharged like a pistol, curling wires zipping through the air and hitting his skin. Then he heard a clacking sound, and suddenly jolts of electricity coursed through him, jerking his body.

A Taser of some kind. They had him.

The dream overtook him. The abstract world consumed him. And he slipped from consciousness.

Chapter 8

WHY DID YOU attack my people?" John Temple demanded, trying to channel as much of Devin Bathurst as he could find inside himself.

Angelo sat quietly in his chair in the darkened office, hands zip-tied. "They're walking into a trap."

"And what if you're wrong?" John replied curtly.

"I'm not wrong. You must believe me when I say—"

"I don't believe you," John retorted quickly. "You attacked Devin Bathurst, terrorized Hannah Rice, and you're going to account for your actions."

Angelo looked away for a moment, then lifted his head. "You don't seem to understand. I'm here to help the Firstborn. I am at your service," he said somberly, dipping his head, "Overseer."

John crossed his arms—startled by the devotion but trying to stay focused. "If you're at my service, then why don't you help us stop the assassination?"

"That," Angelo said, shaking his head, "is the one thing I cannot do."

"Fine." John nodded, turning toward the door.

"Anything else," Angelo added, "anything at all. I am at the Overseer's disposal."

John held at the door for a moment, hand resting on handle. Something compelled him to just keep going—to leave the room.

Angelo must have sensed the hesitation. "I know all about Trista Brightling."

John took a long breath, trying to feel Angelo in the moment, but all that seemed to radiate off of him was a kind of garbled noise. Like television static in the mind.

John considered staying, wanting to stay. Wanting to hear what Angelo had to say, but something deep inside told him to escape.

"I know everything," Angelo continued. "I—"

John opened the door and stepped into the hall and didn't hear any more.

Vincent Sobel walked through the office toward the back room as John Temple was stepping out of the door. The night watchman was standing guard.

"What's going on?" Vince asked brusquely. "Why did you call me in?"

John inclined his head toward the door as he explained. "There's a man in there, Angelo, says he's a Firstborn, but he sees past, present, *and* future. He helped save Hannah from the house fire. But tonight he attacked Devin and threatened Hannah, trying to keep them from fulfilling an assignment. The confrontation turned violent, and I was called in by Devin. Angelo was subdued with a Taser gun."

Vince grimaced. "This guy beat the snot out of Devin Bathurst. *Devin*—tough as nails—*Bathurst*, and you brought him here? To the home office? That wasn't wise, John."

"I know," John said, shaking his head in disgust. "I'm just a little distracted, that's all."

"Distracted?" Vince said, taking a seat next to John. "Distracted by what?"

John was quiet for a moment, staring out the window—like he always did when someone brought up something serious. He was quiet for a moment before he closed his eyes and hung his head. "Trista is getting engaged to someone else."

Grow up, Vince thought. *You've got a homicidal maniac on your hands, and you're worried about a woman?* "Mmm . . ." Vince nodded sympathetically. "John, it's time to let her go."

John didn't move. "I know, I just—"

"No." Vince shook his head. "There's no 'just.' She's moved on with her life. It's time for you to do the same."

"I just—"

Trista is so out of your league, you idiot, Vince thought, but he reached out a sympathetic hand, putting it on John's arm. "John," he said as tenderly as he could, "I'm worried about your ability to be Overseer right now."

"What?" John said, head lifting suddenly.

Vince nodded. "You're letting Trista distract you from God and your ability to make sound choices as leader of the Firstborn. Don't you see that?"

"Do you really think…"

Vince stood, buttoning his suit jacket. "Yes, I do. You've let your obsession with Trista last too long. You don't need any more distractions. It's time to accept that it's hurting you, your work, and ultimately the Firstborn."

John stared at him for a moment. "Is it really that bad?"

"John, you're acting pathetic," Vince said with a loving nod and unbroken eye contact. John looked away. "Maybe it's time to take a break. Reconnect with your faith and move on."

John said nothing.

"Just think about it," Vince added. "For now, let me talk to this Angelo. See if I can gain his trust. Good cop, bad cop, you know." He winked.

"OK," John mumbled.

Vince smiled and stepped out of the room.

John walked to the conference room windows and looked down at the street far below. He rested his forehead against the glass and closed his eyes.

Vince was right. He'd always been right. His obsession with Trista was pathetic. It was so un-Christian to make a woman that much of a priority in his life. Right?

John banged his head against the glass, smacking it with his palms. He cursed loudly, angry at himself for how weak and feeble he'd let a woman make him.

A woman.

He let loose with a vicious string of profanity, grabbing a rolling chair and flinging it across the room. The chair tumbled to a stop.

John slid to the floor and sobbed.

Vince Sobel walked through the hall, past the night guard posted at the door. Nodding, he indicated that it was OK to enter.

The door shut behind him, and he paused—the room going dark. He looked at the man named Angelo. The man sat in a chair. Calm.

Vince pulled up another chair and sat in front of the other man. "It's Angelo, right?"

A set of eyes lifted from the obscurity of darkness. Dark, intense eyes.

"I am who you say I am," he said softly and with resolve.

Vince adjusted in his chair, suddenly unsettled by this man. "I hear you wanted to talk to Devin Bathurst," Vince said with a smile. He leaned, elbows on knees, trying to be friendly. "I hear it…didn't go so well."

Angelo didn't blink.

"So," Vince said with another smile, "tell me about yourself, Angelo."

Angelo said nothing. He stared with dark eyes through the dark room, watching Vincent.

"Listen," Vince continued, still smiling, "this will all go a lot smoother if—"

"You can't let them proceed," Angelo interrupted, face stern.

Vince frowned. "I'm sorry?"

"Devin Bathurst plans to save the politician from being killed. It's a trap. You can't let him."

Confusion was the only thing that Vince felt for several seconds, staring at the other man. He laughed, suddenly and awkwardly, reaching into his pocket for a slip of paper and a pen. "Let me make a note of this," he said, regaining his composure, trying to make Angelo feel like he was being taken seriously. "I need you to explain to me *exactly* what is going to happen."

Angelo blinked. "You don't believe me."

"Of course I—"

"I can feel your thoughts," Angelo said.

"Uh...," Vince stammered, trying to find a way to backpedal.

"You don't believe that I can see the future," Angelo continued, "or the past."

Vince smiled encouragingly. "I hear that you see all three?"

Angelo's head dipped slowly in a nod.

"Like Alessandro D'Angelo?" Vince asked.

"Founder of the Firstborn orders."

Vince shook his head, suddenly concerned, feeling outmatched. "Is there any chance that you're wrong about Devin Bathurst and everything having to do with—"

"I know about your wife," Angelo said with eerie calm.

Vince's body went cold, down to his core. "What do you know?" he said, hesitant, scared, and trembling.

"The man that she met."

Anger bubbled up in Vince. "What did she tell you?"

"Linda? We've never met."

"Then how did you...?"

"You had been married eight years when Linda met him. She told you she had only been seeing him for six months, but it had been more than a year."

"What?" Vince said, feeling all the old feelings—black and poisonous—start to well up in him.

"You say that you've forgiven her. You told her that. And the counselor that. Even your friends—and the pastor you spoke to. But you haven't."

Vince felt any semblance of a smile evaporate. Anger—no,

rage—took over. "That's not true." He launched to his feet, trying to tower over Angelo. "I love my wife, and I forgave her for what she did."

Angelo remained seated and calm. "Do you believe that I see things yet?"

"You could have found out about my wife through a lot of different ways. You're just making up the rest!"

Angelo's eyes became sad for a moment. "I know what you never told the counselor. What you've never told anyone."

Vince paused, watching the calm man. "What do you think you know?"

"That sometimes, when you think about it, you wonder if she would cry if you jumped from the roof of the office building where you work..."

Vince stared.

"...and that sometimes, when you can't take it anymore, you wonder what it would be like to take the letter opener from the top drawer in your study and to stab her with it."

The anger took Vincent over, face burning. He sat, staring at Angelo, tears forming at the edges of his eyes. "I would *never* do that!"

"No." Angelo shook his head. "You don't trust your wife anymore—but you wouldn't ever hurt her. But you and I both know that your imagination has gotten away from you from time to time."

Vince brushed a tear and cleared his demeanor—instantly done crying. "What are you trying to do?"

"I'm trying to show you that I see what is coming—and that Devin Bathurst must be stopped."

Vincent looked away, unable to bear this anymore. "I just—"

"She told you it was a man from work," Angelo added, hesitantly. "That you didn't know him."

Vince turned back to Angelo and glared, gaze intense, face trembling. "It was our pastor, wasn't it?"

Angelo nodded slowly. "Do you believe me now?"

Vincent shook all over. "Tell me everything you know about the future."

Devin was in John Temple's office, Hannah inspecting a cut on his forehead from his fight with Angelo, when John walked in, red-eyed and obviously upset.

"I can't believe this Angelo guy," John huffed, shutting the door behind him before plopping into an office chair. "He doesn't make any sense at all. Why would he warn anyone not to follow after their calling as Firstborn?"

Hannah turned from her work on Devin's forehead and moved to where John was, taking a seat beside him. "I don't know. But something about this assassination attempt has him seriously spooked."

Devin remained at his desk, trying for several seconds to remember what Angelo had said to him before their fight. "He says that it's a trap. He believes that it's somehow connected with the Thresher."

Hannah shook her head, confused. "I thought it was the Thresher that caused Blake Jackson to do the things that he did."

"But," John argued, "he did those things out of a *fear* of the Thresher. That hysteria was *his* trap."

Devin tapped his index finger on his desktop for several seconds. "If it's a threat having to do with the Thresher, then maybe we should pay a little more attention."

"I don't know," John said. "I went to the archives and talked to Jerry Kirkland, our historian."

"We have a historian?" Hannah asked.

"Yeah," John said. "Jerry. He's Prima, like you. He's been collecting and archiving all the known history on the Firstborn—

and he says there have been Thresher scares from our Firstborn ancestors for . . . *centuries*."

"And?" Devin honestly wondered if John might have a point this time.

"And," John continued, "there's evidence that the *threat* of the Thresher has done more to divide and destroy the Firstborn than something dark and demonic actually acting upon us."

Hannah frowned. "Are you saying that the Thresher doesn't exist?"

"No," John mused, leaning forward, elbows resting on his knees. "But he said that the tools of the Thresher are fear, pride, and love of power." He made a pensive face. "Are we actually considering letting this all go because of fear?"

"Or," Devin offered, thinking as he spoke, "are we motivated by pride?"

The room was silent for a moment as they each turned to their own introspection.

Hannah broke the silence. "I guess there's only one thing we can do."

Devin looked down at his hand on the desktop, examining its stillness for a moment. He knew what she meant. And he knew she was right. But it seemed so foreign—to let his guard down. To allow himself to experience that kind of unabashed spiritual nudity.

John and Hannah were already kneeling in the center of the office.

Something like embarrassment or shame tried to keep Devin in his seat. Or, he corrected himself, fear.

Devin stood and walked toward the center of the office. Then he knelt with John and Hannah, completing their circle.

They were totally quiet for a moment—only the barely audible sounds of their collective breathing. Then Devin drew a long breath of his own—

—and let it out.

"Our Father, who art in heaven," he began.

"Hallowed be Thy name," they said in unison. "Thy kingdom come, Thy will be done, on Earth as it is in heaven."

Devin could feel it beginning. Like the tiny murmurings of an infant's heartbeat, building with the recitation of each phrase. Like a thick rumble rising from the earth. Like the heavens splitting. The sensation grew and grew.

"For Thine," they said together, heads bowed, eyes closed, "is the kingdom, and the power, and the glory…"

They went silent.

Devin spoke the last word. Softly. Sincerely.

"…forever."

There was a moment of stillness.

Then it happened. Not images, or sounds, or instincts. Simply a peace.

—an undeniable, unexplainable, completely intangible knowledge—individually derived, communally shared—that this was what they had been called to. That stopping the assassination, finding the girls, fighting the evil, was the only thing that mattered.

They spoke together: "Amen."

John Temple walked into the hall in time to see Vince exiting the room at the far end. John stopped, looking Vince over. He looked like death warmed over—vacant and confused. John approached. "Vince, are you OK?"

Vincent grabbed him by the arm, suddenly aware. He pulled John a few feet away, into an alcove. "You have to listen to him," Vincent declared, making intense eye contact.

"OK." John nodded, confused.

Vince looked like he'd seen a ghost—was a ghost. "He knows

things, John. Things he can't. Shouldn't." Vince looked down, fidgeting. "Stuff I've *never* shared."

"Like what?"

Vince's face snapped upward again. "Things I would *never* share. Things that no one would ever tell me. He knows what he's talking about, John."

John shook his head. "We have to do the best we can—"

A rough hand grabbed John's arm, squeezing hard—eyes blazing. "He says to let the assassination thing go—so we do it. Do you understand?"

A frown began to form on John's face. "Devin and Hannah were called to these things. Not by you and me, but by God. We've prayed about it—and I can say without a doubt that this has to be done."

"No," Vince declared, firm, angry, and unmoving. "You *will not* do that. It's a trap. It has Angelo scared—and that means something."

John took a step back. "Vince, you do remember that I'm Overseer, right? You don't tell me what to do."

Vince looked around, his perfectly sculpted hair shaking free, dangling across his forehead. "John, call them off. You have to. There's no choice."

John Temple cleared his throat. "Vincent, I said it before, and I'm going to say it again"—his voice got quiet but startlingly firm—"I'm not going to tell either Hannah or Devin to back off, and I really don't care what you think about this, because I'm Overseer, and I've spoken." John tried to regain his composure and stepped back—attempting to seem less authoritarian.

Vincent straightened his hair and buttoned his jacket. He looked John in the eye. "Then maybe you shouldn't be Overseer anymore." He walked away.

John stood for a moment at a loss. Then he pushed through

the door of the office where they'd taken Angelo. The night guard was on the floor, knocked out.

Angelo was gone.

Chapter 9

TRISTA STOOD AT the mirror, patting makeup onto the dark circles under her eyes. She'd slept badly after the fiasco with John last night. So bit by bit—with eyeliner, shadow, mascara, blush, and lipstick—she carefully reconstructed her professional face. She would need every bit of cover she could find today, in case she ran into John again at the Firstborn's office.

Outside the sun was lifting behind the Manhattan skyline. A seemingly endless labyrinth of glass and steel canyons. Cold and lonely, a metropolitan jungle filled with people who treated one another as props and obstacles. A forest of human souls that couldn't be seen through the crowded trees of people.

Trista's phone beeped electronically, the red light on its exterior flashing. She moved toward the hotel coffee table and scooped up the phone, answering. "Trista Brightling," she said efficiently.

"Trista," a voice said enthusiastically. "Vince Sobel here. Meeting today. Conference room—noon."

Trista thought for a moment. "Noon? That's the lunch hour."

"Yeah," Vince said slowly, as if trying to think through his next sentence as carefully as possible. "It's a time that everyone else is available and"—another pause—"well... John's out of the office at that time, and we need to talk about some stuff."

Trista felt a sharp sensation of anger stab at her at the mention of John's name. "What do you plan on discussing?"

"Just some concerns for him on a personal level—and some concerns about his work as Overseer too. We think you would have some... insight that might be helpful to everyone else there. Can I count on you being there?"

"Uh." Trista felt her anger blur with a dozen other feelings and was suddenly very confused. "I—yes. I'll be there."

"Fantastic," Vince said with gusto. "And... uh... you wouldn't mind keeping your knowledge about this meeting...*discreet*, would you?"

She knew what he meant. "I won't tell John," she said with a nod, then closed her phone.

Hannah pressed the suburban doorbell and waited. She hugged her arms, feeling the latent chill that still remained from the last few days of rain.

For a moment she tried to talk herself out of it, but it was too late. She'd already pressed the bell. And she had to see for herself. She had to see if Angelo was—

The door opened. "Yes?" The woman who answered was middle-aged and well kept but obviously not looking her best. "Can I help you?"

Hannah was hesitant. "Are you Kimberly's mother?"

The woman's face got serious. "Who are you?"

There was no good answer. Nothing that Hannah could think of to adequately describe who she was or what she was doing here. "I...I'm someone who heard about your daughter, that she hadn't been home. I was wondering if there was anything I could do to help?"

The woman looked at her for several moments, then motioned her into the house.

Five minutes later Hannah was sitting in the living room with a cup of hot tea, listening to the mother—a woman named Peg—talk about her girl named Kimberly.

"She's been gone over two days," Peg said, shaking her head, visibly fighting back tears.

Hannah clasped the boiling hot mug in her hands. "Do you have a picture of your daughter?"

Peg stood, walking to the fireplace. "This is the newest picture we have. It's about six months old—so it looks a lot like her." Peg passed off the frame. "She cut her hair a little since then, and the blonde highlights grew out, but that's her."

Hannah looked at the girl in the picture. She was undeniably pretty and was probably very popular. The kind of girl who would eventually be prom queen. "When was the last time you saw her?"

"She said she was staying at a friend's house Saturday night—but when I called Sunday afternoon, her friend said she'd not planned anything with Kimberly." She shook her head. "After I grilled her, she finally admitted that Kimberly had been sneaking out to college parties almost every weekend."

Hannah tried to make eye contact, her face sympathetic. "But this time she didn't come back?"

Peg began to cry. "Kimberly is our only child, and maybe we spoiled her too much." The woman wiped away tears. "I don't know what we're going to do."

"You did call the police, right?"

Hannah held her breath. *Say it*, she thought. *Tell me that it's all under control. That someone else has taken care of the problem. That I can go.*

"They took a report and put out an alert," Peg said, "but nothing has turned up so far. I've heard that the first forty-eight hours are the most crucial in finding a missing child, and we're past that! I know the police are swamped, but..." She looked up at Hannah. "And how did you find out about her?"

Hannah looked down at her tea, the soaked teabag floating in the ever-darkening brew. She bit her lip and looked up. "I'm on staff with a local organization that likes to help with these kinds of things. I'm not really able to go into detail, but we're a nonprofit organization that wants to do what we can to help, and I've been assigned to your daughter."

Peg shook her head. "Is there anything that you can do?"

Sadness was the only thing Hannah felt on her face. "This

could be very difficult. I can't make any guarantees about how this will turn out."

Peg was on her feet in moments. "Let me tell you about my daughter." She was at the fireplace again, pulling down pictures, stuffing them in her arms. She brought them back, spreading them out on the coffee table. "This was her when she was six. Her birthday party—it was a princess party with all her friends. And this"—Peg pointed to another—"this was when we brought her home from the hospital as a baby. That's her daddy. He never thought he wanted children until we had Kimberly. He held her in his arms, and she's been daddy's little girl ever since."

Hannah didn't know what to say. "Ma'am, I..."

Peg sat down, staring painfully into Hannah's face. "She just turned sixteen years old. She's my baby. But she's out there—somewhere. And she could be in very serious trouble."

Hannah looked the woman in the eyes, studying her face and searching for some way to tell her that her daughter was OK. But she remembered what she had seen in the house before it had burned down. The horrible things that had been done to other girls before. Drugs, violence, and rape. Girls—children—being sold like chattel. But there was no comfort she could offer this woman.

She took Peg by the hands, looking her in the eye. "I promise you, I will do everything in my power to help find your daughter—no matter what."

John was in his office drinking his fourth cup of coffee when his phone rang. He set down his cup and lifted the receiver. "Hello, this is John."

The call sounded garbled with sounds of wind ripping at the other end. "John?" Hannah said through the cacophony.

He leaned forward. "Hannah, where are you? I think we have a bad connection."

"I'm at a pay phone," she said. "Listen, John, I need to discuss something with you."

"What is it?"

"I've started my search for the girls. I wanted you to know that. I met one of their mothers. I didn't mean to go behind anyone's back, but I had to talk to her for myself."

John leaned against his desk with one arm, not certain what to say. Proud of her initiative yet afraid for how things might turn out. "I don't like you working on this on your own. I'm sending someone to back you up."

A long silence. "I can do this without help."

"No," John insisted. "I'm sending Devin, and that's final."

Her attitude seemed to shift instantly. "You're sending Devin?"

"Yes. I wouldn't send anyone else."

"OK," she replied.

"Where are you?"

"I'm near the house that burned down, trying to see if I can pick up on any kind of lead." She gave him the address.

"OK," he said, trying to consider everything, the way a leader should. "Stay there. I'll send Devin as soon as I can."

"Thank you, John. I—"

The pay phone cut off—out of money.

John dialed his phone. It rang for a moment, then the other end picked up.

"This is Bathurst."

"Devin," he said, running a hand through his hair, "Hannah needs your help."

Trista stepped into the conference room. There might have been twenty people in the room, all finding seats. She too found a chair. There were a few men working on the lines that attached to the conference phones in the middle of the table. Someone said something about needing to get a dial tone, and then she heard one buzz loudly from the device.

She presumed that the telephone line was for the Prima who weren't there. She'd been told about how John had set up offices in Domani Financial for the Prima and the Ora to have representatives there full-time. The Ora had taken the offer but apparently wouldn't open their office doors long enough to talk to anyone, and the Prima had simply declined the offer completely—except for an archivist named Jerry who was nowhere to be seen.

Vincent Sobel checked his watch at the front of the room. He spotted Trista and gave her a nod—acknowledging her presence.

The milling dissipated as the twenty or so people found their seats. Laptops opened, and fingers tapped at keyboards. Trista felt out of place without hers.

"Everybody here?" Vince asked, scanning the room.

A reply in the form of nods. Several voices sounded off their presence via the conference phones.

"Everyone know why we're here today?"

More nods.

Vince leaned against the back of the chair, face sullen. "We need to talk about John."

Nods and approving noises.

"Just to recap," Vince said, clasping his hands, "John hasn't listened to any counsel from anyone. He's not doing well as Overseer, and now we're being investigated by the SEC." He cleared his throat and looked gravely at his audience. "And I was just informed that the IRS is officially auditing us and that all our funds are going to be frozen until further notice."

Gasps and sounds of incredulous dread filled the room. This was it. The big one. The bomb that everyone had both feared and expected since the beginning.

"John has made very poor choices as a leader—damningly poor. And on top of it all we now have the Angelo issue." Swiftly, he brought the group up to speed on the previous days' events.

Vince spread open palms to the conference room, as if handing them a final piece of damning evidence. As if wrecking the financial viability of the Firstborn wasn't bad enough. "This Angelo guy knows things. Important things. Now he's asking that we prevent an outbreak of the Thresher simply by giving up a mission—the prevention of the assassination of a known corrupt government official."

Vince's expression took a deathly seriousness as he looked up at them all, eyes narrow. He looked right at Trista. "We've been talking about the Thresher for years. I know my dad talked to me about it when I first discovered my gifting. This is not something small—or to be laughed at. We're dealing with something we don't fully understand, and no one has really understood for nearly a millennium of Firstborn history. And as a result, the Thresher has put fear into the Firstborn for eight centuries. Now this Angelo guy sees it, and he's warning us not to intervene with this one issue—not give up our calling as the Firstborn, but this issue—and John won't pull the plug. At this very minute Devin and Hannah are beginning to work together on preventing this assassination."

Vincent let the room mull it over for a moment as more than twenty people sat in total silence.

Trista watched Vince, waiting for what he was going to say next—fearing it yet needing to hear it.

"Make no mistake; the Thresher will be unleashed if Devin Bathurst and his accomplice, Hannah Rice, proceed with their intentions," he said with a sober nod. "Alessandro D'Angelo warned the Firstborn about it in the fourteenth century. He knew the danger—and the destruction it would cause. He tried to warn us then—and if we don't take that warning seriously today, in the moment, then we're all dead men. Every last one of us is going to be hunted down by this *thing* and ended."

Silence.

Vince stood tall. "I don't think anyone in this room truly believes it's a coincidence that Angelo shares the name of our founder who died hundreds of years ago. I don't think any of us doubt the existence of the Thresher, or the destruction he'll cause us—and eventually the world—when we're out of the way." He put his hands in his pockets. "Why does John?"

The room resumed its quiet.

"It's time for all of us to say what we've all been thinking but none of us has actually had the initiative to say. It's time for me to take over the role of Overseer."

Hannah stood on the sidewalk under an overcast sky, watching the remains of the house smolder. Yellow caution tape surrounded the scene. Black arms of wood protruded from the pile. Brick and metal formed the charred foundation that the smoky wreckage sat upon.

She stared at it all, wondering if bulldozers would come to take away the debris and why they hadn't come yet. She closed her eyes and cleared her mind. She reached out with her heart and mind—toward the center of it all, the source of her gift—to God Himself.

It was like dipping a cup into a well and coming up dry.

Her eyes opened. She had prayed and reached and focused for what now seemed like hours, but she couldn't find the past.

A car stopped behind her and someone got out. "Miss Rice?"

She turned. "Mr. Bathurst," she said with a nod. "Thank you for coming."

Devin wore a gray suit with a tan trench coat. He closed the vehicle door, stepping around the front of the car as he approached her. "John Temple sent me." He looked at the smoldering wreckage of what used to be a house. "Let's get to work."

Trista stared at the slip of paper in front of her as she caught the box out of the corner of her eye, moving toward her from the left as it was passed along.

Yes or no. It was that simple. All she had to do was write a word. Yes, John should be removed as Overseer, or no, he should not. She stared at the ballot in front of her, pen in her hand. The urge to fidget filled her, but she resisted.

Trista tried to weigh the evidence—thoughtfully and scientifically—but there were emotions, ridiculous emotions, that kept creeping into her thinking. She tried to banish it from her thinking—the anger she felt toward John, the way he treated her like she somehow belonged to him, the way he followed her like a puppy, the way he criticized her at the thought that she had met someone else. So much anger. It was deep and visceral and…

…and there was another feeling. One that felt like something else. Just as deep and visceral but not anger. More like…

No. No more feelings.

She tried to think her way through the emotions that muddied the waters, around the pathetic feelings that tried to pull her away from the true question of John's capabilities to lead. The evidence tried to take its place in her mind, easing into an ordered pattern that she could analyze and—

"Ms. Brightling," someone said over her shoulder, the small cardboard box hanging in front of her.

She breathed slowly, trying to make up her mind.

The hand holding the box shook it slightly, indicating the need to hurry.

Decision time.

She held her breath, wrote her answer, and put it in the box.

Hannah sat in Devin's car, watching him through the passenger-side window.

He walked up to the blackened ruins of the house, removed his trench coat, and laid it out over the ground. Then he knelt and clasped his hands, bowing his head—like he always did.

It would be the Lord's Prayer. Exact. Precise. Covering all angles of exhortation and supplication. A perfect blueprint for prayer of all kinds—devoid of the mystery that meant so much to Hannah, but spiritually correct, dictated by their Savior Himself.

He prayed for several minutes, then lifted his head and stood. He picked up his coat, dusted it off with exact motions, then replaced it on his shoulders, arms slipping through the sleeves. Hannah watched him approach the car. He opened the driver's door and took his place at the wheel. "I know where they're going to be," he said, turning the key in the ignition. "We have to hurry."

Vincent Sobel leaned over as a colleague named Drew handed him a scrap of paper. He looked it over, reading it several times to be certain, then looked up at the conference room filled with concerned parties. "We have a verdict," he said with a resolved nod. He folded the paper and set it on the conference table. "Including both the secret ballots collected here in Manhattan, in the main office, and e-mailed responses we have from those of you who are joining us from across the nation via conference call—the numbers are as follows."

The room watched in a kind of morbid anticipation. Vincent let them watch for a moment out of an equally morbid fascination.

"With a combined total of thirty-two voting parties, we have thirty-one votes of 'Yes,' indicating that John Temple should be removed from his position as Overseer of the Firstborn and myself put in place as Overseer. The yes vote has it."

Vince nearly smiled to himself, feeling vindicated to have John Temple ejected from a position he never should have occupied. It was a kind of glee. There was a word for it. German, if he wasn't mistaken, which meant to take joy in the pain of another. What was that word? Shodden-something—

—*schadenfreude.*

That was right. He had enough experience in the film industry to know the idea—the unadulterated glee of watching someone else ground into dust.

But this, of course, was different. John truly had a problem. Maybe he felt relief, even happiness, at the thought that the Firstborn could finally get back on track—but nothing malicious. Vince closed his eyes, escaping the chatter of the crowded room for a moment. A silent prayer, thanking God for the strength to do the hard thing and the grace to take care of John in the light of this difficult news—to be John's friend in the trial that he soon would face.

He opened his eyes and nodded to himself. This was truly the right thing to do. They were all in obvious consensus about it.

Vince spoke to the room. "I'll break the news to John personally. It'll be better coming from a friend." There were nods as the room quieted. "Someone get Devin Bathurst on the line—it's time for someone to officially recall him." More nods as people resumed their chatter, many standing to leave.

Drew approached, extending a congratulatory hand. "That was a difficult thing to do," he said with an affirming nod. "Are you OK?"

Vince gave a pained smile. "I'll be OK. Telling John won't be easy, but"—Vince took a courageous breath and nodded—"I'll be OK."

Drew put a hand on his shoulder. "I'm here if you need to talk afterward."

"Thank you. I—"

"Mr. Sobel?" someone said from behind him.

"Yes," he said, turning.

A woman in her late twenties reached out, handing him a cellular phone. "I have Devin Bathurst on the line."

Vincent nodded, appropriately somber, and took the phone. "Devin?"

The response was crisp and efficient. "This is Bathurst."

"Vince Sobel here. Listen, we were just meeting here at the main office—"

"Did I miss the memo?" Devin asked unflappably. "Anything pressingly important?"

"Actually"—Vince cleared his throat awkwardly—"you weren't invited to the meeting."

A momentary pause.

"I see."

Vince felt cold inside. "You see, we took a vote, and it was decided by an overwhelming majority to replace John Temple as Overseer and—"

"You're establishing yourself as the new Overseer," Devin continued logically, voice free of shock or concern.

"Well, we've yet to decide who is going to—"

"You're the logical choice," Devin said. "You want the position, you have a good reputation, and the only remaining patriarch is Clay Goldstein. But he won't be able to take the position because he has Parkinson's."

Vince was silent, stunned, looking around the room at the myriad people swarming around him. "How did you know that?" Vince whispered. "Clay has been very private about his medical condition and—"

"You're dealing with people who see things," Devin said, free of emotion. "I saw his illness coming six months ago."

"You did?" Vince stammered, turning away from the room,

cupping his hand over the phone mouthpiece. "Why didn't you say anything?"

"I don't tell people they're dying. I see it all the time, but I make a policy of keeping it to myself. I assumed that if he hadn't told anyone, there was a reason."

Vince breathed deliberately for several moments, trying not to lose his calm. "Where are you?"

"I'm driving to an appointment," Devin replied.

"Does it have to do with the assassination?"

"No."

Vince felt it—Devin was telling the truth, if only in part. "Does it have to do with the kidnappings?"

"I'm doing a favor for a friend."

That meant yes. Devin was helping Hannah find the girls—then she would help him with the senator. Vince could feel it in the pit of his stomach. "Devin Bathurst," he said with resolve, "by majority vote you are forbidden from pursuing this issue any further. Do you understand?"

A moment's hesitation. "I understand."

Vince tried to feel him out, attempting to gauge Devin's motives. There was a loud noise from the conference room, and Vince put a finger in his ear, blocking out the sound as best he could. "Devin, can I count on you to do the right thing?"

Silence.

"Devin? Can I count on you to do the right thing?"

"Yes," Devin replied from the other end of the line. "You can count on me to do the right thing."

The line went dead. Vince stared at the phone in his hand, baffled.

"What is it?" Drew asked.

"He hung up on me."

"Is he calling off his action?"

Vince felt something like a spider crawling around in his

stomach—a feeling that told him Devin Bathurst's true motives. "No," he said, shaking his head. "Devin is going to pursue this thing—no matter what any of us say."

"What are you going to do?" Drew asked, face serious.

Vince shook his head, disappointed in Devin Bathurst. "If this is as bad as Angelo is predicting, then someone needs to go and pick him up."

Drew looked around to see if anyone was watching, then turned back to Vince. "Bathurst is a tough son of a gun. He won't give this thing up without a fight."

"Then make sure whoever goes after him isn't alone—and be ready for a fight."

"How far do we take this?" Drew asked, looking Vince intensely in the eye.

"What do you mean?"

"We have to decide now," Drew said evenly, "how far are we going to go to stop Bathurst."

Vince shrugged, still confused. "Follow him across the world if you have to. I'll make the funds available."

Drew cleared his throat again, leaning close. "What if our only choice is to kill him?"

Vince stared at Drew, not having fully considered the possibility until now. "Don't hurt him if you can help it."

"But if we can't help it?"

Vince thought for a moment, then nodded. "Then do what you have to."

Drew nodded. "Understood."

Vince stepped away. He walked toward the conference room window and looked down at the Manhattan street below. He felt numb. Something he hadn't expected. Somehow it all seemed so distant and surreal. Just a game.

Chapter 10

John sat at the deli, eating lunch, Bible open on the table. The pages were spread open to someplace in Psalms—his favorite book of the Bible—and yet he stared out the window at the foot traffic.

Things were going badly. Being Overseer was harder than he'd expected. He missed third-world countries and missions work. He missed the feeling of adventure and the stories he was living—stories he could tell when he came back to the world that others thought of as normal. He missed the smell of noodles cooking on the streets of Southeast Asia and the sweltering heat of the rain forest—so hot your clothes would cling to you in a sopping slick of sweat. He had told them when he left India that he would come back to visit someday. That had been four years ago—and he still had no plans to return.

John touched his forehead, a melancholy feeling flooding him. And there was Trista.

She had left the bubble of the modern world—had the adventures and experiences he had been missing. The thing that made him of most use to God, the thing that made him the most unique among other Christians—his travel—and in the last year she had done more of it than he had. And she had met someone—someone probably better traveled than himself.

He chastised himself for making an idol of her. For wanting companionship beyond that of God.

The situation at hand was dangerous, and Devin and Hannah were counting on him to back them up as Overseer. He had to do his job now and stay focused. He wasn't used to this form of discipline—but he needed to grow and learn both as a Christian and as an administrator.

He thought of Trista—his distraction—and then he felt her.

Somewhere out in the world he could feel where she was and what she was feeling.

She was thinking of him.

John smiled to himself for a second, then realized the depth of her thoughts. And her concern.

She was worried, and she was scared.

John stood, thrust his Bible into his bag, and pushed through the door out onto the crowded sidewalk.

Someone else was thinking about Trista too. With plans of intimidation and hostility.

He surged forward, ducking and shoving his way through the throng of suits and briefcases that marched like ants down the sidewalk. Someone shouted in protest, but John kept running—ducking and weaving through a dark forest of expensive business wear and honking horns as his path spilled into the street. A cab driver shouted angrily, shaking a fist.

That's the trouble with living in the present, he thought—you're always out of time.

He ran as fast as he could.

Trista listened to the sound of her own high heels clacking through the cavernous parking garage, moving swiftly toward her rental car. Not a soul in sight. Rows and rows of empty vehicles left by those working in the surrounding buildings. No outside sunlight—just the tangerine glow of dying overhead lights.

Someone needed to tell John what was happening. Maybe he wasn't the right person for the job—maybe Vince was right…about everything. But it didn't seem right. It didn't *feel* right.

Trista fought herself—now wasn't the time to be swayed by her feelings. She needed to stay solid in some sort of resolve. But she trusted Devin, and she had been impressed by Hannah.

She wasn't doing this for John; she was doing this for them—and the callings they were following.

There was something in her that felt like feelings. The kind that men and women have for each other every day. But it wasn't the kind of thing she and John could ever share. He was too...

Trista struggled for the word. Weak? Yes, weak. And she was a different person when he was in her world. She was a strong woman of business and industry. A member of the Domani. A serious person with serious objectives and goals. But there was something about John Temple that made her forget reason and rationale, that made her trust feelings that made her too weak. There were times when she had wondered if her romance with John had lost her so much credibility with the others, not because she had crossed party lines, but because of the effect he had on her. He pulled her from the steady base of reason and reality and sent her hurtling into a world of schoolgirl daydreams and fantasies.

She moved toward the car—keys in hand. She looked up and stopped.

Angelo.

There was no conceivable way that he could have approached her like that without her knowing he was coming. Or was there?

He was every bit the description she had gotten from Vince at the meeting—dark stringy hair, long black coat, dark pants tucked into army boots. Standing in front of her.

She remained still, saying nothing. He said nothing either. Maybe he didn't see her. Maybe...

Trista took a step toward the car.

Angelo mirrored her, stepping toward the car.

She stopped.

He stopped.

Trista felt the urge to tremble but swallowed it. She lifted her head, looking him in the eye. He spoke.

"Ms. Brightling, I know what you are planning to do."

She said nothing, turning her car keys in her hand, holding them in her fist to use as a stabbing weapon if she needed. Angelo seemed to notice—a look of fear and panic crossed his face, then quickly soured into something...

...wild.

He stepped toward her, ominous and threatening. Her fist tightened around the keys. The plastic fob dug into her skin as he marched toward her.

"Angelo!" someone shouted.

She turned her head—John Temple stood behind her, approaching, breathing hard like he'd been running. Sweat covered his face.

"Angelo," he said again. "Leave her alone."

Angelo tipped his head slightly, like a confused dog—then took another step toward Trista.

"I'm ordering you," John exclaimed. "As Overseer, I demand that you leave her alone."

The confusion on Angelo's face became more noticeable. "I don't understand."

"I'll listen to you," John said, stepping up next to Trista. "I'll hear whatever you have to say. Just leave Ms. Brightling out of this."

Trista watched John step ahead of her, inching his way between her and Angelo.

"I can't do that," Angelo said, shaking his head, slightly more lucid, but still with a rabid edge.

"I am Overseer, and I'm ordering you."

Angelo glanced at Trista, then back to John. He shook his head. "You're not Overseer," he declared.

John turned toward Trista, looking at her, then back to Angelo. "What?"

"There was a meeting," Angelo said, as if all of this were something John should know but had stupidly forgotten. "They voted. You are no longer Overseer."

There was a moment of quiet through the expansive garage, then John turned to her, looking Trista in the eye. "Is it true?"

She glanced at her shoes for a moment, then looked up. "Yes," she said hesitantly, "it was decided that you are no longer the person to fulfill the role of Overseer."

John looked confused and hurt. "How long have you—"

"Moments ago," Angelo interrupted. "You are no longer Overseer, and your instructions no longer need to be heeded." Angelo took another step toward them. "But *she* intends to help Devin Bathurst and Hannah Rice—and I cannot allow that." Angelo's lucidity seemed to continue slipping.

Trista watched John take a step back, then turn to her, speaking swiftly and quietly. "Get in the car," he ordered.

"John, you have to—"

"Do it," he replied firmly, positioning himself as an obstacle between her and Angelo. She didn't budge. "Do it *now*!"

Angelo was approaching again. John stood his ground.

She reached out with the keys, pressing the button on the fob with her thumb. The locks snapped upward with a mechanical pop. The door opened, and she began to step in—

The sound of some hideous violence resonated, and she glanced in the rearview mirror in time to see John's body slam into the back window of the car with a ghastly *thud*.

Trista jammed the key into the ignition and turned. John stood in the rearview mirror, then was thrown aside—Angelo standing directly behind the car, face filling the mirror.

The engine made a shrieking sound as she tried to start it again—momentarily unaware that the virtually silent car was already on. Her hand flashed over the gearshift. Reverse. She jammed her high-heeled foot onto the gas and watched as Angelo's body slammed into the hatchback end of her rental. Her foot came down equally hard on the brake, and he tumbled away with the momentum.

Trista leaned across the center console and opened the passenger side door with her fingertips. John was on his knees, propping himself up—battered looking.

"Get in!" she shouted, watching Angelo rise from the hard garage floor. John glanced toward the back of the car. "Do it!" she shouted again.

John Temple stood, grabbed the door, threw himself into the passenger's seat. He slammed the door.

Trista worked the transmission. Forward. Angelo rushed at the car again. She spun the wheel and punched the gas.

The tires screamed, breaking loose, the car surging forward. Angelo tried to keep up—running fast alongside the car for a split second, then falling behind. He lashed out in desperation—splitting the glass with the side of his fist. John shouted orders at Trista with an edge of fear and frustration. Laying on the gas, she didn't hear what he said.

She saw him pointing forward to the cement wall ahead where the straightaway ended.

The tires shrieked as she worked the wheel, nosing to the right—toward the down ramp. It cost her speed and time, Angelo gaining from behind, following the wake of burned rubber she left on the pavement.

"He's behind you," John said, twisted in his seat and looking back.

"I know," she shouted, temper short.

The car made it around the corner, moving fast, Angelo disappearing from view.

John shook his head emphatically. "He's still trying to follow."

"We're driving too fast for him to catch up."

"He's trying to cut us off."

Trista slowed as she made another turn. "Then we'll deal with it."

John looked around, trying to spot Angelo. "So," he grunted, "when was someone going to tell me I was fired?"

Trista worked the wheel, navigating the garage. "I was on my way to tell you when you showed up."

"Good thing I did," he said.

She shook her head. "I would have been fine, I'm sure." Trista watched as the exit gate approached—two cars ahead of her in line.

"You're welcome," John growled sarcastically.

Trista seethed for a moment, the car rolling to a stop as they waited their turn. She relaxed but still maintained her standard professionalism. "Thank you, John."

"I'm sorry I snapped," he said, shaking his head. "I just can't believe everything that is happening…" He paused, turning his face to her, deeply concerned.

"What?" she asked.

"We can't wait here. This is taking too long." He looked scared. "Angelo is catching up."

"Where?" Trista demanded, looking around with equal concern.

"The stairwell," John pointed past her, and she looked, seeing the stairwell exit just past the chalky-white splintering where Angelo had hit the window.

"How long?" she asked, watching the next car in line pull up to the gate.

"Too soon," he stammered. "We have to ditch the car, make a run for it!"

"We can't," she replied, trying not to lose her cool. "We'll never outrun him on foot." The car ahead of them paid, rolling out as the gate lifted.

Trista resisted the urge to hit the gas, trying to make it out the gate, or to smash through it with the front end of the car—something that only worked in movies and destroyed vehicles when they tried in the real world. She jolted forward, stopping, rolling down her window.

The guy in the gatehouse was watching a television, hardly noticing customers. He checked the total. "Six dollars," he said, eyes transfixed on his screen. Trista reached out with the money, eyes darting to the stairwell exit—

Angelo came bursting through the door, staring right at her. He made a dash in their direction.

The gatehouse guard took the money and hit the switch—raising the gate.

Angelo bolted toward them as Trista moved the car into the street as fast as it would go.

Angelo threw himself at an oncoming car that was pulling into the garage—sliding nimbly across the hood.

Trista pulled hard right and slammed the gas. In a matter of moments Angelo had turned into a dot behind them.

She took a deep breath. "That was too close."

Devin navigated the highway with his left hand, opening his mobile phone with his right. Hannah watched him from the passenger's seat, a look of what might have been disapproval on her face. Perhaps she didn't like the idea of him driving and talking on his phone at the same time. He didn't have time to debate the point.

The other end rang only once before there was an answer. "This is Trista."

"It's Bathurst," he said, signaling fluidly and changing lanes. "John Temple is no longer Overseer. Did you know about this?"

"Yes," she said without hesitation.

"Where do you stand on the assassination issue?" Devin listened carefully for the tone in her voice—regardless of her words, he had a greater need to understand her intentions.

"I'm with you," she said, again without hesitation. "Vince knows that you aren't going to drop this issue, and he intends to have you stopped."

Devin nodded, maneuvering around a large freight truck, pressing the gas. "Extent of countermeasures?"

"It sounds like he's willing to use extreme prejudice in stopping you."

He should have known. Something about Angelo had scared Vince very badly, and when people who saw only the moment get scared, they get desperate—and dangerous. "Understood," he replied. "Where are you?"

"I'm in the city with John Temple. I was about to offer you and Hannah my help when Angelo—"

"Angelo! Did he get to you?"

"No. He tried to stop me from leaving when John showed up and helped. We just escaped him." Her words were crisp, fast, and precise—exactly what Devin was looking for. "Where are you?"

"We're on the highway—headed for Ohio. The kidnappers are going to be there in a few hours, and Ms. Rice and I hope to find their trail."

"And the assassination in Nevada?" she asked efficiently.

"It's more than forty-eight hours away. My first priority is the kidnapping. If I can't take care of that in time, I'll direct my attention to the senator. Until then I'm pursuing this."

"Understood," Trista affirmed. "How can I best support?"

Devin was silent for a moment, considering possibilities—waiting to see if his foresight would take over and tell him to hold back or move forward. He glanced at Hannah, assessing her usefulness to him. Young, motivated, energetic, strongly familiar with the subject at hand. She was all the more help he could ask for with this matter. In fact, it was she who was the real help here, now that he considered it. "I need feet on the ground in Nevada," he said with resolve.

"Reconnaissance?" she asked, instantly understanding his allusions.

"I need to understand the layout—where the senator will be and what is going to happen. Are you equipped to handle this?"

Her reply was quick and unmitigated. "I am."

"Good."

"What do you want me to do with Temple?"

Devin adjusted the phone, navigating through the speeding traffic, the sun starting to make its way out from behind the clouds. "Leave him," he said, shifting gears. "You'll work faster without him."

She didn't reply. Her response was slow, with more consideration than Devin had come to expect from her over the years.

"Ms. Brightling?" he asked, checking to see if they had been cut off.

"He could be useful," she said with her usual exactness. "If something is already happening in Las Vegas, he might be able to see it."

Devin found himself caught by the same hesitation that had held Trista back. "Fine," he said after a moment, "but he's your responsibility. Don't let him slow you down in any way. I need this to go flawlessly, and I don't want any of the unnecessary delays that usually surround him."

"Understood," she replied, quickly again. "I'll take responsibility for the situation."

"Good. How soon can you be in Nevada?"

"Tonight."

Devin nodded. "Good. Keep me informed. You have my cell number."

"Understood."

Devin snapped his phone shut, dropping it in the breast pocket of his jacket.

He couldn't see how this was going to end—but he knew that when it did, things might never be the same again.

"What's the plan?" John asked, watching Trista put her phone away.

"I'm going to Las Vegas to prepare a plan to prevent the assassination."

John nodded, removing the sport coat he was wearing. "And Devin thinks I'm a liability?"

"Yes," Trista replied, devoid of any attempt to soften the news.

A pinprick of hurt plucked at John's chest. "What do you think?"

Trista kept her eyes on the road. "I think you can be reckless." She turned her focus to him, expression unforgiving. "Are you going to be reckless?"

He laughed, trying not to let his voice crack with the feelings of disappointment and hurt he felt. "Reckless is what I do."

"I'm serious, John," she said with a nasty edge.

He laughed again, trying to maintain some dignity in the face of Trista's flagrant doubts. "I haven't taken anything seriously in years," he grunted sarcastically.

Trista angled the car to the right, slamming the brakes hard—the car coming to a screeching stop at the curb. "Get out," she commanded, eyes still on the road, expression stony.

"Trista, I—"

She didn't look at him. "I'm serious, John. Whatever is happening, it has a lot of people scared." Trista turned her attention to him—expression anything but friendly. "I'm scared, John," she said without emotion, "and I'm not going to bring you along if you insist on being a child about this."

"I—"

"Do you understand, John Temple?" she interrupted, as if he were a four-year-old.

John said nothing for a moment, then nodded silently.

"I need to know I can count on you," she said sternly. "I need you to promise me that you'll pull through for me." She glanced past John, toward the street beyond. "Or I need you to get out of this car and out of my way. Do you understand?"

John sat in silence for a moment, examining her face—every beautiful line—then looked out the window at the street.

Trista said nothing, her face serious.

Then John nodded and reached into the backseat, grabbing his sport coat. He opened the car door and stepped onto the street, walking away from Trista and the car. He flung his jacket over his shoulder like a fashion model and moved down the street.

Behind him he heard the car rev and take off. It shot past him—and disappeared around the corner.

She left him. She actually left him.

John looked around. Neither the best nor the worst neighborhood. He didn't know if there was a subway station nearby. He would need to call someone to come and get him. But who could he call? Vince had had him ejected from office—yet another job he'd been fired from. Devin was leaving the state.

He looked at his shoes. He couldn't believe how poorly he'd handled that. Trista was scared and worried, and he'd treated it like a joke. And now…

A car stopped next to him. He looked—Trista. She must have gone around the block and come back for him.

The mechanical window lowered, and she looked at him. "Get in," she said with an indecipherable tone.

John looked around, then got in the car.

Trista put the car into gear, rolling away from the curb. "I'm sorry."

"Me too," he said with a nod, looking forward.

They drove the rest of the way to the airport in silence.

Chapter 11

HANNAH STARED OUT the windshield, watching the sun sink farther behind the horizon as they drove down the highway. What state were they in now—Ohio? Had they really been on the road that long? They'd left the house in New Jersey around lunchtime, and now the sun was setting. She hadn't looked at the signs or bothered to keep track of the miles. It had apparently been longer than she had realized.

Devin sat silently in the driver's seat. They hadn't said anything in hours. Perhaps there were things to talk about, but Hannah kept her focus tightly clenched on the road—feeling the world pass through them, the past swirling around her. She could feel something like a warm current as they stayed on the right path, cooling only when they deviated. But she had to stay aware of it—with a quiet mind. Whatever small talk they might have would only have been a distraction.

Devin didn't seem to mind the quiet. He kept still and silent, navigating the road as if he were gliding across ice. Whatever he had seen was leading him forward as well—making him equally consumed by his own calling.

Hannah felt the path start to cool. Chills ran up her arms. She hugged her arms and felt it—

Exiting the highway. Into the gas station.

"There." Hannah pointed toward the exit.

Devin nodded, switched on the turn signal, and aimed the car at the exit.

Hannah sat up in her seat, excited. This was it. This was where the girls had been brought. This was where…

She could feel herself losing touch with the past.

No—she couldn't give in to the overflow of thought and chatter. She had to clear her mind—let it all wash over her with clarity of thought.

"The gas station," Devin said with a nod. "This is it."

Hannah nearly wrung her hands, squirming in her seat. Stop it, she thought, settling in. The car came down the off-ramp, nosing into the turn—into the parking lot.

"This is wrong," Devin said, shaking his head. "It's too dark. They were here when there was more light."

"We're late?" Hannah asked, fighting her worry and concern.

Devin looked around as if he were trying to confirm his hunch—then nodded. "We're late."

"How late? Do you think they might still be here?"

He pulled the car to a stop just outside of the gas station, rolling into a parking space. "Maybe twenty minutes." He parked the car and turned off the engine. "I'm going inside. I'm going to ask some questions. You stay here. Understood?"

She bit her lip with nervous energy. "Yeah."

Devin stepped out and moved toward the glass doors. He stood in line, waiting to talk to the man at the counter.

Hannah pulled in a lungful of air and held it. This was ridiculous. The girls—the kidnappers—they had been here. They had been *here*. If they had gone into the store for any reason they would have used those very same doors. The only thing that was missing was time. They were late.

The idea seemed incomprehensible. Everything seemed so interconnected—so closely tied. How could a few minutes be enough to lose them?

No, she thought. It was all connected. Every piece. Every fragment of the universe. All one complete whole.

She closed her eyes.

Her mind wanted to talk to God—to beseech Him for help. But not with words. Nothing so limited and invented as words. She reached out with…herself.

Her mind cleared. Her thoughts went blank.

Her brain told her to open her eyes and search…but

something compelled her to stay in the silence a moment longer. To let it…

The dragon—in the gas station.

From the door to the truck—opening the rolling freight door.

The girls—ripped from the truck, thrown into a van.

Doors slamming. Girls screaming silently through bindings and duct tape.

The van pulling away…

Up the ramp to the empty highway.

Gone.

Hannah opened her eyes and stepped out of the car. She couldn't see Devin inside—but she didn't wait. The truck—had it left yet? Was it still here?

She circled around to the back of the building into the darkness—a single light positioned above the station's back door, flickering from a dying bulb.

The truck. It was still there.

It looked like a moving truck, some corporate logo on the side—for hauling milk, maybe?

She could feel the footprints on the ground, circling from the gas station—still warm in her mind. Hannah paused for a moment, glancing side to side. Maybe there was someone still in the truck.

She silenced her mind and marched forward—resolve thundered in her chest like a physical sensation. The truck thirty feet away—then twenty—then ten. She reached out, touching the handle to see if the back was locked—

The door moved effortlessly against her touch, swinging out a few inches.

Hannah stopped. There was no way to know what was beyond that door.

She took a deep breath and opened the door. The metal squealed quietly as the hinges ground against themselves.

The doors opened.

Hannah stared into the darkness, eyes adjusting. Just plastic crates, stacks and stacks of them rising all the way to the ceiling, only a few feet in.

A dead end?

This wasn't right. This was where the girls had been kept—she could feel it down to her core. This was where they had been placed and held and moved from. But there wasn't enough room to carry three girls, was there?

Despite the concerns of her logical mind, Hannah climbed up into the back of the truck. The compartment dimmed as the truck doors swung slowly back into place. Darkness covered everything for a moment, until her eyes had a chance to adjust, working with the minuscule fraction of light that came in from the crack in the door.

She examined the crates, then let her breathing slow.

The latch that they had used—between the crates.

Hannah reached out, putting her hand between the crates. She reached wrong, adjusting. The crates should have shifted, or at least moved some tiny amount. Instead, they stayed stuck in place—a solid wall of crates. Her hand adjusted and found something cool and metallic—a dead bolt, running vertically.

She lifted the metal nub, and the wall of crates—only a few inches deep—swung out to reveal what was behind.

Devin waited for the big man who reeked of cigarette smoke to finish paying for his latest pack and move to the door. Devin stepped up to the counter, set down two bottles of water, and reached for his wallet.

"Just the water?" the attendant—a short middle-aged woman with dark hair and bad teeth—asked in a gravelly voice.

He nodded. "I was supposed to meet someone here," he said, putting a ten-dollar bill on the counter.

"Oh yeah?" she said absently as she rang up the water and opened the register.

"He had a tattoo on his arm—a green dragon. Does that sound familiar?"

She nodded. "He was just in here. He was with that guy that just bought cigarettes..."

It hit Devin like a brick:

Hannah ripped from a truck—beaten bloody—in mortal danger.

He stepped away from the counter.

Hannah stared at the walls—close and claustrophobic—foam pads spread across the floor with bundles of mildewed blankets.

Here. They had been here.

Whoever owned this truck knew who had taken them—and maybe where they were going. Her heart raced, trying to form a plan from thin air.

The back end of the truck dipped slightly, and there were footfalls. The wall of fake crates pushed the rest of the way shut—and she heard the dead bolt drop into place.

She rushed to the fake wall—pushing hard, but it didn't budge.

Then she heard the outer doors to the truck slam shut—and latch.

Devin bolted from the front door of the gas station, his expensive shoes moving as quickly as they could carry him, trench coat billowing against the air he pushed through.

Out the door. Around the corner. Behind the station.

The truck—roaring to life, taillights flashing.

He surged toward the vehicle as it started to roll. Devin shouted with the utmost fury he could muster, waving an arm.

A cloud of dust swirled around him as the truck accelerated and its taillights shrank exponentially in fractions of a second. Devin skidded to a stop, then spun—heading back to the station—back to the car.

Moments later he was in the driver's seat—the gas station attendant staring at him with confusion through the big glass windows. He started the car and threw the vehicle into reverse, working the gas and the clutch in a smooth motion—the car ripped backward in a turn, the front end swinging. The shrieking of tires and the burning of rubber attacked his senses—

And he took off into the night.

"We have a lead," Drew said from across the line.

Sitting in the Overseer's office, Vince Sobel rubbed the back of his neck. "Yeah?"

"It's John Temple."

Vince sat up, eyes suddenly open, leaning into his desk that used to be John's. "What have you got?"

"We have a hit on his bank account."

"The Overseer stipend account we set up for him?"

"Yes. He made a withdrawal at the airport."

"How much did he take?" Vince asked, not really worried about the dollar amount as the percentage.

"All of it," Drew said with certainty. "He drained all the funds from the account."

Vince winced. "Why didn't we close that account?"

"That's what I was doing when I found this."

"OK," Vince said, accepting it with a nod. "The airport," he said, moving to the next subject. "Any idea where he's going?"

"We can only speculate," Drew said, somewhat resigned.

"Contact Trista Brightling; maybe she has a lead on his whereabouts."

"We've been trying to get in touch with her by phone and

e-mail," Drew reported. "So far we haven't been able to contact her."

Vince thought for a moment, eyes fighting to stay open after such an eventful day. "Keep trying. Any word on Angelo?"

"I'm sorry, but he seems to have simply…vanished."

Vince turned his chair, looking out the window at the city's lights in the darkness. "Keep me informed," he said with authority and ended the call. He stared out into the evening.

So this was what it was like to be Overseer.

John Temple woke suddenly as the voice on the intercom announced that they were going to be landing soon. It was dark out the window, and it was hard to see where they were the few times he had looked out.

Twenty minutes later they were on the ground, and as others were trying to unload overhead luggage, John simply stepped off the plane—no luggage or carry-on to speak of.

He couldn't remember if he or Trista were supposed to land first. She'd explained it to him several times, but travel to him had always been more about winging it than well-fleshed-out logistics. They hadn't been able to get flights together and so had flown on different airlines, with different flights at different times. The result was confusion—and a very real chance that Trista was avoiding him entirely.

John stood in front of the arrivals board, staring blankly at the circus of letters and numbers that were supposed to represent flights. Hundreds of planes from all over the country—and the world—all pouring into Las Vegas, the city of sin, in a steady stream.

"My flight was held up," Trista said as she stepped up next to him.

John looked at her and nodded. "How was your flight?"

"Bumpy. Yours?" she asked, cordial but uninterested.

"I slept."

"Hmm." Trista looked ahead. "Let's go get the rental car."

Devin screamed down the highway in his car, watching the stream of red taillights approach and disappear behind him—the dotted line between lanes flashing past the car in a flickering parade.

Hannah. His mind narrowed on her, trying to stay focused.

Why had she left the car? She knew better. Couldn't she see what would happen? Her future leapt into his mind:

Hannah—ripped from the back of the truck.

The truck—she was in the truck—wherever it was that it was going.

A violent punch to her face—nose broken, spilling blood.

He focused his eyes through the darkness, scowling at the night. Devin didn't pray with words—but he prayed that this stretch of highway wasn't being patrolled, that there were no police to pull him over, to slow him down, to lose Hannah.

Grabbing her by the hair—dragging her across the dirt.

The future could always be changed. But it was never easy. And time was always running out.

The slick leather gearshift moved under the direct control of his hand, the mechanism gliding from one gear to the next. He signaled fast, changed lanes, pulled ahead of the last car in the pack, and saw the vehicle ahead of him.

A truck. Like a small moving truck of some kind.

He recognized the back doors—this was it. Behind those doors Hannah was waiting—trapped.

There were only a few options—try to run the truck off the road and risk Hannah being hurt in the back, or follow until the truck came to a stop.

Devin shifted gears and settled in behind the truck.

Hannah sat on a foam pad, back against the cold metal, trying to think. She reached for one of the blankets. Ignoring the smell of dirt and mildew, she wrapped the thick material around her shoulders.

The truck hit another bump, jostling the entire interior again, shaking up and down, from side to side.

She held the blanket close, the smell nearly overpowering. Hannah pulled the blanket away and sniffed the air—the odor of sweat, salty and bitter. The girls had been here—the three of them, at least—

Crammed into the space like canned fish, moving down the highway in the sweltering heat of the packed metal box.

More girls—others. Two Latino girls, older than the others, pulled from the truck at an earlier stop.

The three girls, taken to another place. Stripped to their underwear—pictures snapped of them.

Thrown back into the truck and taken to the gas station—pulled from the truck again and thrown into the van.

Hannah opened her eyes. Wherever she was being taken wasn't where the girls were going. But maybe it was where they had been.

There was still a chance to save the girls.

But who was going to save her?

Devin watched the truck pull off the highway.

The middle of nowhere. A single structure under a bright light at the top of a pole. A ring of dead bulbs, several winking on and off, outlining the edges of a dim sign: Roadside Motel. Rooms available. Hourly rates.

The truck's taillights rounded the back of the motel and came to a stop. Devin slowed his car and turned off the headlights, trying to navigate the car through the dark. He pulled the car to the side of the road and stepped out—hunching down as he moved toward the motel.

The driver must have been doing something in the cab because it took him several minutes to step out into the night. Boots hit the dirt—crunching dirt under his heels. The driver looked around. Devin ducked around the corner, trench coat swishing softly. His back pressed against the side of the motel wall as he tried to stay out of sight.

Devin listened to the sound of the driver walking toward a door, jingling keys and a clicking lock. He peered around the corner: the driver was gone, weak light glowing through the glass doors where darkness had been before.

There was a moment of waiting—to see if the driver was coming back soon—and Devin stepped out. He moved toward the truck as he glanced at the light that glowed from a back room beyond the front desk. He looked a little closer at the front desk and saw something he didn't expect—

A handgun. Semiautomatic. He couldn't determine the make or model through the poor light, but it sat there on the desk, waiting for someone.

Devin considered stepping in and taking the gun but glanced at the truck—his first priority was Hannah.

He moved toward the truck. His hands touched the doors, and he looked up and down: a long bar ran the length of the door, clamped in place at the base with a heavy-duty padlock.

He examined the mechanism, trying to determine if it was a lock he could defeat without the key—something he was fairly certain he could do, if he had a proper lock pick. That or bolt cutters. Either way, it was an obstacle he would have to deal with before he could even consider getting to her, and he didn't have the tools on his person.

His attention swung back to the glass doors and the warm

glow. He stepped toward them. After a few quick strides, he reached for the door handle—

Devin stopped. A silhouette of a man, from the light—

The driver.

They stopped. Held. Stared. Just for a moment—the driver's attention flicking quickly to the side, looking directly at—

The gun.

There was a sensation of weightless that swelled in Devin for a moment—like the apex of a tall climb before a diving plunge.

The driver launched toward the gun. An ancient bell jingled as Devin threw the door open.

The driver grabbed the gun and spun toward Devin. Their bodies collided, slamming into the front desk—the service bell sounding off in the darkness as the counter rocked.

The front end of the gun was Devin's concern. He slammed the driver's arm down, absorbed the retaliating blow.

A gun blast—the glass door splattered with opaque cracks.

Devin reeled—a punch to the jaw. Twisting the driver's arm, he hurled him into the wall—plaster caving. The gun hit the padlike carpet.

Devin pinned the driver at the chest, trying to hold him there. The driver fought—struggling, straining, then reaching down. The driver's arm behind the small of his own back, suddenly snapped forward—Ka-Bar combat knife, old marine issue. The dark black blade faded into the darkness, serrated teeth only visible as a silhouette against the ambient light on the walls.

A slash at face height—Devin shoved away, preparing for the return.

Nimble fingers teased the handle of the combat knife, flicking it in quick tremors. The driver was an expert.

A slash at Devin's throat, missing. Half a dozen slashing strokes came at him, Devin swatting them away with swift and skilled jabs. The footing shifted, moving through the front room like a violent dance.

A wrong step, Devin losing his footing—the knife slicing too close. He dropped his shoulders, shedding the trench coat from his back into his hands. The driver, mad with ferocity, swiped with the knife, pressing the advantage.

Devin swung the coat like a bullfighter, catching the charging beast, razor-sharp tip thrusting. Three flicking stabs, slicing through the coat, cutting it to pieces—sounds of ripping cloth.

They slammed into one another—hitting the wall, tumbling to the side—smashing through a shoddy wooden door—into a motel room.

A punch to Devin's face and the driver was at him, holding the knife. Devin kicked him in the face and the Ka-Bar hit the floor. The bloody-faced driver recovered—attacking, grabbing at the slashed trench coat, ripping a long strip free.

Grappling. They rolled across the floor—struggling for advantage. A swift move and the driver was behind Devin, wrapping the coat scrap around Devin's neck, throttling him.

Devin tried to stand—the driver's weight pulled him down by the neck. A swift lurch and Devin slammed the driver into a mirror, smashing it.

They hit the floor again—the noose tightening around Devin's throat. The driver's knee in Devin's back for leverage, pulling hard.

The blood pumped in Devin's ears—a screaming like a teakettle getting higher pitched with every second. The makeshift garrote cut into Devin's flesh, stinging painfully.

His bleary eyes searched the floor: across the carpet, the crumpled clothing, a spilled bag of potato chips—*the Ka-Bar.*

He grabbed the big knife with one hand, the taut remainder of the garrote with the other—slashing.

The driver tumbled back—hitting the floor, then stood and charged like a wild animal.

There had been gunshots—something bad was happening.

Hannah worked at the crack in the door, trying to find a way to lift the securing latch. Her fingers hurt from digging into the cold metal, trying to fight the door open.

Nothing was working. Nothing at all.

She couldn't stay here. The engine had stopped—the truck was just sitting there. She could feel how much the girls who had been here before her had feared it. When the driver came for them, pulling them from the truck toward—

Her work became more furious as she let the panic touch her. Then she stopped, breathing deeply. She had to be calm—to work with her surroundings, not against them.

But there was something in her that wanted to fight. To scream. It all reminded her of when she had been kidnapped. Stuck in that basement for days on end in the frigid wastes of wherever it was they had dragged her to. But she couldn't let that cloud her judgment. There was more than her mental well-being on the line.

Then she heard it.

The sound of the lock clicking on the outside of the doors—swinging open beyond the false wall. Someone reaching for the latch, metal working free.

Hannah looked around. There had to be something she could use as a weapon, right? Nothing. She took a place at the back wall, ready to make a running start at—

Too late. The doors were opening. They swung open, and she saw him standing there: a tall slender silhouette behind a bright wash of white light.

"Miss Rice?" Devin said.

And she exhaled with relief.

Devin motioned to her without speaking, and Hannah followed him into the motel.

"The place is clear," Devin said definitively and efficiently. "We're going to rest here for a few hours." He looked at her commandingly. "I want you to get some sleep."

Hannah looked around. "Where did the driver go?"

Devin pointed to the credenza—something sat on top of it, propped against the wall—a white sheet thrown over the form. She disregarded the object for a moment, then did a double take. Legs dangled from beneath the sheet, arms hanging limp to the sides.

"Is that…?" She looked at Devin.

He didn't reply.

She pulled the sheet aside and saw the driver—a knife blade buried in his chest, the handle sticking out.

Sleeping after seeing that was going to be hard.

No matter how many dead bodies a person steps over in life, she thought, it still can keep you up at night.

John Temple brought the bags into the hotel room and looked around. Anything would have seemed top-notch in comparison to his "living in huts and hovels" missionary life. But this was especially impressive. A gleaming kitchenette with granite countertops. A huge flat-screen TV. A view overlooking the blinking lights and outsized casinos on the Strip. A fake Eiffel Tower, lit up like a Christmas tree, caught his eye. Bright, flashing billboards were everywhere below, filling the night with an electrifying promise of adventure.

He glanced back over his shoulder. Trista had evidently retreated into the bedroom of their suite. He approached, considered knocking, then stepped away. If Trista didn't want to see him, there was no point in waking her up. They'd both had a long and confusing day.

He sank into the couch and picked up the remote, turning on the television. He keyed the volume as the set came on too loud. The television was set to the hotel's main channel. He began flipping through channels, looking for something to fill the void—an overwhelming sensation of need for human contact.

The Firstborn had disowned him, and his closest friend in the Ora, Vincent, had spearheaded it. Devin still didn't trust him, and Hannah didn't need him.

John glanced at the bedroom door.

And Trista.

He turned back to an infomercial, a miracle cure to boost every man's confidence in the bedroom. He changed the channel. A music video with a twenty-something coed dancing in next to nothing. He changed the channel. A television talk show with women discussing "technique." He changed the channel. An after-hours premium cable show—soft-core pornography. John lifted the remote control to change the channel, then paused, watching the screen.

He felt the sense of loneliness leaving him. Something held him there as a beautiful brunette winked at him through the screen.

Beyond the conventions of society and small talk, he looked at the screen and saw something.

Intimacy.

Scripted, cheapened, and pumped full of plastic. But there it was: a sense of personal prowess and belonging. There was another word. What was it?

Acceptance. As if the woman on the screen—who had never, and would never, meet him—was smiling directly at him.

He lifted the remote, turning the television off.

"Nothing good on, anyway," he said to himself as he lay back on the couch. The sensation of loneliness returned, and he stared at the ceiling for a moment.

John looked around, reached for the Gideon Bible in the desk, and flipped it open.

"God," he said to himself. God was the cure to all loneliness. And the only way to connect with God was through the Bible, right?

To read a book that had been penned thousands of years ago on another continent, in a different culture.

He read a chapter from the psalms and told himself that he felt better.

John stared at the ceiling for what felt like hours. Finally, he fell asleep.

Chapter 12

THE SUN HADN'T come up yet.

Devin had slept only a few unsettled hours. He hoped Hannah had slept better in the room next door. He'd found two rooms with made beds that seemed more sanitary than the others and slept above the covers, hands clasped, pistol under his pillow. It wasn't the most restful sleep he'd ever had, but sleep, he reminded himself, was a crutch anyway.

He got up and found a shower, checked for clean water—undressed and stepped in. He set the pistol on the edge of the sink, only a foot or so away, keeping an eye on the cracked door as he bathed as quickly as possible. He dressed, his suit feeling better after he'd had a chance to hang it out for a while. Devin smoothed the few wrinkles in a mirror and decided to make a second search of the motel.

The place was dilapidated. Obviously built sometime in the late fifties and abandoned. Who knew if the people who had been using it actually owned the place or not—it wasn't like anyone was going to check on them in this rat-infested heap. Nearly every room looked as if it had been rampaged through by a herd of wild animals—clothing, sheets, and even mattresses were tossed everywhere. The windows were open in a few rooms, letting the outside world tear in.

Devin stepped into another of the empty rooms—the smell of dirt and mildew, just like the others. He approached the closet and opened it: intimate apparel, video camera equipment, a cardboard box filled with lewd paraphernalia. He pulled on a pair of leather gloves from his car and pushed some of the items aside, cautious of the health hazards involved.

A box moved, and there was a jingling sound as something hit the wooden floor of the closet. He reached down, searching carefully. Devin had found used needles in several of the other rooms and had no interest in finding another one—especially not by the exposed tip.

The last of the debris shifted, and he saw what made the noise: a tiny ring with a set of small keys. Devin picked them up and looked them over. He scowled in thought. They didn't belong to anything in the closet. He scanned the room again, stepping toward the nightstand.

Nothing in the drawers. He went prone, looking beneath the bed. There was a wadded shirt that someone had forgotten—and a box. Devin reached in, pulled the box out by the handle, and set it on the bed.

A large, fireproof lockbox. Heavy-duty construction. He tried the key in the lock, and it turned with ease.

Devin opened the box.

These people were more dangerous than he'd realized.

"Hannah."

She shifted slightly, suddenly becoming aware of her body again as she awoke.

"Hannah," Devin said again, stepping further into the room.

Her body unfurled from the curled position she had slept in. Still in her clothes, on top of the covers of a motel room bed. She stretched as she watched Devin walk up to the night table and shove the items off of it.

Hannah sat up, yawning. "What is it?"

Devin spilled the contents of a fireproof box onto the table.

"Guns," he announced, describing the dumped contents. "Two Magnum revolvers, a Sig Sauer with the serial number filed off, and two MAC-10 submachine guns."

Hannah blinked; she knew the name. "MAC-10?"

Devin picked up one of the submachine guns. It looked like a smallish metal brick with a stubby barrel and small grip.

An ammunition clip that was almost as long as the gun itself protruded from the base of the grip.

"The MAC-10," Devin said as he looked it over. "Rickety little submachine guns used by street gangs. Fully automatic with a high rate of fire, made out of stamped metal—inaccurate to the point of unusable."

She rubbed her eyes, looking over the firearms. "How is that bad?"

"It means that they're trying to intimidate more than girls."

Hannah stared at the small pile of guns, her breathing getting slower.

"What do you know about human trafficking?" Devin asked, waiting for Hannah to reply.

She thought for a moment, still focusing on the weapons in front of her. "I've heard some things about it. In other countries mostly. Why?" She studied the lines on the dark gun metal of the Sig Sauer compared to the glint of light on the silver-looking revolver.

"Hannah," Devin said from another world.

She was used to guns. She'd grown up around rifles and shotguns and cousins who liked to hunt. But the weight of a firearm—the precise construction of such a brutal mechanism always seemed to startle her.

"Hannah, look at me."

It never seemed real until she touched them. Even now it all felt like a dream from some other—

"Hannah," Devin said firmly. She turned her head, looking at him—commanding in his suit and perfectly fastened tie. He pulled up a chair next to the bed and sat down, closer to her than she had expected, eyes focused and unblinking. "Do you understand what you're getting yourself into?"

Hannah studied his serious face. She answered with honesty, shaking her head. "No."

Devin remained still and silent for a moment, as if he were preparing his words with precision and care. "Human trafficking is the illegal buying and selling of unwilling human beings into sexual slavery."

Her breathing stopped. She knew that. But to say it? That was something completely different somehow.

"Every day girls and"—he was careful to add—"boys are captured, tricked, and cajoled into the hands of traffickers who sell them as sexual slaves. In fact, eight thousand human beings are bought and sold in the United States alone every year. It is real, and it is dangerous."

Hannah nodded without speaking.

"It is, by some counts, the second-most profitable illegal trade in the world, directly following after the drug trade." His face became sober, looking her deep into her eyes. "Do you understand what I'm saying?"

She didn't respond.

"Selling human beings into a life of rape and captivity is more lucrative than money laundering, counterfeiting, loan-sharking, and the international arms trade."

Hannah blinked. "The international arms trade?" she repeated.

Devin nodded. "More money is made from the trafficking of human beings than from the sales of every single firearm sold illegally to every street punk, terrorist, and third-world dictator on the face of Planet Earth."

Hannah's heart rate seemed to change—not faster or slower, but somehow painful, as if it were trying to tear itself apart. "Are you trying to scare me?" she asked.

Devin held up a MAC-10. "I'm trying to ask you how firmly you believe this is worth it. Because these people are criminal. There is no government regulation on the human sex trade. There are no receipts, returns, or unions. There is no Better

Business Bureau for the buying and selling of twelve-year-old boys as perverse playthings—there's only this." He tapped his index finger on the submachine gun.

Hannah nodded.

"People get shot every day over meth deals that have gone bad. It's the nature of the black market. But these people aren't cooking meth in their basements so they can sell it to kids on the street—they're selling the kids on the street into other people's basements—and they are not interested in losing their investment. And they'll chop you into slices of meat if they catch you. Do you understand?"

Something seemed to rumble inside of Hannah. Like a tremor exploding from inside of her. Some part of her wanted to cry—another wanted to scream. But she held it in—a fireworks display of emotion escaping in the solemn phrase: "I understand."

Devin looked over her face for an inordinate amount of time, studying her, trying to pick up on any hint of hesitation or fear that might work its way to the surface. Hannah focused on her breathing—pushing every thought out of her mind, dwelling as much as she could in the stillness and serenity of single-mindedness.

"Good." Devin nodded. He stood up and walked toward one of the grimy windows. "We need to do one last sweep of..." He stopped dead and stared out the glass.

"What?" Hannah moved from the bed and came alongside Devin at the window.

He pointed with one hand, grabbing her arm with another. "That's them."

Hannah followed his pointing finger to a tiny dot on the distant highway—a mile or two away. A car or truck—impossible to tell at such a distance.

"They're coming back here," Devin announced, pulling her away from the window. "They're on their way now."

"Now?" she repeated, shocked. "How long?"

"Two minutes. Maybe."

Hannah felt panic stab at her. *Help me, God*, she prayed silently in the recesses of her mind—then chastised herself. Now wasn't the time to tell God what to do but to listen to what He had to say. She focused on the stillness.

Devin moved to the table, picked up the Sig Sauer handgun, and began stuffing magazines of ammunition in his pockets. One magazine locked into place in the grip as Devin threw his back into the wall, handgun clenched at the ready, head peeking out the window.

Hannah was suddenly overcome by the rashness of his actions. "Do you plan on shooting your way out?" she asked skeptically.

Devin paused, obviously digesting some kind of vision he was having. "No," he said definitively, "there are too many of them, and they're too well armed. We have to get out of here." Devin pointed to a nightstand. "Get my car keys."

Hannah rushed to the nightstand, seeing the keys lying there. Her hand reached out, and something stopped her.

The girls being photographed.

The pictures uploaded onto a computer.

The images on the Internet—advertising to potential buyers.

Logging vital information.

Stashing the laptop in the room.

Hannah stopped, fingertips barely touching the keys. Her focus shifted to the right.

"What are you doing?" Devin asked, firm.

"The laptop," she said with purpose.

Devin's attention flashed to her. "What laptop?"

She moved to the wardrobe against the wall, pulling the doors open, searching through the clothing hung there. "I have to find the laptop," she said without hesitation.

"There isn't time," Devin said roughly, grabbing the keys

from the table himself. "We have to go."

"No." Hannah shook her head. "They stored information on the laptop—where they're keeping the girls. How and where they're going to sell them!"

Devin moved alongside her, pulling objects from the wardrobe with less care than Hannah, trying to help.

"I need you to get the car," Hannah said, pulling the drawers open.

"But there's no time. We have to—"

"I'm sorry," Hannah interrupted, "but you have to get the car. Bring it around. If I'm not there when you come around, you have to leave without me."

Devin shook his head. "No. The point was to rescue the girls they took, not give them someone else."

She rummaged through to the bottom of the drawer, then pulled the entire drawer out of its place, tossing it onto the bed. "Please, Devin. Go now. I need you to get the car!"

Devin backed away, not taking his eyes off her.

"Go!" she shouted.

He turned, leaving the room.

Hannah turned back to the wardrobe, pulling open the bottom drawer, rifling through it. The laptop wasn't anywhere to be found. Maybe they'd taken it with them. That's what she would have done. It made the most sense to her. But she wasn't going to give up on it if it were still here.

She heard a car engine outside. Devin? Or the others?

What if they did grab her? What if she did become their next piece of cargo to buy and sell? What if…?

She silenced her mind. Speculation was useless. The future hadn't happened yet. It was only squawking birds that muddied any wisdom she might pull from this place.

She looked at the mess on the nightstand.

The nightstand.

Hannah dropped to her knees, pulling open the bottom drawer, pulling it completely free. Beneath the drawer, resting on the carpet.

A cloth case.

She grabbed it, dragging it from beneath the bed, pulling the zipper with a ragged buzz.

The laptop.

Hannah pulled the zipper shut, standing. She moved to the window, shouting, "Devin, I—"

A heavy-duty pickup truck pulled up next to the window.

Not Devin.

Haggard men. One with a tattoo.

The dragon.

She turned, ramming through the doors at the other side of the room, uncertain if he'd seen her. Through the hallway, into the room with the front desk. Another vehicle pulled up to her left.

A midsized silver sedan.

Devin.

Hannah shoved the glass doors open—the jingle of the door's bell announcing her presence with a chiming that froze her blood in her chest. She rushed outside and threw herself at the door.

"Get in!" Devin shouted pointlessly as she leapt into the passenger seat.

"Go!" she ordered with a kind of harsh whisper.

Devin didn't hesitate. His foot slammed on the gas, and the car took off—a billow of dust lifting after them, obscuring everything behind them.

"Are they following us?" Hannah asked.

"I don't know," Devin barked. "I can't see anything through this dust!"

Hannah spun in her seat. "What do I do if they're following?"

"Here," Devin said, shoving the Sig Sauer at her.

"Devin, are you sure?"

They hit the pavement hard as they climbed up from the gravel they had been screaming across and took off across the paved road, toward the highway.

In the distance Hannah saw the figures disappear into the motel. They hadn't figured out what was happening yet. But that would change soon. They would find the body, know that someone had ransacked the place. And then they would come tearing after.

The motel vanished beneath the horizon as the speedometer reached seventy.

"We got away?" Hannah asked, incredulous.

"Maybe," Devin nodded, looking in the rearview mirror.

Hannah scanned the paved horizon behind them. "Will they come after us?"

"Absolutely."

"Will they find us?" she asked, tapping her finger against the trigger guard of the pistol in her hand.

"They're certainly going to try."

Hannah set the gun next to the gearshift and pulled the laptop from its case. "Then there isn't much time."

Chapter 13

JOHN MOVED QUICKLY along the Las Vegas Strip, passing the statues of Caesar's Palace and the fountains of Bellagio, daylight scorching every patch of unshaded world. His feet, fettered in dress shoes, ached. Yesterday's dress pants and shirt—unbuttoned and flapping as he moved through the still, nearly nonexistent air. His shirt was soaked. Despite the fact that he'd ditched his sport coat, he was still boiling.

He had always been quick to adapt to new temperatures—rain forests all over the world had been his home in six- to eight-week stretches for years. But the quick movement—racing along sidewalks at the fastest pace one could without drawing attention—was enough to melt him from the inside out. They passed a fake volcano near the street, and he could swear he felt even more heat radiating off of it.

Trista, on the other hand, was unfazed. She'd been able to change her clothes but was still in women's dress slacks and a red knit top. Her shoes, while no longer high heels, were not what John would have considered to be sensible either.

None of this stopped her. Or even slowed her down.

She marched forward with purpose and resolve, head snapping side to side as she looked at every possible thing that might be of interest. Eyes darting from the kitschy Eiffel Tower to the glass pyramid of the Luxor. Her judgments were almost instantaneous—look, assess, move on. Every few minutes she would cast her head over her shoulder toward John, speaking quickly, saying something that was of interest.

The same stretches of pavement they had been walking along for nearly an hour and a half were all starting to blur—in part from repetition, in part from the speed with which they blasted past. The only thing that changed were the swirls and swarms of passing pedestrians that walked, moved, and sauntered across the same stretches of sidewalk and pavement—oblivious to any coming trouble.

Trista stopped on the sidewalk, looking at John.

"This is the place—that's for certain." She glanced at the buildings that surrounded them: the MGM Grand on one side of the street, the Excalibur on the other. "What about you? What have you felt?"

"I..." He had nothing to add, he realized. John shrugged. "I've got nothing."

Trista glanced at a car, then back to John. "Devin is tied up with Hannah, trying to find the girls that were taken. He needs our help establishing the scene while he's away. OK?"

John nodded.

"I need you to focus. Do you understand?"

He nodded again, more slowly this time.

Trista cleared her throat. "I'm sorry if I sounded impatient. You know how stressed I can get on a deadline." She forced a smile. "Do you need to take a break?"

John sat on the edge of a planter, hung his head to rest it for a moment, then looked up. Flocks of people from all around the world moved both ways along the busy sidewalk. Just beyond them the street was jammed bumper to bumper with cars. A truck passed slowly—a moving billboard, taking deliberate advantage of the nearly stopped traffic. On the side of the bright red truck was a picture of a woman—wearing next to nothing. "Full escort service," the truck said in big yellow letters, a phone number located just below.

The woman was smiling—at him? It was all so much easier than dealing with a flesh-and-blood woman—someone with needs and feelings, someone who was so easy to fail. He averted his eyes, looking at the fountains of Bellagio that swayed in the distance.

"Are you going to marry him?" John asked without thinking.

"Do you mean Holden?" Trista asked.

He nodded without looking at her, wiping a river of oily sweat from his taxed face.

Trista turned to him, arms crossed. She walked toward John and sat down on the planter beside him. "Do you really want to know?" she asked without looking at him.

"Yes," he said, taking an anticipatory breath, "I do."

Trista was silent for several minutes as a host of Las Vegas tourists passed by. "I told him no," she said without emotion. "I told him no before I ever left Belize."

John didn't speak for several minutes, trying to feel something—but it was like his heart was frozen in a block of ice, so prepared to hurt that it wasn't ready to do anything else. "Why did you tell him no?" he asked after several minutes.

She stood, avoiding a retired couple in matching T-shirts as they walked by, arms filled with bags. "Does it matter?"

John stood. "I guess I just…"

Something soured in his chest—a feeling of disgust. There was something dark and impenetrable nearby. Not just a feeling. A face. Like someone was watching for them.

Then he saw it with his mind's eye.

Angelo.

What had been a steady marching of his heart was interrupted by a furious flame, the tempo skyrocketing in speed.

"Trista!" He stepped toward her, grabbing her arm, eyes shifting side to side as he looked for the mysterious figure.

She seemed surprised, eyes focused sharply on John. "What are you—?"

He yanked her away from the place where they had stopped, pulling her as fast as he could.

Angelo's eyes remained closed.

Sweat slipped across his body. Down his face. His back. Through his hair.

The hot sun on his black clothes. Black jacket.

He could feel the past. Amorphous and clouded—his personal memories wiped away. Somewhere in the past were needles and flashing lights. Corruption and confusion. And now he stood, feeling it all happening around him, heading straight back into the living hell that had no name or form. Something he dreaded—it was all happening again, and none of them would be safe.

His mind searched for them.

Trying to find—

His eyes snapped open.

They were in the street below. Beyond the glass of the shop he stood in. In the midst of the crowd.

They knew he was here.

They would run.

He would catch them. And stop them.

"What's happening?" Trista demanded, confused by the hand that was holding her arm so tightly. John pulled her through the plodding mess of tourists. "Where are we going?"

"Angelo," John said again—face sullen, voice serious.

"Here?" she asked, face snapping side to side, looking for the mysterious—

John spun suddenly and thrust a finger as if it were a spear tip, jabbing toward a building across the street. Tall glass for walls—a figure in black, ragged and unkempt. A wild drifter. Angelo. Rushing down the stairs, visible through the glass, racing toward the bottom floor. Toward the street.

"John!" she exclaimed, as if he didn't already know what was happening. Trista looked back at him.

His face was serious—rough, almost angry. "Come on!" he ordered, pulling her with a swift jerk to her arm.

They moved through the crowd, pushing through the windows in the crush, worming their way as quickly as possible through the forest of swishing tourists. Their speed was hardly faster than a walk despite the fact that they were passing everyone else as if they weren't moving at all.

A truck horn, low and blustering, let off a set of angry beeps. Trista's vision blurred for a moment as her attention raced toward the commotion. It was Angelo, rushing across the street, through the traffic. Another beeping horn as he got in the way of another already delayed vehicle.

She heard John's voice before she felt his firm grip jerk her along: "Run!"

Trista took off after John as he pulled her along for the first few steps, then let go. They charged forward, her feet pounding out a rapid rhythm as they weaved and dodged through the ever-shifting maze of humanity.

Someone shouted behind them. A woman and her bags toppled onto the sidewalk. Trista stole a glance back and saw what she feared: Angelo ramming his way through foot traffic like a charging bull.

One pedestrian blurred with the next as the whole world became a flashing tumult of people, sunlight, and reflective glass. Trista's feet thundered against the ground—faster and faster. John was ahead of her, his hand reaching for her every few seconds, grabbing at her, tugging her in one direction or another, then letting go so she could maneuver faster. Every step her pace increased, and with every increase in speed John became harder to make out through the crowd.

"This way!" John announced, shouting as he grabbed her wrist, pulling her into traffic.

A car horn screamed as her feet hit the pavement, weaving through cars—all virtually stopped. Across the lanes, dodging polished vehicles—most, freshly washed rentals.

Trista followed John along the side of a big red truck, watching him disappear around the front end.

A second behind. She turned the corner.

"*John!*" she shouted over the traffic noise, the truck horn reprimanding her with a harsh blast of loud noise. John Temple was nowhere to be seen.

More honking. Her glance stole to the traffic light down the street.

Green.

Every stagnant car in the street began to shoulder its way forward with as much speed as possible.

Trista found herself between lanes, cars rushing forward to either side. The truck passed and she looked back, the red curtain of the trailer pulling away.

A raucous symphony of car horns and profanity.

Angelo—climbing over car hoods, rushing through the obstacles ahead of him with uncanny speed. Trista launched herself across the last lane, hand raised to warn the oncoming traffic.

She clambered across the median, plunging into another rushing stream of cars trying to make it through the green light. She was halfway through the second lane when she heard the sound of a human voice over the blaring of car horns.

"Trista!"

She recoiled, swinging for John's throat before she realized who had grabbed her arm. He pulled her between the vehicles, her feet touching the sidewalk after just a few short moments.

There was a scream of tires as momentum propelled a car forward. A human scream. A sickly sound:

Thud!

They turned just in time to see a black sedan hit Angelo as he plowed across the lanes. His body thrown to the ground.

The world seemed to stop for a moment.

Traffic halted. The sauntering tourists paused, watching the spectacle. Trista held, John coming up beside her.

The driver got out of the vehicle, walking toward the badly damaged front end.

Trista swallowed, uncertain how to feel. She turned to John. "Is he . . . ?" She didn't finish her sentence.

John shook his head. "I don't know."

The gathering crowd leaned in for a moment around Angelo—obscured by cars and people—then stepped back. Surprise covered their faces. The top of Angelo's head—covered in long grimy curls hanging from his bowed shoulders across his downturned face—lifted.

Trista's heart stopped.

"John," she stammered, trying to think of what to do next.

He grabbed her arms, squeezing hard. "Trista." His expression was sharp with a ferocious seriousness. "The room!" he barked. "I'll draw him off. Go!"

She tried to speak—to protest—to tell him that she would be fine and that she would stay with him—

Angelo stood in the street, eyes lifting—making contact with Trista's.

"Go!" John shoved her, sending her back hard, nearly falling over. He stabbed down the sidewalk with a fingertip, pointing the direction to go. "*Run!*"

Angelo shoved his way through the surrounding people, pushing past cars.

Trista ran and didn't look back.

Angelo's vision was still blurry.

What had happened?

There had been cars. Lots of them. He'd shoved his way

through traffic. Something had gone wrong.

He caught sight of a car's front end. He'd been hit.

His vision swished side to side, trying to steady on one particular thing. Someone was trying to talk to him—like voices beneath the ocean surface. Sounds took shape like blurring images sharpening under the twisting focus of a camera's lens.

"You need to watch where you're going!" someone growled.

Angelo braced his weight against his knees, pushing himself up.

More voices: "You should get to a hospital, buddy."

"You're lucky you aren't dead."

Luck didn't factor into it. At least it wasn't important. Nothing was important. Only Temple and the woman—*Brightling?*

The sidewalk. He looked. Two bleary figures through the haze of his eyes—a man and a woman.

Angelo took a step forward, nearly toppling. Someone tried to help him, but he shoved them away. People hung from their car windows, shouting obscenities, demanding he get out of the busy street.

He looked up again, vision clearing. The woman was gone. Run away? Temple stood there—staring. Then ran.

An instinct took over and he charged after—powerless against the impulse.

Like a bobcat, he thought, the way they took off after hikers and runners. Chasing after anything that would run away.

He was over a car hood in a flash, tearing after John Temple, chasing him down an alleyway.

A wild animal, Angelo thought to himself, coolly. He was a wild animal with tunnel vision. He noted how true this seemed—the way his mind seemed to narrow into a fixated tunnel. As if John Temple—his quarry—were the only thing that existed.

Through the blistering hot alleyway. Around the corner—into a parking garage attached to the back of one of the numerous hotels on the Strip. Up a ramp. Higher and higher.

He could feel Temple. He couldn't let him go. He was so close. Just around—

Angelo rounded the corner.

And never saw it coming.

John backed away.

The third floor of the parking garage. Angelo on his knees—knocked to the ground from the solid kick he had delivered to the small of Angelo's back. He moved in to kick again—leg cocking back.

"Wait," Angelo said, lifting a hand to ask for a moment.

John stopped, confused. Just a moment ago he was being chased by something wild and unpredictable. Now he was staring at a seemingly lucid individual, asking for patience.

"What do you want?" John shouted, overcome with panic and anger.

Angelo began to raise himself, crouching—then lunged forward, wrapping his hand around John's throat, slamming him into a cement wall. The shockwave rippled through John's body and along his arms, hands grasping at his choking throat.

"I was just hit by a car!" Angelo spat. "Do you think that *kicking* me will do *anything*?"

John tried to fight loose, hands groping.

"Stop struggling," Angelo ordered, staring into John's eyes. He seemed to lose patience in an instant. "*Stop struggling!*"

John stopped, staring at Angelo, realizing suddenly that he wasn't strangling.

"I'm not here to hurt you," Angelo announced firmly.

"What?" John asked, confused.

"I'm here to warn you."

John looked over Angelo with suspicious eyes. "I don't understand."

Angelo let go, taking a step back. "I obviously can't stop you, so the least I can do is warn you."

John grabbed his knees, taking long and deliberate breaths, recovering from both the run and being pinned to the wall. "Warn me about what?"

"How much do you know about the Thresher?"

John shook his head. "Not much. I know the older Firstborn get spooked when they talk about the idea. He—it—whatever the Thresher is, it's bad."

Angelo nodded, stepping away from John. "The Thresher is a simple thing. As long as the Firstborn are divided and useless, the Thresher stays dormant. But as the Firstborn come together, it wakes—and is unleashed, allowed to do greater evil."

"What are you saying?" John asked, wiping sweat from his forehead as he sat on the concrete.

Angelo crouched in front of John, face getting close. "The last time the Thresher was unleashed was in the first half of the twentieth century. There had been a serious attempt to unify the Firstborn in Europe, and it almost succeeded, but as a result they were nearly wiped out. To this day there is still next to no Firstborn on the European continent. And the evil they restrained was set free."

John studied Angelo's intense face, trying to remember what Jerry Kirkland had told him about the history of the Firstborn, trying to see if it all worked together. But it was too vague to make it work in his mind; he needed more. "What evil?"

"The evil that plunged us into world war and slaughtered millions."

"That can't be right," John stammered. "That's not possible."

"The Firstborn," Angelo said, standing, "are not possible. But here we are, talking about unseen evils and visions of an otherwise unknowable future." He took a step back, as if to leave.

"Wait," John said, raising a hand. "You said you came to warn me. About what?"

Angelo straightened his long dark jacket. "Beware of the Thresher. God isn't the only originator of visions. The Thresher can make you see things too."

"You think we saw something false?"

"One of us must have," Angelo asserted. "And I know what I saw."

"So do I," John replied. "Which means that it's my perception of reality against yours."

Angelo nodded. "Which has always been the problem with people and faith. Something the Thresher is going to exploit."

"What is the Thresher anyway?" John demanded.

"The Thresher?" Angelo said with a nod, obviously preparing to share whatever he knew. "The Thresher is a job, a vocation among demons. Whichever demon is chosen to be Thresher is charged with destroying or containing the Firstborn. When you started to come together, they got rid of the old guy—he was too gentle—and they got somebody new. A demon who was meaner and more aggressive. This demon has been given permission to take you out with extreme prejudice."

John thought for a moment, trying to see if Angelo's sincerity showed any sign of cracking. "The Thresher has been unleashed."

"Yes," Angelo agreed. "And the Thresher can trick you, trap you, and kill you."

John considered for a moment. "And the Thresher wants to kill me?"

"Not you," Angelo said, turning his back, walking away. "Trista Brightling."

Chapter 14

THEY SAT IN a coffee shop they had found in a small town off the highway. The sign had said "Free Wi-Fi," and that was something they might need.

Hannah stared at the screen of the confiscated laptop, looking up occasionally at Devin, who glanced at his own personal laptop between casual and paranoid looks at the door.

She watched a progress bar race across, fill with green, then turn over onto the next screen demanding a password. "Uh-oh," she muttered to herself.

"What is it," Devin said casually, still watching the door.

"I need a password to get in."

Devin nodded. "That's expected."

"You were military intelligence," she said, shaking her head. "What do I need to do?"

"I was HumInt—human intelligence—that's a SigInt question."

"SigInt?" she asked, staring at the password screen.

He took a sip of coffee. "Signals intelligence. Try *password*." Devin taped at his own computer. "It's the most common password."

Hannah typed in the word, hitting the enter key. She shook her head. "No good. Anything else?"

Devin didn't look up. "Birthdays, nicknames, hobbies. Those are all common mistakes. But those are weak passwords—the kind that people can figure out. Professionals don't make those kinds of mistakes."

"Then what do I do?" she asked.

Devin glanced naturally at a window. "Pray they're amateurs."

She typed in *dragon*.

Nothing.

She tried *girls*.

Incorrect.

She typed several random dates. Place names—it was all grasping in the dark.

"I'm trying everything I can think of," Hannah said, shaking her head. "I think we already established that these people are professionals. I don't think I'm going to be able to guess this."

Devin looked up, making contact with piercing eyes. "Then you have to find it."

"What do you mean?"

"The password is buried somewhere in the past," he said. "You're the one who can see that."

Hannah looked down for a moment. "It doesn't work like that. We don't get to choose what to see; we only see what we're shown."

"True," Devin said, looking her over for a few moments. "But it can't hurt to ask."

Hannah thought for a moment, then nodded. She stared at the screen. Some part of her wanted to plead with God, but instead she simply made a small, silent appeal—then closed her eyes.

She focused on her breathing—listening for the quiet voice of eternity.

Then she felt it.

The past was quiet. No pictures. No sounds. Just the feeling of the keyboard. She lifted her hands, setting her fingers on the keys.

She felt the motion, her finger moving from its resting place to a key—then struck. Then another key. She could feel what had been done before—so many times, as if warmth were rising from each key. Hannah tapped away—a string of more than ten letters and numbers—a code that meant nothing to her, a total jumble no person would ever guess.

She struck the enter key and opened her eyes.

The screen went black.

Her breath caught in her throat for a moment. The desktop loaded, icons populating the field as they appeared intermittently in a jagged pattern.

Hannah let out a small sigh. "We're in."

Devin stood, coming around behind her.

Her hands continued, feeling out the warm path backward through time. The mouse cursor glided effortlessly across the screen, her finger gliding toward the image that seemed to rise up in her mind.

Double-click. A desktop folder opened. Another set of clicks, another opened folder. She didn't even have a chance to read the label on the digital folder—images of the process unfolded in her mind like a tutorial, taking her through the steps.

A document opened. Not a Word document. Something else.

"Devin," she said slowly, "what am I looking at?"

He eyed the screen over her shoulder for several seconds. "These are source files for a Web site."

Hannah looked over the images: pornography. Naked bodies of young girls—their faces all cropped out of the image. Hannah felt embarrassment and discomfort, even though it wasn't much different than some of the things she had seen hanging on dorm room walls back at school. She frowned. "Why aren't their faces in the pictures?"

Devin was silent for a moment, his eyes turning up toward the counter now to see if any of the management had noticed what they were perusing. "They're minors," he said, voice strained.

"How do you know?"

He groaned to himself. "Because in the eyes of the law it's not considered child pornography unless the face is showing."

Hannah's stomach tightened in a bad way.

Devin continued, "And if you're going to have a public Web site advertising what you have in your possession, you don't want to make the girls identifiable to begin with, and you certainly don't want to get hit with child pornography if you are caught. The courts don't like it, and fellow inmates don't take well to it either."

Hannah nodded, focusing on her breathing and her stillness. "Do you think these are our girls in these pictures?"

"Does it matter?" Devin asked. "We're still dealing with very horrible people."

"But will it help us find the girls?"

Devin reached for the touch pad, moved the mouse cursor, and clicked on a link. He read for a moment: "Jackpot."

"What?" Hannah asked, not bothering to read the screen.

"It looks like the girls are being auctioned off at a private residence in another state."

"Where?" Hannah asked, searching the large block of text on the screen. Then she saw it. She wasn't as surprised as she might have suspected.

"Las Vegas, Nevada," Devin said with a nod. "Everything is pulling us there."

John Temple walked the halls of the hotel, nearing the room.

He was tired. He was beaten. His body ached.

Had Angelo been right? Was Trista Brightling going to die? Could he stop it? Was Angelo even lucid enough to know the difference between fact and delusion?

His world seemed to float. Arms, heavy and fatigued, swung at his sides as he walked. Each step seemed to land with a strange certainty. Ahead he saw the room. A few more steps. Standing in front of the door he reached for the key card. John swiped the black magnetic strip, the light flashed green, and the lock slid away with a thud.

He reached for the door handle, but it turned on its own. Someone inside opened the door and threw it open:

Trista.

Her eyes were wide—scared? Excited? It didn't matter.

She threw her arms around his neck, pulling him into the room, the door sliding shut behind them.

"John," she stammered, almost tearful, "I was scared to death. You ran off, and I came back to the room and you weren't here." She pulled away, smiling at him. "I'm just glad you're all right."

John stared into her eyes. Big and beautiful.

"Are you OK?" she asked.

He shook his head, eyes never leaving hers. "Why?"

"You're just looking at me like…"

He pushed a blonde strand from her face with one hand, cradling her cheek with the other. "Trista, I want you to know something."

Her expression changed to confusion. "What?"

"I'll protect you," he said with a sincere nod. "No matter what happens, I'll do everything to protect you."

Her eyes seemed to soften, more vulnerable than before. "Are you OK?" she asked, still confused. "What about Angelo? What if he finds us again? Do you think he's trying to kill us?"

"I'd die for you," he said, holding her face gently. "You know that, right? You know that I'd—"

She kissed him.

John stared at her. "Why did you do that?"

"Shut up," she seethed. "Shut up and kiss me." She moved close to his face. "Kiss me before I come to my senses."

Lips touched. Like static, John thought, mind racing—world vanishing. Her arms around him, pulling him close. He pushed back, lips working in tandem, pressing her into the wall.

She muttered his name, and he moved to her neck.

"John," she said.

His teeth worked gently on the soft skin of her neck.

"John," she said again, "stop."

He pulled back, looking at her face, lipstick smeared. "What?"

"Stop," she stammered, pushing him away.

"I'm sorry, Trista," he said, trying to think of what to say to make it right.

She wiped her lips with the back of her arm. "I'm sorry, John. I never should have done that."

"Trista," he pleaded, stepping toward her, "talk to me."

She put up her hands. "Stay back, John, OK? Just leave me alone for a while. It was a mistake. That never should have happened."

He opened his palms to her, pleading. "Why not? Will you just talk to me?"

She shook her head, backing away. "We can't be together, John. We can never be together—not ever. I'm sorry to make things more difficult for you. I really am. I'm sorry for leading you on, but it was a mistake. It was always a mistake."

"Trista," he called toward her as she moved into the suite's bedroom, "wait."

The door shut. The lock clicked. And John Temple stood in the hotel room by himself. He walked to the bedroom door and knocked. There was no reply.

He waited thirty minutes, then left.

Devin stepped out of the coffee shop, moved to the trunk of his car, and popped it open with the remote on his key fob. Hannah was still inside, using a restroom.

His phone chirped in his jacket. "Hello?" he said, phone at his ear.

"Devin Bathurst."

Devin frowned in confusion, recognizing the voice. "Mr. Goldstein?"

"It's been awhile," Clay Goldstein said from the other end of the line, voice enigmatic and strangely neutral.

"It has been awhile," Devin said, trying his best to get the other man to betray something in his tone. “The meeting in San Antonio, right?”

“That sounds about right,” Clay Goldstein said with his usual casual tone. “It was the night everything went bad. Morris Childs went missing, and there was the incident between Henry Rice and Blake Jackson.”

“Blake Jackson killed Henry Rice,” Devin said unceremoniously, seeing if his lack of finesse might draw something out in Clay’s voice.

“That’s right,” he replied, strangely jovial, “but I didn’t call to reminisce.”

“OK,” Devin replied, hesitantly, still deeply confused. “Then how can I help you, Mr. Goldstein?”

There was a belly laugh from the other end of the line.

Devin cracked an awkward smile, feeling like the butt of some kind of joke. “Is something funny, sir?”

“Don’t call me sir. My father was sir.”

“Very well.” Devin nodded. “Mr. Goldstein.”

“And don’t start that either,” he said sternly. “It’s Clay, got it?”

“OK.” Devin paused. “Clay. How can I help you?”

“I don’t need your help,” Clay said with a certain charismatic warmth. “I’m calling because I am going to help you.”

“Vincent Sobel made it very clear that—”

“Vince,” Clay grumbled, “is getting a little ahead of himself.”

Devin shut the car trunk. “What do you mean?”

“We can discuss that later,” Clay assured. “Right now you need to get to Nevada, and you need to get there fast.”

Devin glanced from one side of the street to the next, seeing if anyone was watching him. “What makes you think I want to go to Nevada?”

Another solid belly laugh. “You forget that I see things as they’re happening. I may be in California, but I can still see you in the moment. And I know what you want.”

Devin looked around the street, trying to spot anyone who might be watching him. A man glanced up at him from a park bench across the street.

"That guy doesn't work for me," Clay said.

Devin shook his head. "I don't know what you're talking about."

"Yes, you do." Clay laughed. "And why do you shake your head when you're on the phone?"

"What do you want?" Devin demanded, turning his back to the street, speaking intensely into his phone.

"What about you?" Clay asked. "What do you want? The sale is the day after tomorrow, and driving will take too long."

"You don't see the future," Devin said sternly. "How do you know when the sale is?"

"Because you know. And I also know how to use the Internet." Clay laughed. "This is the twenty-first century, you know."

Devin considered for a moment. "And you want to buy me a plane ticket to Nevada?"

Another enigmatic laugh. "How does a charter jet sound?"

John Temple wandered the halls of the hotel. Thoughts of Trista filled his head—none of them fully formed or coherent.

How long had the thought of her been haunting him? Like his own shadow. He couldn't seem to shake the thought of her. The desire that he had tried so hard to pray away, think away, wish away—escape. He knew that the only way to ever rid himself of his desire of her was to find comfort in God. To turn to the Word.

"God," he muttered the address. There was no auditory response—but God didn't work that way. God spoke to his soul. Right?

He stepped into the elevator and punched a button with his thumb.

The thought of Trista's touch. Her skin. The smell of her hair. God's love for him was so much more real than all those things—the taste of a kiss, the feel of her arms—all of that was less meaningful than believing in a very real, very personal God.

Wasn't it?

Wanting anything more than his Savior was a sin. Idolatry.

Wasn't it?

"God?" he said again, nearly pleading. He couldn't feel anything.

The elevator doors opened, and he walked into the casino, walking through the jumbled forest of sensations. Jingling bells. Bright lights. The smell of alcohol and cigarettes.

The kaleidoscope of sensations passed him by as he walked through the thicket. More hallways passed, a nagging feeling of need filling him and gutting him all at once.

A hotel restaurant—he wasn't hungry. That wasn't what he needed. His attention moved: a hotel bar.

John stopped, staring at the establishment. Whatever it was that he needed seemed to pull him toward the place. He took a step forward. The place was dimly lit with a circular bar surrounding a spirelike collection of alcohols in white-lit glass. Dark brown wood covered the curved walls, though they could hardly be seen through the dim light.

He tried to remember the last time he'd had a drink. He drank lightly in foreign countries at times when it would be considered rude not to, but he'd avoided alcohol ever since he'd overdone it in college. But now he felt a desire to wash away every feeling. Everything he'd spent so much time longing for being thrown, literally, into his arms—then torn away.

He sat down at the bar—empty except for a man in a white suit, sitting around the corner.

"Can I get you something?" the bartender, a college-aged guy with a goatee, asked.

John stared at him, wanting to order something that would make him forget.

He shook his head instead. "I'll just have a Sprite."

The bartender nodded. "Anything else in that?"

"No." John shook his head again. "Just the soda."

"OK," the bartender acknowledged, reaching for a plastic cup.

John Temple hung his head, staring at the bar, running fingers through his hair.

"You," a bright voice with a slight country twang laughed from the end of the bar, "must be the only other liquor-free man in this entire city."

John looked up to see the other man, dressed in a white suit, looking at him. "I guess so," John replied with the most sincere smile he could muster at the moment.

The man got up from his bar stool. "My name is Dalton," he said with a cheerful smile, moving toward John. "Dalton Waters." His hair was styled, jaw square. Midforties. Blue shirt with an open collar under his pristine-white jacket. A handsome man with a big smile and a mouthful of dazzling teeth. He thrust out a hand for shaking.

"John Temple," he replied, reaching out. His hand was pumped by Dalton's viselike grip.

Dalton let go and sat down next to John. "So what brings a nondrinker like you to the city of sin?"

John shifted awkwardly in his seat, not entirely certain he wanted company. "I'm here to help a friend."

"Now, that is neighborly," Dalton said with his distinct country charm. "What kind of help?"

The bartender handed John his drink in a smallish plastic cup, three-quarters full of ice. "It's kind of personal," John said, not making eye contact.

Dalton laughed. "There's a lady involved," he said with a self-assured nod.

John cleared his throat, hiding an amused smile, studying Dalton's amused smirk. He waited a moment, debating in the recesses of his mind, then nodded. "Yeah," he said, taking a sip of his soft drink, "there's a woman in the equation. What made you think that?"

Dalton shrugged. "You're alone in bar—which a nondrinker would only go to for a couple of reasons—a temporary crack in his resolve, or serious boredom. Both are the result of avoiding something."

"And how do you know that reason is a woman?" John asked, confused.

"Just a hunch, really," Dalton said with a shrug. "And you still have a hint of lipstick on your face, which I'm doubting is native."

John laughed nervously and wiped his face with the back of his arm.

"You'll have to forgive me," Dalton said with a continued smile. "I was a pastor in another life. I'm used to seeing people who need to talk."

"And you think I need to talk?" John asked.

Dalton smirked. "You've been kissing a woman, yet you're sitting in a bar all alone. I'm supposed to believe that everything went according to plan?"

John smiled, took another sip of his soda, and realized it was already half gone. "So you were a pastor?"

"Seven years," Dalton said with a nod. "I'm an accountant now but still a deacon for my church. But you're changing the subject, John." Dalton leaned close, suddenly a bit more serious. "May I call you John?"

"Sure," John said.

"So," Dalton asked as if it were all obvious, "what's on your mind?"

"I just feel stupid," John said, shaking his head.

"OK," Dalton said.

"I should find fulfillment in my relationship with God, right?"

"Ah," Dalton said, nodding. "So you're a religious man?"

"Sort of," John acknowledged. "I'm a follower of Christ."

Dalton clarified. "So, Christianity is your religion?"

"Well," John said seriously, "Christianity isn't a religion; it's a relationship."

"Oh," Dalton said, taking a casual sip of his own drink. "And what makes you say that?"

John frowned, not certain what this guy was getting at. "My belief in God and my practice of faith is the product of my relationship with Christ, not some list of dos and don'ts."

Dalton laughed for a moment, then leaned in, touching John on the shoulder. "Son, Christianity is a religion. It's on the list of world religions, and it got on that list for good reason. And your failure to recognize that, son, is where you're running afoul."

"No." John shook his head. "Following Christ is a relationship, and that's what makes it different from every other religion on the face of the earth."

Dalton leaned back, spreading his hands grandiosely. "Christianity is not a religion; it's a relationship?" He shook his head. "That's a slogan, son. A PR statement designed to make a religion more pleasant to the unreligious."

"But Christians respond out of God's love for them," John argued, "not out of an attempt to earn it."

Dalton cleared his throat. "Son, it doesn't matter if you pray to the east, feed rice to a statue, dance for rain, or have a 'quiet time' with God and sing bad acoustic rock songs—they are all actions meant to worship a god or gods."

"I don't agree." John frowned, wondering how he'd gotten drawn into this. "Christians—true Christians—aren't motivated by the same things."

"Maybe"—Dalton shrugged—"but probably not. What you're spouting is a list of slogans and bumper stickers."

John thought for a moment. "Christian chic," he said absently, remembering the phrase from somewhere else.

"Christian chic." Dalton smiled. "That's a good term for it. But Christianity is better because it's the truth. And you've really got to get to the basics—the fundamentals and beyond—to really *follow* God through religion, or He is *never* going to be able to use you."

John sat for a moment, thinking, considering everything that was being said to him. "Do you think that's my problem? That I haven't embraced religion enough?"

Dalton was quiet for a second. Then he took the last sip of his soda and set the empty plastic cup on the bar. "I think God brought you here, to this moment, and it's my job to tell you what the Lord told me—that He wants to bless you. But you've followed Him only so far and stopped short."

"Where do you think I've fallen short?" John asked, studying the other man.

"I just met you"—Dalton shrugged—"your walk with the Lord is between you and Him. All I know is that there aren't any riches or blessings or glory in wandering into a bar with a woman's lipstick smeared on your face."

John let his forearms rest on the bar, shoulders relaxing as he considered what was being said to him. This man knew that God had brought him here, knew that something was wrong. Perhaps this was the place where he needed to be. Maybe this was what he needed to learn. Maybe this was his chance to truly listen to counsel. Not just on personal things, but also on the nature of God and faith. "What do I need to do?"

"You need to follow the Lord more nearly," Dalton said definitively. "We all do." He tipped his cup back, crunching a cube of ice. "You can always do more. Give more. Sacrifice more."

"Like what?" John asked, feeling as if he somehow belonged—that he'd found someone who understood him.

"Read your Bible more. Tithe more. Serve more. Sacrifice more of the worldly things that distract you from the Lord. Do more good and less evil," Dalton said in a nurturing tone. "It doesn't matter who you are—there is always some way that you are holding back from the Lord—and you will never be of any use to Him until you're willing do *everything* that He asks of you."

John found himself hesitating to agree. "It's just that now is such a—"

"We always want to put things off. But when the Lord comes back—and it's going to be soon—and you're standing before Him, what do you want to hear: 'Well done, good and faithful servant'? Or 'You could have done more'?"

John sat for a moment, letting it all sink in.

Dalton spoke before John had any response. "Of course you want to be right with God. That's why you're here—now. You know you're holding out on God, and you're slapping Him in the face and mocking His sacrifice of Jesus on the cross by not being your absolute best for Him."

John felt something in the pit of his stomach—a sickening feeling. He felt a kind of disgust—a feeling he couldn't find a word for. Conviction, he thought. The feeling was conviction. It was God telling him to do more—that was it; it had to be. Regardless of his personal feelings, it was still counsel. Important counsel on an important issue.

He thought of Angelo's warning about Trista, that the Thresher was seeking to kill her. Maybe this was the answer. Maybe this was the way to save her—to renew his devotion to God.

He turned to Dalton. "What about you?" he asked. "How are you following God more closely?"

Dalton's smile seemed to fade a bit. "I'm following God with everything I've got." His tone became more somber with every word. "There was a time when I gave God only the table scraps of my life—but then I started to follow Him. Truly follow Him." Dalton turned his head, watching the hotel foot traffic pass outside the bar. "Then I stepped onto a narrower path and *felt* the presence of God for the first time ever. But it faded over time. But each time my path narrowed a little more I started to feel Him again."

"And?" John asked, still searching for the answer to his original question.

Dalton continued to look out of the bar. "And now I'm getting ready to make the biggest sacrifice of my life."

Whatever it was that John felt, the sensation was growing stronger. He studied Dalton's features for a minute: an intense look of resolve. John spoke. "What do you hope to do?"

Dalton traced the grain of the bar's wood with his ring finger. "I've come here to fight the devil," he said with a grin.

John tried to process the words. "How?"

"Ancient monks," Dalton said, "used to come out into the desert—what they referred to as the wilderness—with the specific intention of doing battle with the devil."

"Really?"

Dalton nodded. "They believed that the demons lived in deserts—not unlike the one we're in right now. They swore off the civilized world and went out into the wilderness to test their strength. I'm doing the same."

John thought for a moment, reevaluating everything about Dalton Waters. And yet he seemed fully together—handsome face, perfect hair and teeth, pristine suit. He seemed sane enough. "How?" John asked.

Dalton smiled—small and discreet, almost mischievous. "You have time to go for a walk?"

"I'm still not certain I understand," Hannah said as they pulled up to the small private airport.

"Neither do I," Devin said without taking his eyes from the road, maneuvering his car gently.

She sat quietly while Devin parked the car, watching him steer with precision. They were walking toward the paved airstrip when she finally spoke. "Do you think this might be some kind of trick?" she asked, hoisting a duffel bag over her shoulder.

"It may very well be," Devin agreed, placid as ever.

Hannah didn't want to seem critical or rude, yet she spoke her mind as tactfully as she knew how. "Does it seem wise to do this if you have doubts?"

The small charter jet, parked on the landing strip, seemed to grow in size as they got closer. "There's obviously tension between Clay Goldstein and Vince Sobel. I don't know if Clay is trustworthy, but this may still be an opportunity."

Hannah kept walking. "The enemy of my enemy is my friend?"

Devin nodded without saying anything, arriving at the jet's open hatch.

"Mr. Bathurst?" the pilot asked. Devin nodded again. "Right this way." They stepped onto the plane and were shown to their seats.

Hannah sat, buckling herself in, one of the flight crew taking her bag. The contents included a change of clothes that Devin had bought her at a department store and the handguns that he had found at the motel—something she was hesitant to see in the hands of someone else. Her attention shifted to the jet door as it was lifted up, her last chance to get off the plane slipping away. One of the crew pulled the door snuggly into place, then latched it. Whether she liked it or not, she was committed now.

Devin took a seat across the aisle from her. Hannah looked him over, then spoke without thinking. "I hope you know what you're doing."

He buckled himself into his seat and looked absentmindedly out the window. "So do I," he said with a nod. "So do I."

John Temple walked along the outside of the hotel pool next to Dalton Waters. The area was a courtyard, the sun searing down on the people from above—all trying to cool off in the pool. Palm trees surrounded the long meandering pool that snaked around the trees, teeming with people. Children squealed and splashed, sending a nearly unending series of droplets cascading into the air. Adults chatted at the bars. The smell of chlorine hung in the air. Women wearing virtually nothing seemed somehow ubiquitous.

"Las Vegas," Dalton said, hands in his pockets, "is not a place for a moral man."

John pulled his eyes away from a twenty-something redhead in a bikini. "True," he agreed.

"Strip clubs, showgirls, escort services, and legal brothels." Dalton scoffed. "They hand porno out in the streets—folks on street corners just passing it out, leaving it everywhere. This country used to be great. Founded on Christian ideals with the Bible as our true guiding star—and now look at us." He waved a hand through the air. "We're falling apart. The value of the dollar is dropping like a rock, our economy is tanked, our enemies are walking all over us. Seriously," he asked, "where did we go wrong?"

John sidestepped an incoming splash of water, shaking his head. "I don't know."

"I'll tell you where we went wrong," Dalton said firmly. "The children of God are no longer in control—and the children of Satan have taken over."

"Children of Satan?" John asked, confused.

"That's right," Dalton said. "The Bible tells us that God made His children, but the Bible is also very clear—Satan has his children too. And they are among us; they are…" Dalton stopped himself, muttering something inaudible. "Well, there are some of us who believe very firmly that what the Bible is saying is that God made His race of people here on Earth, and the spiritual war we fight is against Satan's children."

"Who are also a race of people here on Earth?" John asked before he'd really thought it through.

Dalton nodded, unable to make eye contact—as if what he were saying might cause trouble. Then the weight of it came over John. "Do you mean like actual *ethnic* races? You don't really believe *that*, do you?"

Dalton stopped walking, smiled awkwardly, and turned to John, putting a hand on his shoulder. "I never said that," he declared jovially, flashing big sparkling teeth with a charismatic smile. "The only thing that matters is that the Almighty Lord demands excellence—proof of a life transformed by grace—and that means you can't hold out on Him any longer. Do you understand?" He squeezed John's shoulder and bowed his head. "Let's pray."

John automatically lowered his head.

"Lord," Dalton said quickly, "grant my brother in Christ, John, the heart to follow You more closely and to make greater sacrifices and commitments to You with each new day. In Jesus's precious name—"

The amen came in unison as they lifted their heads. Dalton let go of John's shoulder, giving it a manly smack. The sounds of children playing in the pool seemed to rush back.

Dalton looked at his watch. "Now, I've a meeting I need to get to, but I'll be praying for you—OK?"

John nodded, strangely thrown by everything.

"I'd give you my card," Dalton smiled, "but all my information is about to change—so there wouldn't be much point. Regardless—quit giving God your table scraps. Got it?"

John nodded again, traded farewells, then watched Dalton Waters walk away, heading back into the hotel.

Everything seemed so confused. And something seemed very wrong.

Chapter 15

THE ENGINES ON the charter jet droned.

Hannah sat at the laptop, looking for whatever she could find. For the most part it appeared that the computer was used for building the Web site. It all seemed distant somehow. Perhaps that was the only way to deal with the fact that human beings—young people, minors—were being held against their will, forced to do unspeakable things.

She closed the laptop, unable to continue, and slid it into the seat beside her. Outside the window the sky slipped past—an ethereal thing with no shape or boundaries, only possible to see the clouds that floated lazily by, defying intuition, marking the distance traveled like yellow dotted lines on the highway. Her attention stayed on the sky for several minutes more before looking across the aisle to her traveling companion—Devin.

It took her a moment to realize his eyes were closed. He sat perfectly still in his seat, good posture, head only tipped back a few degrees, if even that much. His eyes opened, and he turned his head toward her. "What's on your mind?"

"Nothing." She turned back to the window.

"You put the laptop away," he noted. "You haven't done that since we left the ground."

She watched a puffy cloud, so wispy that she could nearly see the water droplets that made up its shape. "How does this happen?" she asked quietly.

"Flight?"

"No." She looked back at him, pointing to the laptop. "This kind of exploitation."

"Greed," he said without hesitation. "Where there's a demand for something, people will do horrible things to profit off that demand."

Hannah unbuckled herself, pulling her bare feet onto the

seat with her, hugging her legs. "I mean the demand—why do people...?" She trailed off.

Devin's eyes closed again, staying shut. "Anomie. The feeling of isolation—cut off from others and the feeling that we can't really connect with true relationships."

"The inability to connect?" she asked, confused. "How does *this*—?"

"Anomie," he said again. "That's where it starts at least. Then it gets worse."

Her mind worked through his words. "How?"

Eyes still closed, he spoke as if it were all obvious. "Human beings aren't designed to be alone—not really, not forever. We need to connect. When our real relationships fail us, we turn to alternatives—things that aren't real. The more we grasp at the emptiness, the less real it feels. And then comes abuse, the desperate hope that we've made some impact, some kind of impression. And then it really starts to get ugly."

Hannah thought about the hundreds of people out in the world whom he was alluding to, all searching feverishly to find some sense of connection. "And that drives people?"

"That only explains it on one level. At the end of the day, you're dealing with a black-market commodity. People want something, whatever the reason, that they can't get legally. An illegal supplier will always arrive to make money off that demand." He adjusted his head and closed his eyes again.

Hannah sat quietly. The cabin of the small private jet was silent, except for the hum of the engines. She evaluated herself, her feelings. The sensation that Devin was talking about made sense. The feeling of needing to reach out and really, truly *connect*. "Do you feel isolated?" she asked, wondering if the question might be too personal.

"I like being alone," he said softly, putting no effort into speaking. "There's a difference between being alone and feeling isolated."

She took a long breath, relaxing into her seat. "I don't like being alone," she mused, wondering if she was going to stay alone for the rest of her life. It was something she had found herself thinking about more and more in the past months, the possibility of getting so caught up in her life as one of the First-born that she would never find someone to share it with. "Can I ask a personal question?"

"Certainly." Devin nodded without opening his eyes.

Hannah took a moment, trying to think of how to ask. "Are you ever sorry that you never got married?"

His eyes didn't open. "I've been married," he stated casually.

"Really?" Hannah asked, surprised. "I mean, I'm sorry to hear that," she backpedaled. "Did she pass away?"

"She left," Devin said, detached. "I came home from a weekend exercise when I was in the army to find a note."

"Oh my gosh," Hannah stammered, feeling invasive. "That must have been horrible."

Devin shrugged. "She didn't like being alone either, it turns out. So she married someone more exciting than me, a minor-league baseball player. Someone who wasn't so structured and serious all the time. Someone reckless like…." He didn't finish.

Hannah listened to the engines for several moments more. "Where is she now?"

"Alone," he said quietly. "It turns out that reckless and exciting aren't everything either." He was quiet, shifting in his seat. "She confused excitement and stimulation for connection and relationship. As a result she got neither."

Hannah watched him sit in silence, eyes closed. "Do you miss having someone?"

Devin opened his eyes and looked out the window for a moment, then tipped back his seat and closed his eyes again.

"I'd rather not talk about this anymore."

Hannah turned to her own window and looked out, thinking about what they must look like to those on the ground—if they could see them at all. Just a tiny speck in a cloudy sky.

Still chattering with his associates, Dalton got up from the table. He patted his full stomach, and someone made a joke about him having a paunch. Ribbing aside, Dalton was in great shape for a man of his age, but the famous Vegas buffets could fill him full enough to think he might blimp any day. He had always been a sucker for a good steak—which he'd had in abundance over dinner, avoiding all those foreign foods like the plague. Chinese food, in particular, had always smelled like a latrine to him.

The seven men followed him out of the restaurant and into elevators. They stepped in and the doors closed.

"When is the press conference?" one of the men asked.

"Ten a.m." Dalton watched the floor numbers climb. "I'll cover the details in the room."

The doors opened, and he led his entourage into the hall, walking in a loose herd.

"You're sure of the time and the place?" another man asked.

"Yeah," Dalton assured him. "My visions were backed up by some reliable sources. I'm not alone on this; it's been covered in prayer." Dalton looked up toward the door of his hotel room and saw someone coming his direction. "John Temple?" he said with a smile. "What are you doing here?"

John seemed equally surprised to see him. "Dalton?"

"That's right," Dalton smiled, reaching out and shaking John's hand. "These are my associates." He motioned behind him to the seven other men. "We're just heading back to my room for a meeting."

A look of amusement. "This room?" John motioned to the correct door.

"That's right."

John laughed. "I'm right next door," he said, pointing to the adjacent room.

"Well," Dalton grinned, "isn't that a coincidence? I told you God brought you to me, didn't I?"

John nodded sheepishly. "You sure did. So what kind of work are you guys discussing?"

Dalton paused—thinking of Senator Foster and the next day's press conference. And the things that they needed to do. Dalton shrugged. "Nothing interesting."

The smile seemed to fall from John's face as Dalton spoke, as if the young man could read Dalton's thoughts. "Hmm," John murmured, distracted. He stared at them for several awkward seconds. "Well, I should let you get to it then."

"Yeah," Dalton agreed. "We've got a lot to discuss. But it was good to see you again."

"You too." John nodded and turned to his own hotel room door.

"I'll be praying for you," Dalton assured with his usual pastoral warmth.

John's expression had a kind of seriousness to it that Dalton hadn't seen before. "I'll be praying for you too."

Then John slipped into his room.

"John," Trista said to him as he entered the room, "where have you been?"

"I'm sorry," he said, shaking his head, "but I can't talk." He walked to the wall, put a hand to it, and rested his forehead on the back of the same hand. Eyes closed, he listened, murmuring an almost silent petition to God.

"What is it?" Trista asked, coming up beside him.

He hushed her gently, listening, focusing on the thought of Dalton Waters and what might be happening in the next room.

"What do you hear?" Trista prodded.

He stopped. Stepped back from the wall. Blinked. "Nothing," he said, shaking his head. "Nothing at all."

She was beside him. "What is it? What do you think you've found?"

His face turned to her, concerned. "Something connected to the Foster assassination, I think." He turned back to the wall, resting his forehead against the back of his hand again. Thoughts strained to hear whatever it was that he thought he might hear.

It was like trying to push back a curtain of thorns. There was nothing but a thicket of his own ignorance, nothing to hear or see. Darkness in the mind's eye. "Please, God," he begged, "please show me something... *anything*."

Whatever was happening in the next room was continuing on without him. Whatever window there had been was closing; whatever opportunity there had been was slipping. Every second there was something new, he thought, something that might save lives, that he couldn't hear or see. He snarled to himself, pressing his forehead harder into his hand until it hurt.

Something touched his hand.

He didn't look. He knew the feeling, the touch, the sensation of another hand touching his own. He knew the hand, the feel of her skin and the smell of her hair as she came closer.

Trista.

She held his hand with one of her own, holding on to his arm with the other.

His body relaxed. His mind quieted. His words silenced. And he felt them. A room of them.

"M14 rifles," Dalton was saying, pointing to the bag. "Fully automatic, American made." His finger pointing to a map. "Three crews. The van crew—here, then two other crews, shotguns and M14s. I want you in the bathrooms. When the shooting starts, Foster's security will bring him in off the curb—their first desti-

nation will almost certainly be the security station... here. We need to cut off that route, cut off the exits, encircle, and kill.

"If we get him and you're still breathing, then the getaway cars are going to be here and here. Worst-case scenario—there is the monorail that leads through Vegas and an access to it through the back of the hotel lobby. But we all know that this is a suicide mission."

Nods of understanding and approval.

"We are very blessed to have been offered this chance by such well-connected people."

More agreement.

"Gentlemen, we're going to make America safe for decent white folks again."

Hannah stretched as the charter jet touched down. It was time to get up and move around again. The wheels dragged with the usual screech, rubber and runways tearing at one another. It took several minutes for the plane to slow and taxi to its destination. The plane stopped, and there was a sudden sensation of loss as the tiny vibrations of the vehicle stopped and the engines went quiet.

Devin stood, took his cell phone from his pocket, and set it on his seat. He rubbed the back of his neck, then disappeared to the back of the plane, presumably into the lavatory. Hannah stretched again, and the phone chirped. She looked to the back of the plane—Devin was nowhere to be seen. The ringer sounded again, the vibrate function causing the tiny device to glide across the seat toward the edge. She reached for the phone, picked it up, and looked at the incoming caller: John Temple.

Hannah opened the phone. "Hello?"

"Hannah?" John asked, obviously confused.

"Devin is busy. What's up?"

"I think I've found our assassins."

Hannah's heart hopped. "Where?"

"They're in the room next door."

She scoffed, incredulous. "You're kidding."

"No. I even went for a walk with the leader before I realized what was going on."

Hannah shook her head. It was surprising how normal horrible people with horrible plans could be. Or seem, at least. It always made her wonder if she was the strange one. "What are you going to do?"

"They make their move at ten a.m. tomorrow morning. I have an address and everything."

The door opened, letting bright yellow light into the plane's cabin in a vibrant splash. A man in a dark suit with a mustard-colored tie stepped up into the plan. "Miss," he said without emoting, "you need to put down the phone. Mr. Goldstein would like to see you both."

She nodded. "Just a second." Devin returned from the back of the plane and Hannah reached out, handing the phone to him. "It's John. He has a lead." Devin took the phone and began to talk. Hannah turned to the man in the suit, following him down the steps of the small jet.

The Nevada heat—dry and blistering hot—hit her like a wall. The sky was blue, the searing sun getting low in the sky. Yellow sun bounced off of everything in globular swells of light, making it virtually impossible to see anything until her eyes adjusted.

Their jet had been parked twenty feet from another jet that looked nearly identical, noses pointed toward one another. Men in dark suits, sunglasses, and mustard-yellow ties seemed to swarm around her—ten of them? They were security, that was certain.

"This way," one of the security guards said, leading her to a folding table two-thirds of the way to the next plane. "Please put your personal belongings on the table."

Hannah unshouldered her bag, setting it on the table. "Are you security for the airport?" she asked.

"We're Mr. Goldstein's personal security," the man said with a nod. "Please empty the contents of your pockets and turn them out for me," he continued.

Hannah reached into her pockets, emptying anything that fit that description, turning them out as instructed. A security man with a metal detector wand approached, waving the device over her. Two others were looking through her bag.

"Are you certain of the deadline?" Devin asked, talking into his cell phone as he approached from behind. He made acknowledging sounds both to the phone and to the guards as he passed through their security measures. He finished on the phone and handed it to a guard, them emptied his pockets.

Devin lifted his arms over his head. "I have an FN Five-seveN pistol at the small of my back," he announced, "and two more firearms in the bag."

A security guard reached behind Devin's back and removed the gun, taking the magazine out and ejecting the final round from the chamber. "Do you have any more weapons, Mr. Bathurst?"

"No."

They didn't seem to believe him. They continued to pat him down, running the wand over every inch of his body twice. When they were satisfied, they moved him over to where Hannah stood. They were instructed to wait and were left standing in the harsh sun for several more minutes.

Hannah mopped sweat from her forehead, wondering how long she'd been standing. She was about to ask when a women in her thirties, a very beautiful Latina, came down the steps of the second jet and approached. The woman wore a dark suit but no tie. On her lapel was a yellow pin; the sign of the Firstborn—the triquetra over an upside down crown.

"My name is Nina, head of Mr. Goldstein's personal security," she said with a kind of authority. "Do you understand what is about to happen?"

Hannah shook her head, confused. "I don't know what's happening."

"You're about to speak to Mr. Goldstein. This isn't a common occurrence, so you need to understand the basic guidelines."

"Understood," Devin agreed.

Nina continued. "While you are with Mr. Goldstein, there will be no quick movements. I will be in the plane with you, and I will maintain control of the situation. If Mr. Goldstein considers you to be a threat at any time for any reason, the meeting will be over. If I consider you to be a threat at any time, the meeting will be over. All of my colleagues and I are armed. Do you understand?"

Hannah's mind swam. What kind of people was she dealing with? What kind of meeting was this? Had everyone and everything suddenly gone completely crazy?

"Understood," Devin said without hesitation.

Nina looked them over. "Good," she said. "And one more thing."

"What's that?" Hannah asked.

"Mr. Goldstein is the patriarch of the Ora. Meeting with him is an honor. I expect you to treat him with the utmost respect. Do you understand?"

"Understood," Hannah said with a nod.

Nina turned to Devin. "Mr. Bathurst?"

"We'll see," he said with a snarky smile. "Lead the way, Nina."

Hannah followed the woman up the steps to the plane, climbing into the cabin.

The interior of the plane was dark, the shades pulled shut. A man with a beard and a short-sleeved Hawaiian shirt sat at the back of the jet. His seat was a cushioned bench facing the aisle. "Devin," the man said happily, standing, motioning them to sit across the aisle.

"Mr. Goldstein," Devin said, motioning for Hannah to sit first.

"And you must be Hannah Rice," he said, looking at her.

She nodded. "I am."

"I knew your grandfather Henry. He was a good man. I'm very sorry about what happened to him in San Antonio. I was in the city the night that happened."

"So was I," Hannah said, not making eye contact.

"You were in San Antonio?" he asked, then continued. "I'm sorry we didn't have the chance to be properly introduced. But after the meeting, things went horribly wrong, I'm afraid."

Hannah nodded in agreement.

"Do you two want something to drink? Soda, mineral water, anything?"

Devin spoke first. "No, thank you."

"Are you sure?" He turned to Nina. "Could you get me a bottle of water?" She nodded. "And bring one for each of my guests as well." Nina nodded and turned away, walking to the other end of the plane.

"Thank you," Hannah said. "I didn't expect—"

"Hospitality?" Clay Goldstein asked with a grin. "You've just been dealing with my security. They take themselves a bit too seriously, but there's no reason we can't have a good chat."

"Too seriously?" Devin asked.

Clay Goldstein shrugged. "A bit."

"Do you still believe that the Domani killed your sons?"

Clay paused midsmile, looking awkward. "Well..."

"Your water," Nina said, setting a small glass bottle on a table next to Clay's seat.

"Thank you," he acknowledged.

Nina handed Devin and Hannah their bottles, sweating chilly condensation in the Nevada heat. Clay cracked his open and took a swig.

"Why are you helping us?" Devin asked, leaning back and crossing his legs.

Clay set down his bottle and was quiet for a moment. "I'm sick," he said without prelude, watching their faces to see their reactions. "I have Parkinson's disease."

"I'm so sorry," Hannah said, genuine in her empathy. "Are you OK?"

Clay cleared his throat. "Parkinson's is fatal. If the disease doesn't get you, a heart attack will. Which means my days are numbered."

"I'm sorry to hear about your diagnosis," Devin said unsympathetically, "but that still doesn't answer my question."

Clay looked them over. Nodded. Leaned forward and clasped his fingers, elbows resting on his knees. "Vince Sobel is my subordinate in the Ora—or at least he's supposed to be. The position of Overseer should have come to me, but Vince doesn't think I'm well enough."

Devin spoke up. "So you're helping us to spite him?"

"No," Clay said with a dark laugh, "I'm helping you because Vince isn't going to stay Overseer for long. He's going to have to pass it on to me at some point. I just have more experience and more vision."

"You're going to undermine Vince and have him replaced," Devin continued, "the same way he did with John Temple?"

"Meh." Clay balked. "You make it sound so dramatic. So cloak-and-dagger. I'm the one with the background in the film industry."

"Then what is it?" Devin asked.

Clay's face got suddenly serious. "There are people already working on getting me into the position of Overseer. It's just a matter of time. But," he continued slowly and carefully, "I want you to know whose side I'm on when I get there."

Hannah thought of the various possibilities. "What do you mean by that?"

"I want people like you and Devin—people with initiative—to know that you can trust me."

"To owe you favors," Devin retorted.

"I want you to trust me," Clay said without any trace of weakness. "And I want to be able to trust you. If I'm going to lead the Firstborn, that leadership needs to be built on mutual trust; don't you think?"

Hannah thought for a moment. Perhaps this man was the right man for the job. "That sounds reasonable."

Devin didn't seem as convinced. "And what's going to make you any different from Vince Sobel or Blake Jackson, or even John Temple on his bad days?"

"Because," Clay continued, "I have a vision."

"Meaning?"

Clay seemed to relax, his body moving effortlessly into what he said next. "Why do you think the Firstborn exist?"

"To serve God on Earth," Hannah said without hesitation.

"But why do we have these gifts? Gifts that no one else has. Why would God do that?"

Hannah paused. "I hadn't really thought too much about that."

Clay smiled. "I have. And why else would God put us here: people with the ability to see everything and fix everything? Because that's exactly what we're meant to do."

"To fix everything?" Hannah asked.

"To fix the world," he said with an almost magical twinkle in his eye. "Just think about what a united Firstborn could do. With John Temple in charge, we haven't been nearly as effective as we should have been. In less than a year he's plunged the Firstborn into very serious financial problems."

"The IRS?" Hannah clarified.

"Yes!" Clay declared. "The people who were able to send Al Capone to Alcatraz for life when nobody else could touch him. The people who put away Mickey Cohen, the mob boss of Hollywood, in the fifties. The big, mean hammer of the federal government that hangs over everybody. And because of John it's coming down—and it could come down hard." Clay took a breath, looking at them with a kind of intimate sincerity. "It's time for a change."

Hannah looked at Devin. He said nothing and made no expression, simply listening. "Continue," she insisted.

"God put us here to change the world. To fix the problems around us. Think about the Ora—the ability to see and feel things in the moment. We could negotiate a lasting peace. We could solve the world financial crisis, facilitate discussion, end nuclear proliferation, end exploitation of women and children worldwide, bring all American troops home, cure the diseases of the world. Just think about everything we could do if we would stand together. If someone would just *lead* us together."

Hannah watched Clay Goldstein's face. He was serious as a heart attack. "You really think the Firstborn could do all of this?" she asked.

"I do," Clay said with a nod, "and we will."

"How?" Devin asked bluntly.

"We get the SEC squared away and the IRS off the Firstborn's back," he said with a rehearsed polish. "Pursue profitable enterprises that really bring back the vitality. Play it smart though. Not just going with knee-jerk reactions like John Temple did. I've spent the last few years buying up media companies. We've become a leader in the field of mass media and communications. We do that to make the money and increase our influence. Then we start in on politics—and we shape foreign and domestic policy."

"You're joking." Devin scoffed.

"No," Clay said with a smile, "I've been talking to my people. We can do this. If we pool our resources and our abilities, we can be up and running in no time. Every Firstborn on a central payroll in constant contact with one another."

"You're going to turn the Firstborn into a corporation," Hannah stated.

"Yes." Clay nodded.

"Isn't that a little tacky?"

He shrugged. "Sociology 101: It's the natural progression of things. First comes religion, then politics, and then business."

Hannah frowned, not buying it. "What do you mean? Religion hasn't gone away."

"True," Clay conceded, "but the religious elite are no longer the ones who dictate values to the most people. They used to be—the Vatican, the theologians, the clergy—but then the Enlightenment came and government became the new leader in ideas." Clay laughed to himself. "I mean, look at the Founding Fathers. They were practically deified in early America. The prophets of the new age. But"—he waved his hand airily—"all that has given way to the profits of the modern economy. It's our corporations and advertisers who dictate our values now. But that doesn't mean we can't still make those Christ's values."

"How so?" she asked.

"There are more ways to follow God than just going to church and doing religion. A person needs to make a difference in the world if they're really going to live out their ideology—and that means growing out of religion and into a body that can make a change."

"Politics," Devin interjected.

"Yes." Clay nodded. "But you have to pay for it all, which means business. It's a natural progression of importance and social growth." Clay took a drink. "One of the best examples is in Salt Lake City. The tallest building in a city is usually considered the most important, and in the beginning the Mormon Tabernacle was the tallest building in the city. That was back when people valued the opinions of their religious leaders. But times changed and society grew, and they built the capitol next door."

"And it was taller," Hannah agreed.

"And then came business, and those buildings tower over everything." Clay paused for a moment of effect. "Power shifted. And if we want to be relevant in the world, we have to shift with it."

"You're serious," Hannah uttered, her mind finally wrapping around the concept.

A shrug lifted Clay's shoulders. "Sad fact, kiddos: while an individual may do a better job of having meaningful insight than large groups, individuals will never be able to accomplish anywhere near as much." He took another drink, wiping his mouth with the back of his forearm. "With unity and coordination—with a central vision at the core of our leadership, we can fix the world. We can change everything forever—and we can lead the world to a new era of peace and prosperity. We can bring the kingdom of heaven to Earth!"

Devin cleared his throat. "You really think that it's our place to 'change' the world?"

"We can *save* the world," Clay said with a nod.

"And what if the world doesn't want to be saved?"

Clay waved a hand at Devin. "You're just being a contrarian. Of course people want to be saved—and I'm going to make sure it happens."

Devin shook his head. "I don't understand. How does this involve us?"

"I want you with me," Clay said, raising his bottle of water to them. "I want the best and the brightest of the Firstborn to be with me in this endeavor—this crusade. Can I count you in?"

Devin was quiet for a moment before he spoke. "A lot of very terrible things have been done in this world while attempting to do something good. What you're talking about sounds very risky." Devin was quiet again for a moment. "I'm not ready to commit to your cause, but I do appreciate your help."

Clay sat back, letting the subject drop for the moment. "Of course I'll help. Vince is scared of this Angelo guy."

Hannah spoke up. "And you're not?"

Clay shrugged. "Why should I be? I've caught glimpses of him skulking around for the past few years—nothing serious. He knew some private details about Vince's wife and the affair she had with their pastor. Tough stuff. It scared Vince, but I'm not that kind of guy."

"So you have no problem with us stopping the Foster assassination?" Devin asked.

Clay shook his head. "Not really. I think you're wasting your time with small stuff, yes, but I see no reason to try to stop you like he has."

"Small stuff?" Hannah queried.

"Yeah," he said casually. "Truth be told, Senator Foster is a slime. If these guys don't get him, somebody else will—and the world won't be too sad without him. It's not like he was any good as a senator anyway."

"It's still wrong for people to try to kill him," Devin said with resolve.

"What about the girls?" Hannah asked. "Do you think that's 'small stuff' too?"

"Human trafficking isn't going away," Clay said. "Sadly, eight thousand girls were shipped into this country last year, and next year will be the same. There's a demand in this country for sex without strings, and that's not going to be solved by saving a few girls." Clay turned his palms out. "Besides, I have reason to believe it may already be too late. But if you believe in this, then I'm not going to stop you. I'm just going to ask that you be darn certain this Angelo guy was wrong."

Devin spoke. "I don't understand."

"Are you certain he's wrong about the Firstborn being torn

apart?" Clay took another sip of water. "Sure, he's crazy. He's seeing past, present, and future all at once, and it's burning up his mind. It's too much for any normal person to handle. But are you so certain he's bonkers that you're willing to risk the future of the Firstborn?"

"If you're so concerned," Devin asked, "why are you letting us do this?"

Clay shrugged. "I've always been more interested in the present. In the moment. The future doesn't bother me very often. Maybe he's right; maybe he's wrong. I wasn't too fond of the way the Firstborn were anyway."

"So you'll let terrible things happen if we're wrong?" Hannah asked, amused by the concept.

Clay remained casual. "I'm dying. My mortal life is going to be over sooner than I'd like to think. That's changed my priorities. A year ago I was mostly an administrator. But today I have a vision of the way I'd like to leave the world."

"A legacy," Hannah added.

"Yes," Clay agreed, "a legacy. And while saving a few girls is good, I'd rather bring an end to the whole practice of sexual predation for profit. Does that make sense?"

"Yes," Hannah nodded, "it does."

"But if you believe that you can save these girls, I'm not going to stop you. Just be aware that Angelo may still be right—and you don't want that to be your legacy, do you?"

She thought for a moment, then shook her head. "No."

"If you want my advice," he said, putting the cap back on his water, "go to the sale tomorrow, and if that doesn't bring everything to a happy conclusion, then drop it. Let it go. There's no point in burning precious time chasing after one incident, and if you have any doubt about doing this stuff, then that's a good deadline."

The cabin of the plane was quiet for several long seconds.

"Is that all you wanted to discuss?" Devin asked.

Clay thought for a moment, then nodded. "Yeah. I guess it was. Mostly, I want you to know that I trust you."

Hannah smiled cordially. "I'm very flattered."

"You should be," Clay agreed. "I don't trust people very well anymore. Not since my two grown sons were killed." He eyed Devin for a moment, waiting for some kind of response, then turned his attention back to Hannah. "I've left Napa Valley only three times in the last two years. One of them was the night your grandfather was killed. One of them was today."

"And the other?" she asked.

"The doctor's appointment where they confirmed that I'm dying," he said with a morose edge, "so I guess it's all tied together." He forced a smile. "Now, I have a car for you two—silver, midsized sedan. Just the way you like, Devin."

Clay stood. "I did some checking," he continued. "The sale information got updated. It looks like your product might already be sold. The girls may already have gone to a different buyer."

Hannah stood. "No," she said, incredulous.

"I told you things might not go so well." Clay shrugged, then reached into his pocket. "This is an address. This is where pickups are supposed to take place—where buyers get their girls. That's what my visions say, if you trust them. I don't know what you'll want to do with this information, and maybe I don't want to know, but here it is."

"Thank you," Hannah said, nearly tearing up.

"And," Clay continued, taking out another piece of paper, "this is the information for a bank account. There's thirty thousand in there. My sources say that should be about enough to buy back three girls from these people."

Hannah accepted the piece of paper, looking over the routing number and its associated information. Without thinking she threw her arms around Clay's neck. "Thank you," she whispered. She let go and stepped back.

"And you," he said to Devin. "I really do think that John Temple has the information you need."

Devin went to speak, surprise on his face.

"I know," Clay continued. "I never expected John to get anything like this right either. Now, you had best be on your way," he said, leading them to the door. "And Godspeed."

Chapter 16

JOHN SAT ON the hotel suite's couch, hunched over the coffee table, sketching as fast as he could, trying to remember every possible detail of what Dalton and the others had discussed—the layout of the hotel's lobby and the security station they were going to try to cut off. The escape routes—possible or otherwise. Even the monorail train. Were they serious? How could they escape on something that moved that slowly, with that much glass and that little cover? Maybe the plan could be more intricate than he realized.

The harder he thought, the faster he scribbled. The faster he worked, the more quickly it all seemed to slip from his mind—one piece at a time, all of it slipping. He had to get it out. He had to get it on the page. Devin would need the information to stop the assassination, and he needed to do this for himself—and for God. There was always something more he could give to God, he told himself. There was always something he could do better, faster, with more virtuous intentions.

Yes, what Dalton planned was evil—but that didn't eliminate the power of his advice, or the overwhelming sense of conviction that had flooded John at hearing Dalton's words. As far as he was concerned, Dalton had been speaking on behalf of God. Sure, he had his priorities all wrong, but his understanding of God was spot on. It was what John had embraced for so many years in the mission field. It was what he had lost and forgotten as Overseer. Maybe he'd let people like Devin influence him too much.

His best, he told himself. He had to do his best. His first-fruits were all that God deserved—and if he could please God, then maybe, just maybe, God would spare…

Trista sat down next to him. She put a hand on the back of

his head, running fingers through his hair. "Are you going to be OK?" she asked.

He stopped, noticing her fingers in his hair for the first time. John nodded quickly and emphatically. "I just have to do this. I can't cut corners. I have to get this right."

John turned back to his pad, pencil lead pressing hard against the stationery. Then he stopped. That was it. That was all he could remember and re-create. After that there was only blurry recollection, and John had never been good with the past.

Trista lay her head on his shoulder and his eyes closed, his body crackling as every muscle relaxed in a ripple that moved from the top of his head to the tips of his toes. Whatever she was doing, it was a distraction. "Trista, I—"

"Shh." She hushed him gently, taking hold of his arm.

"I don't understand," he said, letting his head rest on hers. "I thought you couldn't be near me."

She nuzzled his arm. "Maybe," she mused, "but right now I think we need each other."

"I can't let anything distract me from—"

"I know," she interrupted softly, "but let's just pretend for a second that you can."

He felt her push him gently back into the couch, and he rested there, her head on his chest. It was everything he could have hoped for. Everything he had hoped for, and yet there was something that wasn't right in his mind—real or imagined.

John breathed deep and let it out.

Some part of him couldn't help but relax at the feel of her touch. Something kinetic and elusive. Something felt so perfect and yet so perilous.

And then he felt something else—something beyond himself. Like his visions of the present. But this was something else. The future. The same way he had seen the events of the other room while holding Trista's hand. She could feel it too; he knew it. A shared sense of what was to come.

Trouble. Difficulty. Struggle.

John waited for Trista to say something. But she didn't. Instead they closed their eyes and pushed it into the back of their minds.

Time passed. Maybe minutes. Maybe hours. But eventually, there on the couch, they drifted into sleep.

Devin drove the car down the streets of Las Vegas—away from the Strip, into the suburbs. The places where life was "normal" and the people with families lived to keep their kids as far away as possible from the bright lights and dark alleys of the city of sin. The city sparkled in the distance—the night sky giving contrast to its thousands of bright bulbs.

"Take a right here," Hannah said, looking at the laptop. They'd stopped for directions, pulling up the route from the airport to the sales location on the Internet. She'd unplugged the computer, and they were a long way off from any kind of Internet hot spot, but the map and its directions were still on the screen. Hannah was in the passenger seat next to Devin, finger moving along the screen, presumably following the list of directions. "It's up here," she said. "Right-hand side of the street."

She gave him the address again, and Devin watched the street numbers approach, lit up by the headlights, until he saw the one they were looking for.

"This is it." Hannah pointed.

It was a suburban house that looked identical to every other home in the neighborhood. Like cracker boxes, Devin thought to himself. The color was unique: a sage green, compared to the brighter-colored houses surrounding it. There was a lawn, but it looked sickly despite the rotating sprinkler in the yard. A squatty palm tree grew up out of the middle of the brown grass, a yard gnome at its base. For the most part, the house looked, for lack of a better word, normal.

Devin pulled up in front of the house, putting the car in park and killing the engine. He looked the place over one more time. "You're sure this is the place?" he said.

Hannah checked the screen again. "Yes. This is it."

Devin breathed, nodded, then reached for the pistol at the small of his back. FN Five-seveN, gray, with a rounded back end. The underside of the barrel had an accessory rail where things like tactical flashlights and laser sights could be attached. The rail was jagged and looked to Devin a bit like saw teeth. A full magazine of twenty bullets was locked into the grip.

He pulled the action back just far enough to see the brass casing of the bullet lodged in its proper place, but not so far as to run the action the way people always seemed to do in action movies—a behavior that would eject a perfectly good bullet. Devin let go of the slide, allowing it to snap back into place. It had been drilled into his brain years ago that proper gun safety was to treat every gun as if it were loaded. He had also learned that basic gunfight safety meant treating every gun as if it were empty—and double-checking before putting yourself in a situation where an unloaded gun could be a disaster.

He turned to Hannah. "I'm going in to speak with these people. I think it's best if you stay in the car."

"Why?" she asked without hesitation.

"Because," he said, eyes on the front door, "the nature of this business makes you a potential commodity, which could make rescue of others difficult. Stay here and keep your eyes open. I put another of the handguns in the glove box in case you need one."

She opened the glove box and looked at the gun: dark metal with a short barrel that tapered up toward the muzzle.

"That's a Sig Sauer," Devin instructed. "Do you remember how to use a pistol?"

She nodded, checking the action the same way Devin had with his FN Five-seveN. "I do."

"Good. Now stay put, and be ready to make a move if something goes wrong."

She didn't look happy about it, but she nodded in acknowledgment. Devin didn't worry. Hannah Rice wasn't the type to go back on her word or do something reckless. It simply wasn't in her nature. He returned the FN Five-seveN to its place at the small of his back. "What was the name of the man you made contact with—the one with the dragon tattoo?"

"Dominik," Hannah replied, not hesitating.

Devin repeated it to himself. "Dominik." Then he climbed out of the car and stepped lightly across the crackling lawn to the front door. He rang the doorbell.

There were several long seconds of silence, then the sounds of someone approaching the door, which opened after another moment. An overweight, middle-aged man with a craggy face stood in the threshold. "What do you want?"

"My name is Alex Smith," Devin lied. "I'm an associate of a man with a dragon tattoo, goes by the name of Dominik. He said that I should speak to someone here about making a purchase."

The overweight man looked Devin over, slightly aloof, then motioned with his head for Devin to follow him into the house.

Devin looked back at Hannah in the car, sitting perfectly still. He really hoped he wasn't going to need her. Then he turned and followed into the house.

A television blared noisily from a living room that Devin was led into, passing through a curtain of beads. The place was not well maintained and had a distinct 1970s look, with brown shag carpet and wood-paneled walls.

"Mr. Scarza," the overweight man announced, "this is Alex Smith. He says he's a friend of Dominik's."

Mr. Scarza was a man in his late twenties—probably

good-looking, except for his bloodshot eyes, scraggy beard, and unkempt hair. He wore a paisley bathrobe and slippers, a gold chain around his neck. "Yeah?" he said with a slight New Jersey accent, confused. He sat on a pea-green couch, watching television a moment longer before he picked up a remote control, pointing it at the television and muting his overloud show. "How do you know Dominik?"

"I was involved in some things he had a hand in around the New Jersey area," Devin said without missing a beat. "He recently picked up some girls in that area. Three of them. These three," he said, pulling a computer printout from his pocket, "to be exact."

Scarza took the printout without getting up, rubbing his eyes as he looked it over, wiping a running nose with the back of his sleeve. The man was obviously high, probably cocaine. He looked at Devin through bloodshot eyes. "What did you say you wanted again?"

"I want to buy these three girls," he said with the same businesslike demeanor he would bring to any deal.

Scarza eyed him, obviously trying to think through some kind of chemically induced haze. His look shifted to the overweight man. "I'm going to have my friend Scud here search you, OK?"

Devin nodded, lifting his arms. "I have a handgun in the small of my back," he announced. Scarza's eyebrow lifted. "Just thought you should know."

The man called Scud reached into the small of Devin's back, removed the gun, and handed it to Scarza, who in turn set it on the coffee table between them. Scud continued to pat Devin down, checking him twice. He was getting sick of being searched today.

Scarza lifted a pack of cigarettes off the table and pulled a cylinder from the box. "How come I've never heard of you?" He tucked the cigarette between his lips and reached for a shiny lighter, cupping it in his hands as a flame flashed to life.

"I'm new to this part of the business," Devin said.

A long drag on his cigarette pulled the glowing embers a visible quarter of an inch down its length. Scarza blew out a lungful of smoke, setting down the lighter. "How come Dominik has never mentioned you?"

Scud stepped away, finished with his search, and Devin put his hands in his pockets. "Are you worried I'm a cop?"

A shrug was all Scarza gave before taking another drag. "That would make more sense than anything. Even though cops don't tend to worry about this kind of business."

"The human trafficking business?" Devin asked pointedly.

Scarza tapped the ash off his smoke into a crystal tray before sitting back. He eyed Devin, one arm resting on the top of the couch. He seemed to fight some kind of internal debate, then spoke. "I don't know what you're talking about."

"You don't?" Devin asked, feeling the whole venture melting around him. "You aren't aware of the fact that Dominik—the man with the dragon tattoo—works in picking up girls and making a profit off of selling them?"

The cigarette collapsed like an accordion as Scarza crushed its ember. "This has been a really interesting meeting, Mr. Smith, but I really don't know what you're talking about. So, it's time for you to go." Scarza turned his attention back to the television, handing the FN Five-seveN to Scud. "Give that back to him once you've escorted him off my property."

"I can pay," Devin interjected, trying to get Scarza's attention, who said nothing, reaching for the remote control. "I have thirty thousand at my disposal right now, and I can get more."

"Good-bye, Mr. Smith," Scarza said with a flippant wave of his hand, pointing the remote at the television.

"I'm good for the money," Devin assured.

Scud grabbed his arm. "Come on."

Devin made his move, twisting Scud in a way he wasn't expecting, dropping to his knees, the FN Five-seveN in Devin's hand in an instant. He kicked Scud in the chest and came at Scarza fast. "Where are they?" Devin shouted, the pistol thrust toward Scarza. "Where are the girls?"

Panic covered Scarza's face, blitzed out of his mind with drugs, and scared out of his wits with fear, his hands lifted, nearly climbing out of the couch and up the wall.

"Where?" Devin shouted, grabbing the lapel of the paisley robe, gun in the nape of Scarza's neck. "Where are you keeping them?"

"I don't have them. They're not here," Scarza stammered.

"Where?"

"I don't have them. They're not here!" he blithered like a mantra. "I don't have them. They're not here!"

"If they're not here, then where are they?" Devin shouted, angry, teeth bared. A fleck of spittle hit Scarza's cheek, just below the eye. "WHERE?"

"Ukrainians," Scarza stuttered. "People Dominik used to work for. They have an operation going through Mexico. They bring Ukrainian girls here, usually, but they had a deal with a client out of the Middle East. They wanted an American girl—young, that was their order. Under sixteen. Blonde. Nonprofessional. Virgin." Scarza was nearly crying. Whatever drugs he'd been taking were screwing with his mind, turning him into a blubbering mess.

"What about the other two?" Devin demanded, jamming the pistol roughly into Scarza's chest.

"The Ukrainians—same operation." Scarza whimpered, trying to pull away, bound in place by Devin. "They needed American girls—maybe for private buyers, maybe for the circuit. I don't know what for, but they bought from us!"

"Are they OK?" he demanded. "Did you hurt them?"

"What?"

"Did you rape them?" Devin shouted, leaving nothing to the imagination.

"No!" Scarza assured him. "Not *them*. First-timers can bring a lot of money, and the Ukrainians were specific."

"Why did you cancel the auction?"

"What?" Scarza asked dumbly.

"The auction, of the girls—why did you cancel it?"

Scarza was starting to calm down. "We were only doing the auction because it looked like our order with the Ukrainians might fall through, but they pulled it together last minute."

Someone—Scud—grabbed Devin from behind, ripping him backward, away from Scarza. Devin hit the floor, landing on his back. Scud flashed a gun, yanking it from his belt. Devin pulled the trigger, blasting him—the big man flailed back and hit the floor. Scarza reached for the end table—a gun of his own. A second shot from Devin's pistol and Scarza slammed back into the couch—a bullet in the side.

A split second of silence passed between the sound of the last gunshot and the sound of Scarza shouting hysterically, hands groping at the wound. The man shouted in pain and fear as he pulled open the top half of his robe, looking at the wound. A hole the size of a dime punctuated the smooth surface of Scarza's skin as he tried to put pressure on the wound. Blood poured out of the puncture, drenching the robe and the couch.

Devin pulled himself to his knees, then stood. He checked the Five-seveN; he hadn't fired it before and had worried in passing about its ability to perform. Devin took his finger off the trigger and walked toward Scarza. "Where did the girls end up?" he asked again.

Scarza's hysterics deteriorated to a kind of macabre giggle. "They're gone. They're long gone. They're all gonna get fed to perverted strangers who are going to violate them in ways you've never dreamed of." A shudder ran through Scarza's dying body.

The front door came open fast. "Devin," Hannah's voice said from behind him, "I heard shots. What. . . ." She trailed off, apparently taking in the carnage of the scene.

"Where are they?" Devin demanded again, jamming the muzzle of his handgun into Scarza's eye socket. "Where are they, you *sick*—?"

"I'm already dead." Scarza laughed, a malicious grin crossing his already paling face. "And you'll never find out what happened to those nubile playthings."

"What?" Hannah demanded, rushing up next to Devin, grabbing at Scarza. "Where are they?"

Devin stood, backing away. He'd been through this. And this sicko was going to let the whole thing die with him. Hopped out of his mind on drugs he bought with the suffering and misery of others. Devin watched the intensity of Hannah's actions, begging Scarza to tell her where the girls were, but there was no point—the trail and Scarza's body went cold at the same time.

Then the sirens started.

The police were on their way. The neighbors had heard the shots, and the police would be there in seconds. "Hannah?" he said gently.

"Where?" she asked the dead body, the grin gone from the man's face.

"Hannah?" he said again, a hand on her shoulder, "we have to go."

She stood, backing away, seething with anger.

"Hannah," he repeated, "we have to go."

She looked at him, turned, and followed him out the front door.

John Temple's eyes opened, and he saw Vincent Sobel standing in front of him.

"Hello, sleepyhead." Vince smirked.

"Vince," John said, moving to sit up, realizing that Trista was still resting her sleeping head on his chest, "how did you...?"

Vince sat on the coffee table, eyes meeting John's. Trista started to stir, waking. "You know I don't support this," he said.

John glanced down at Trista, her waking face surprised by the presence of Vince. "Vince?" she said.

"I don't approve of the two of you, either," he said, rubbing his hands together, "but I'm here about Senator Warren Foster and your disobedience."

John looked around and saw three other men in the room, all wearing suits, though none as expensive as Vince's. "How did you find us?" John asked.

Vince nearly rolled his eyes. "We're all members of the Firstborn here. It was just a matter of time until one of us saw where you were. And there are more of us that are opposed to what you are doing than those that support you. A lot more."

John looked down, working the heels of his hands into his forehead. "What do you want?"

"We're here to make sure you don't try to pull anything having to do with the Senator Foster press conference tomorrow." He reached into his jacket and removed something, setting it on the table—a silenced pistol. "And we really do intend to keep you here. No matter what."

"Even if that means letting a United States senator die?" John asked, looking up.

Vince didn't reply.

Chapter 17

Hannah must have nodded off. Her eyes opened, feeling the sting of dawn light creeping in. A few seconds of recollection: She was in the car, passenger seat. They had left the house in a hurry—Scarza dead on the floor. They hadn't talked at all, not a word between them as they drove in circles. Hannah's mind had been a furious tumult of thoughts, fears, and conjecture. Plans made themselves and unraveled at their seams as she had tried desperately to will the girls out of captivity. And then, at some point, she had succumbed to the exhaustion that worry and anxiety brought.

Devin was outside, leaning against the hood of the car, a silhouette against the horizon and the keen slashing rays of the dawn sun lifting over it. His arms were crossed, face turned slightly down—caught up in a kind of stillness that was inhuman. Hannah hunched her shoulders, stretching, then reached for the car door.

The car was parked at a higher elevation than most of the rest of the city, giving a good view of the city below. The kind of place people always seemed to name Lookout Point or something ridiculous and cliché. Tan dirt and short dry plants were all that was anywhere near them.

"Hello," Hannah said to Devin, walking toward his place at the front of the car. A tip of the face as a subtle nod was all she got in return. She took a place near him, leaning against the hood. Hannah crossed her arms, feeling cold, forgetting that the desert could get so freezing cold at night. "Where do we start looking for the girls?" she asked after a moment.

Devin moved for the first time in a truly noticeable way, stepping away from the car. "We don't," he said with a sigh.

Hannah blinked, then stepped toward him. "What do you mean?"

He turned from her, walking toward the edge of the bluff, once again a silhouette against the golden bloom of the morning sun. “It’s too late,” he said, shaking his head as he put his hands in his pockets.

“Devin,” she chided gently, “you can’t be serious. They’re just girls—barely into their teens. We can’t give up on them.”

“Clay Goldstein might have been right,” he mused, eyes transfixed on the city below. “Maybe it is time to give up on the girls. They’re not here, and we only have a few hours before they’re supposed to attempt the assassination.”

“But,” Hannah started, sounding more desperate and weak than she believed she was capable of anymore, “the girls—”

“Are gone,” Devin interrupted, turning to her, face stern. “They’re gone. Sold. Out of our reach. At least for now.” He shook his head morosely. “Maybe later. Maybe sometime in the future we can resume the search. But right now there’s nothing that we can do to—”

“No,” she sneered, backing away from him. “I can’t believe you’d just let this happen. I can’t believe that you would let them…” She winced, trying not to think about the possibilities.

“We just don’t have the time.” Devin balked. “Don’t you see? We have to choose—and the assassination is about to happen. There just isn’t time right now.”

“So.” Hannah took another step back, appalled by what she was hearing. “You’re just going to give up on them? Forever?”

“No.” Devin looked away. “Just until we make sure the senator is safe.”

“The window is closing,” Hannah argued, crossing her arms, “and if we wait, they’re going to be gone. Forever. Or might as well be.” She wasn’t used to arguing. She hadn’t done it much, and she had never liked what little she had done. But she found herself emphatic. Impassioned. Angry.

"We can't just let these thugs kill a United States senator," Devin said, voice raised, tone angry.

"These girls have mothers. Fathers. We can't let this happen!" Hannah argued back, matching volume, posture pitched forward, tone shrill and desperate to be understood.

Devin threw his arms out to the sides, posture equally emphatic. "They're going to kill a senator! We've wasted enough time trying to save these girls!" he shouted, mad.

"Wasting time?" Hannah demanded, face red.

"They're gone, Hannah!" he yelled, jabbing a finger at the dirt. "It's too late. Why can't you see that? It was always too late!"

"But we have to keep trying!"

"Later," he shouted, balling his fists, "maybe. But not now. Not with so much at stake!"

"Like what?" she demanded. "A senator?"

Devin pointed a finger accusingly. "You're being an irrational child!"

She took a step back, furious. "I am *not* being irrational, and I am *not* a child!"

"You're emotionally involved," he growled. "You see yourself in the people you're trying to help—young, vulnerable girls!"

"And you're not?" she fumed, "Trying to save an authority figure who just happens to have the same skin color as you?"

They stopped.

Devin's expression dropped.

Hannah trembled, suddenly realizing what she was saying. "Devin, I'm so..."

Devin sighed. "We're always pitted against each other—forced to choose between two goods."

"Devin," she stammered, "I'm sorry for the things I said. I'm sorry I lost my temper." She pushed a drop of blurry mist from the edge of her eye. "I'm so sorry."

"That's the problem when people work together," Devin said

with a kind of resignation. "They become more caught up in what's happening between them than what they set out to do in the first place."

She turned her head toward the sun, the sky starting to turn blue now in a fully formed morning. "We're going to have to do these things alone, aren't we?"

"No," Devin said, putting a hand on her shoulder, "because I'm not going to let you do this alone."

"But the senator—"

"If there's one thing I've learned living a life in the pursuit of moral and spiritual wholeness," Devin said gently, "it's that if you try to do it all by yourself, you won't last a minute. Working together has its problems, but it beats working alone." He took out his phone. "Besides," he smiled, "there's already someone who can deal with this."

Trista Brightling sat in the hotel suite. Their intruders had kept a close eye on them, restricting their movements to the point of paralysis. Vincent Sobel had tried to make small talk with her and John, but neither were willing to engage with him. The other three "guards" had taken turns sleeping and going to the restroom, occasionally opening one of their laptops to check e-mail.

Trista sat on the couch—the same place she had sat and slept for hours now. She was watching Vince, standing at the window, looking out at the city, when John's cell phone went off in one of Vince's jacket pockets. He had collected their phones, making it that much more difficult for them to contact anyone in the outside world. Vince took the phone from his jacket, checking the caller. He frowned and hit a button, silencing it, before putting it back in his pocket.

She looked at John, slouched in his place, looking beaten and sad. "Are you OK?" she asked, certain she knew the answer. He seemed to think for a moment, then looked her in the eye.

"I am," he said with the hint of a smile.

Trista frowned, thrown. "Why?"

He looked at her hand, taking it in his. "If everything has to go wrong," he said with a fully blossoming smile, "then I'm just glad that I can be here with you."

Trista felt something warm in her chest, a feeling that urged her to return John's smile. "Me too," she said without thinking.

The cell phone rang again in Vince's pocket. He checked it again, silenced it, returning it to its place.

Trista looked at John again, trying to think of something to say.

"I love you," he blurted softly, without any kind of pretense.

She felt the urge to say something back, to reply with something that might come out disastrously similar. Yet she somehow managed to stay silent.

"I always have," he continued, "since I first met you in Barcelona—it feels like it was years ago."

Trista laughed quietly, almost to herself. "John—it was years ago. Two, at least."

"And I've never stopped," he whispered, eyes sincere and intense. "I ran halfway across the world, but I never stopped loving you."

"John, I—"

"I told you I'd die for you," he said with all seriousness. "If it comes to that, I promise I will."

Her threshold of comfort diminished in an instant. "What are you saying, John?"

"Angelo," he said, unblinking. "He said that the Thresher wanted you dead. That's what he said to me in the parking garage yesterday, before he disappeared."

"And you believe him?" Trista asked.

"I don't know," he said, looking like he might cry, "but you have to promise me that you won't do anything to put yourself in harm's way. Do you understand?"

She stared at him, transfixed, trying to find some crack in his resolve, some indication on his face that he didn't believe what he was saying—not really, at least. Did he?

The phone in Vince's pocket rang again, and John stopped, like a dog that caught the scent of something. "It's Devin," he said, suddenly realizing. He raised his voice and said it again. "It's Devin."

Vince looked at him intensely, then reached for the phone.

Devin heaved an internal sigh as the phone finally connected to someone.

"Where are you?" the voice on the other end asked.

Devin frowned. "John?"

"Where are you?" the voice asked again.

"Vincent Sobel," Devin said, recognizing the voice, suddenly concerned. "What are you doing at this number?"

"I caught up with them," Vince replied, his tone casual.

"You're keeping them locked down," Devin stated, "so they won't interfere with the assassination."

Vince didn't speak for a moment. "We should talk about this," he suggested, "over coffee. Where are you?"

"I want to talk to John," Devin said, edging toward ordering.

"Just a second, then."

There were a few seconds of rustling as the phone was passed from one person to the next.

"Hello?" John asked.

"John? Are you OK?"

"I'm fine," John replied, hurrying to add something else, but he was cut off by more rustling and the sounds of protest as the phone exchanged hands again, apparently against John's will.

"There," Vince said. "Now why don't you come and meet me?

Put down your guns and let this Foster thing go. OK?"

Devin turned to Hannah, standing with him there on the dusty bluff. There was something in her face—she understood what was going on.

"You've made me the only person who can deal with the assassination," Devin stated, realizing the fact himself for the first time.

"Yes," Vince agreed, almost as if he'd realized it for the first time himself, "and I promise you that I'll do everything in my power to make sure—"

Devin hung up on Vince midsentence and put his phone into his pocket. He turned to Hannah.

"Do I need to do this alone?" she asked with an unmistakable air of courage.

He didn't speak for a moment, trying to find a way—some chance that they, mere mortals, could know beyond a doubt what they should do. By saving the senator, he could well be dooming Hannah's mission—and Hannah herself. He groped for some perfect answer to all the questions that flitted through his mind and pricked at his conscience. Discernment. He prayed for discernment. Just having visions wasn't enough.

Then, looking into her resolute face, he found his answer.

"I don't want you to do anything until I can help," he ordered, stepping toward her. "I told John I wouldn't let you act alone, and I intend to keep my word. Don't make contact, don't try to rescue, and don't confront. And whatever you do—don't get caught. Do you understand?"

She shook her head. "What do you want me to do, Devin?"

"You're right," he said, feeling an abstraction of the future. "If you don't go right now—right this instant—and find out where these girls are, then we'll never find them."

Hope seemed to flood her face, filling her features with life. "You're saying I'll find them?"

"I don't know," he said, shaking his head, somehow confused by his own words, "but I do know that the only chance they have is for you to find them now. And when you do, call me. If I can come, I will be there."

"If you're done," she acknowledged. "If you're still alive."

It always sobered Devin after the fact that he could have died in a particular situation. But it was the kind of thing he pushed off until after, then dismissed as being a part of the long lost past. "Yes." He nodded. "If I'm still alive."

Hannah was silent for a moment, the breeze tousling a hair. Stepping forward, she hugged him.

"Dear God," she muttered in Devin's ear, standing on her toes to reach it, "protect my brother and friend, Devin. Give me stillness. Give me peace. But give him safety."

Devin leaned down toward Hannah's ear. "Lord, watch over Hannah. Protect her and keep her. Forgive me for not being able to be with her, but keep her safe!"

And then, without an amen, he pressed the keys to the car into her palm, stepped away from her, and walked toward the road.

Chapter 18

SENATOR WARREN FOSTER stood on the balcony of his hotel room, looking out over the city. Las Vegas was made for the night, when it could be its own evening sky, filled with colored lights. But during the day the place seemed dirty, grungy, and run-down. Vegas had been torn down and rebuilt several times over, and now with the current economic woes, it looked as bad as ever. Empty parking lots, devoid of their nighttime visitors. The kind of uninhabited wasteland that most places had to wait until two in the morning to become.

He was ready to leave. Not that Vegas wasn't a charming place in its own right, but he was ready to sleep in his own bed.

He was tired. The scandal and the accusations had been more than he was ready for, and the nature of the situation had caused more than its share of controversy. It was hard on his marriage, hard on his kids. It was all more than he wanted to talk about or deal with. And then there was the issue of security.

As a senator, he didn't have a Secret Service detail, not usually. Someone had made sure he had security, though. Private contractors who were supposed to keep him safe if something happened. Mostly he just found them a nuisance.

He'd spent the last two days touring Las Vegas, "investigating" for human trafficking activity. It was important; he knew that. Prostitution was legal here, like it was in Amsterdam and parts of Germany. In Europe, legalization of prostitution always seemed to be justified by the notion that it would protect women, allowing them insurance and medical care, and bring revenue to the state. The result was government programs that weren't being used by the women—many of whom were too embarrassed to go on the record to say they'd made a living that way for a short period of time. Most of them didn't plan to live that kind of life any longer than they had to and weren't about to do something that would let their friends and family know they had taken up that kind of vocation.

But Nevada's European counterparts had only really served as a means of hiding illegal trafficking in a forest of legal prostitution. The demand for girls was simply too high, and not enough of them actually *wanted* to make a living that way. The result was a flood of girls from all over the world, mostly the Ukraine, being bought and sold against their will, into a trade that would ruin their lives.

The point of the investigation was to see if the same things were happening here in Las Vegas, which was something he could hardly establish in just two days. But it was a publicity stunt. A series of photo ops designed to show people he was a good senator worth reelecting. And there had been something else that had made his associate, Mr. Crest, so interested in coming to this place.

Warren Foster took a long, deep breath of morning air. He wondered if he could change the time for the press conference, maybe catch an earlier flight back home. He could get some sleep on the plane and be home in time to see his wife.

"Senator?" someone said from behind him, and he turned.

"Mr. Crest," he acknowledged. The man had a first name, but Foster couldn't bring himself to use it. Crest was tall and very thin with round glasses. Yet there was something commanding about the man. The kind of thing that made first names inappropriate.

"I'd like you to take a look at the plans for the security," Crest said, approaching with his briefcase.

"OK," the senator said with a resigned nod, telling himself that he just had to get through this and then he could go home.

Hannah Rice drove the car through the streets, still miles away from the house where Devin had shot Scarza. She wondered if there were police there. Was it a crime scene? There was always the question of justification when killing someone. Devin had feared for his life, they were going to shoot him, but was it self-defense? It was the kind of question she wasn't good with.

She prayed. That was what other people called it, at least. A term that had little to do with the reaching of her soul into an ever-sharpening path toward God. She said nothing.

The car moved slowly, yet the passing of the neighborhood around her seemed to be a flickering of color. Everything seemed to be going faster than it really was. Her world seemed to blur, her eyes starting to relax. It was the kind of thing that didn't impair her ability to drive yet let the muscles in her body relax.

A thought came to her—that these were the same streets the girls had been taken down. The relaxing of her body continued, the trees and houses blurring together in a faster and faster display of color and motion.

Then she felt it.

The girls in the truck. Dominik at the wheel.

She was on the trail. This was where they had gone, and she could follow it to where they were going.

Her vision became crystal clear. She knew where to go now. She was on the scent, and she would follow after these girls—even into the hell they were being taken to.

Devin walked down the road, almost marching. Time was slipping by. No matter how fast he tried to reach the future, it was always down to the wire, it seemed.

He felt the bulk of the FN Five-seveN in his belt, the weight of the magazines in his jacket. He'd been sure to grab the ammunition from the car after he left Scarza's house. He'd feared that there would be more of them, and maybe they had followed. Luckily his fears had not come to pass.

Now he was simply glad to have them on his person. Stopping an assassination was not an easy task. He would, of course, do his best to involve the police. But it was always the same—the lesson you learned early as a member of the Firstborn—if you see things that others don't, then you'll be seen as crazy. Especially by government organizations like the police. Devin had no problem with the police, but he knew better than to turn to them as a first line of defense, and he certainly knew better than to expect them to understand.

There hadn't been any cell phone reception when Hannah had taken off in the car, and now the battery was dead. It made calling for help difficult. But he still had time. Enough to make it.

He had been walking for miles, and already his feet hurt. His shoes were hardly made for walking, and they were torture to his feet. A fact he would never reveal. But he wasn't there yet. He had a long way to go—and no idea if he would make it in time.

Dalton Waters got up and started getting dressed. He picked up a plastic cup from the bathroom counter and put it under the faucet, turning it on. His hand shook as he held it under the stream.

Whether he lived or died didn't matter; this was going to be an important day. Respectable white people should have made a stand a long time ago. It wasn't safe for them anymore in this country. Power was shifting, and those of different races were breeding them out like crazy. And white people were getting less and less representation. Even those who had voted for the current president based on race knew that—because he was bringing representation to his race.

Dalton took a sip of water and splashed some more on his face.

The white population of America was giving up. Soon they would be a minority, and the country they had started, that had been great, would wind up just like the countries those other races had come from. America would be no better than Africa or South America or Mexico. Rat-infested places, all.

He walked to the bag in the corner and opened it, looking at the M14 rifle inside. A beautiful piece of equipment. American made. The design had come about after the Second World War, when the army decided to take all the best features of the Browning assault rifle, the Thompson submachine gun, the "grease gun," and the M1 Garand and put them all together into one rifle—the M14. Of course it looked like a normal rifle, wood stock with a traditional shotgun grip, so it looked old. As a result, the army had chosen to change to the M16 during Vietnam, and Dalton couldn't help but think that was the reason the whole thing had gone so badly.

But it was a quality rifle. So good that navy SEALs were dusting them off by the boxload and taking them into the deserts of Iraq, refusing to let such a good service rifle die. Dalton liked that. The understanding that some things will just always be better than others—and that the truth of the inequity will always be made evident. Lucky for him, the people who had approached him and asked him to do this job knew where he could get a whole crate of the Korean War–era rifles.

His phone rang. "Yes?" he asked, snapping it open.

"We're ready. Everything is a go."

Dalton closed his eyes and let his shaking stop. Today they were going to make a point. A profound one. White men weren't going to take orders from less-advanced races. Not in this country.

A beautiful view, Clay Goldstein thought as he sat on his balcony.

His mansion was a place he always felt safe. Security was tight and maintained. There were enough cameras on the grounds to film *Ben-Hur* twice, enough personnel to fight a small war, and enough fence that he sometimes joked that it could be seen from space.

He breathed deeply and took in the view. The Napa Valley

never ceased to amaze him for its beauty. Rolling hills, vineyards, greenery, and sun.

"*Nessun Dorma*"—the famous aria from Puccini's *Turandot*—played on a small MP3 device nearby. He reached for his bottle of wine and poured himself a glass. The wine was from a local vineyard he owned. It always pleased him to think that he was the owner of a vineyard, even if he did none of the work himself.

He held the glass up to the sunlight. The red liquid swirled at an angle, its residue gliding down the sides in a perfectly measured pace indicative of its sugar content. A quick swirl under his nostrils, breathing in the dry bouquet of the merlot—then a sip.

A staggering moment of epicurean completion. Wine, music, and scenery blending together as the aria's hero, Calaf, declared his victory in love, over and over in climactic, soul-tugging glory through the timeless language of opera.

Clay leaned back breathing in the clean air. Taking another sip of wine, he held it on his tongue before swallowing the dry nectar. It was good to be alive—even if only for a while longer. The Parkinson's would be fatal, they had told him, but he would probably have a heart attack first—a common finish to the disease. But the wine was good for his heart, he told himself, and drank happily.

The music faded to silence, and for a moment there was nothing to listen to but his thoughts. Thoughts of things that were far away. It was strange the way his ability to feel the present had grown keener since the first symptoms of Parkinson's set in. He hadn't started shaking or freezing up, but the effects on his mind were starting to slip insidiously into his life. Simple things that he never would have forgotten before were suddenly starting to evaporate. Concepts that would have once been simple were now impossible to decipher. Not all the time, of course, but every once in a while. The doctors said it was the early onset of dementia—something that came along with his type of Parkinson's. And while his ability to reason in the real world had suffered, his ability to see what others could not had only grown. And his gifts as a member of the Ora were considerable to begin with.

Then something changed—the feelings of things far away. The indulgence of the moment was replaced with a different sensation. He could feel them all:

Hannah Rice, weary from driving, nearing her destination. Devin—striving toward his own objective. John and Trista—kept in place by Vincent.

He heaved a sigh. Peace and quiet might have to wait. It was time to make the call.

Hannah watched the signs as she drove through the desert. She'd gone south into Arizona. Hours had gone by, but she knew what she was following, and the time had evaporated.

The area was like a hideous lunar landscape with light brown dirt and flat ground that stretched out in perpetuity. Dark patches of desert shrubs dotted the flat landscape and were the only things that really appeared to pass by at all out here. A road sign approached as she accelerated. Besides the road itself, it was the only sign of human life out here that she could find. Hannah slowed the car slightly and read the sign.

Apparently she was somewhere in the vicinity of Yuma, Arizona. She knew that name, something about an army or air force base in Yuma. Or was it in that Nat King Cole song about Route 66? She continued looking over the sign; she was less than thirty miles from the Mexican border. If they were planning on moving the girls across national lines, then she needed to act fast.

The trail shifted, and she turned right, down a dirt road. There were shallow ruts in the road, meaning that someone still used it, but there were no signs of life. Hannah focused, silencing her mind, making certain she wasn't just imagining it all. No, this was the direction.

Another five minutes of tense driving, worrying that she had gotten off track and that she was following some kind of wild goose chase. There were warning signs declaring the place private property, but there was nothing to protect it as far as she could tell.

And then she saw it. A church, old and brown, all its paint rotted off. It wasn't the old Spanish mission-style church she would have expected in this part of the United States. Instead it was the decaying remains of a traditional American church building. A tall steeple with a bell, steep roof, and dirty broken stained glass. It was little more than an outline in the distance.

Hannah stopped the car a quarter of a mile away, pulling off the dirt road into a slight dip, hoping the car would be slightly less obvious there. She reached for the handgun Devin had given her; what had he called it? A sour? Regardless, the pistol looked lethal in its tightly packed structure of dark gunmetal. She double-checked the magazine and pulled back the slide just enough to check the action.

She stepped out of the car and waited for a moment, checking her surroundings before moving forward, staying low. If she was going to call Devin, she had to have something to say. And she wasn't even absolutely certain this was the right place. Scouting the area was what made the most sense.

The old church looked completely abandoned at first, but as she got closer she realized that it was surrounded by tire tracks and modern amenities. There was a shed with a shiny new latch and padlock that someone was maintaining. There was a bright red air compressor and even a satellite dish, presumably for getting cable television. As she continued her circuitous approach, she saw a collection of vehicles parked at the back door of the old church.

This was it. This was the place.

Devin had been specific that she was supposed to call, not to do anything without him. Hannah crouched in the dirt near some kind of dry shrub, sharp rocks and desert plants jabbing at her knees. She took the cell phone out of her pocket and opened it.

—No signal—

Hannah lifted the phone into the air, watching the reception bars fluctuate from few to none. She looked back at the car, realizing how poorly hidden it was, then back to the church. Perhaps the best thing to do was to get in the car and drive fast toward someplace civilized where there was cell phone reception or a pay phone. She could call for Devin and wait for him to arrive. It had taken her the better part of four hours to get here, so it would probably take Devin as long. She would have to wait. Get a cup of coffee or take a nap.

But this was the place.

She could contact the local police. Get them to come out here. Working with the authorities as one of the Firstborn was a dicey thing at best, she knew, but maybe this time it would work out.

Either way, it was a terrible idea to go in there alone, without any hope of backup. Especially as a young woman. It was the worst thing she could possibly do, and Devin had known that.

She stood to go. Something else would have to be figured out.

Hannah waited a moment, then as she was turning to leave she heard something. It was faint, coming from the church. The sound of something human.

—screaming.

The stillness in Hannah's mind shattered, and her thoughts were filled with the ravings of a madhouse.

She tried to tell herself to listen to what Devin had said. To do the wise and sensible thing. To do the calm and realistic thing. But all that filled her heart and mind were passion. Anger. Fear. The thought that those screams were coming from a human being.

Another scream. Louder. A woman. Pain.

Hannah held her pistol tight and charged, racing toward the church in a frenzy of steps, plowing through the dirt.

Around a shrub, over a sagging barbed-wire fence, past the shed, up the steps, to the door—throwing it open.

Gun raised, she stepped in, door closing behind her. Hannah stopped.

A collection of five or so people in folding chairs sat in the sanctuary around a television, backs to her, watching a game show. They turned, almost in unison, staring at Hannah.

Two very attractive women and an older woman with white hair were among them. Their expressions were confused, like someone who had accidentally stumbled into the break room at a local super market.

The older woman, mid to late sixties, with short white hair, frowned. "Who are you?" she asked with a thick eastern European accent.

Hannah stood, holding the handgun, feeling more embarrassed than anything. Had she heard the television?

The scream came again. Louder. More immediate.

Hannah turned her attention to a door to her right, throwing it open to see a set of very steep stairs disappearing into the basement.

"Stop!" was the word she heard the female voice cry.

Hannah rushed down the stairs, smelling heavy mildew and perspiration. The stairs took a sharp turn, then stopped.

The basement. Dark with no windows and only a single overhead light bulb. A cement floor covered in mattresses and filthy blankets. Nearly a dozen girls and a couple of little boys stared back at her from a far corner. To her right was a woman, fully clothed, pressed against the cement wall, arm trapped in a hammerlock, screaming in pain. Her captor barked in her ear in another language—Russian, maybe.

Hannah recognized the man.

The dragon tattoo.

Dominik.

She stopped, staring at him.

Hurried footsteps came down the steps behind her, coming to a stop.

"What is this?" the older woman jabbered, hands gesturing emphatically as Hannah turned around. "This is private property! You cannot just be here!"

Hannah tried to think of something to say. Something strong that would guarantee that she was understood, that would make them all realize that she had a gun and that she was in control of the situation. All of that was overridden by the absurd urge to apologize.

She lifted the gun, pointing it at the older woman. The woman's expression soured, looking offended. The woman said something in her native language, including one word that Hannah understood.

"...Dominik..."

Hannah looked behind her where Dominik had been, turning just in time to see his fist.

Chapter 19

THE LAS VEGAS city bus rolled along the streets, off the Strip, near some of the seedier portions of the city. Faux skylines of New York and Paris were somewhere ahead in the distance.

The mammoth vehicle stopped, its doors opening. A handful of passengers got up and made their way to the exit while several climbed aboard.

Devin glanced out the window, then at the bus map he'd found crumpled on a nearby seat.

Almost there.

He checked his watch. Not much time.

Almost there.

Those getting on the bus found their places. A passenger sat across the aisle from Devin. He caught a passing glance in his peripherals as he looked out the window, then did a double-take.

"Mr. Bathurst," Angelo said, currently lucid.

Devin looked up, preparing himself mentally for a fight. "Angelo," he replied.

John could feel the urgency from the next room.

Dalton Waters standing, duffle bag in hand. A bulletproof vest and rifle inside the bag, along with ammunition, a mask, and various other items.

Going to the door.

Leaving. Heading for . . . somewhere.

"You have to let us go," John Temple said, standing in the middle of the hotel room, stepping toward Vince.

"No"—Vince wagged a finger—"not a chance. You're staying here. Things are going to play out naturally. No interference from you two."

"We know there's going to be an act of violence," John snarled.

"We have to do something. We have a moral obligation—or it's the same as killing that man ourselves."

"No, we don't," Vince rebutted. "We don't have to get involved. It's not our fight—and some things simply have to be allowed to play out. This is one of those things."

"John's right," Trista said from her place on the couch. "I don't know the extent to which each individual should be expected to take care of everyone else, but we're called to this. This is something that we have to do. Otherwise John wouldn't be getting the visions he's getting."

"No." Vince shook his head. "Devin Bathurst was called to this, and he put it on you to finish it for him."

"But someone *was* called," John said.

"Yes," Vince agreed, "but he chose a different calling and left this one."

"Fine." John could feel the situation coming together, time slipping through his fingers.

Dalton Waters and his associates making their way to their respective places—bags filled with weapons and scads of ammunition.

John turned toward the door of the hotel room. "I'm leaving."

"Whoa!" Vince ordered, stepping in front of John, the other three guards getting up from their places. "You're not going anywhere. Do you understand?"

"Or what?" John stepped up to Vince, eyes focused on the other man's pupils. "Are you going to shoot me?"

Vince pushed his sport coat open and put his hand on the grip of the pistol he'd tucked in his pants. John took another step, and Vince pushed him back with his left hand, reaching for the pistol with the other.

"Back!" he shouted, pistol pointed downward but ready to be raised.

John glanced at Trista, sitting on the edge of the couch, then back at Vince. "I can shout and scream at the top of my lungs," he said smugly, "and when the neighbors complain about the noise—"

"They'll call the room," Vince interjected, "and I'll tell them it was my kids and that I'll keep them quiet."

"But when the noise doesn't stop, they'll send someone."

"By then"—Vince shrugged—"it'll all be over, and we'll all just go our separate ways."

Dalton Waters getting into a van, tossing a bag of guns onto the floor. The driver starting the engine.

"How long have we been friends, Vince?" John asked, looking him in the eye.

A sudden look of sobriety crossed Vince's face. "A long time."

"Kind of a stupid thing to end a friendship over, disagreeing on whether or not to let a United States senator be assassinated."

Vince shook his head, sincerely apologetic. "I'm sorry, John."

"I'm sorry too, Vince," John said sadly. He lunged forward and punched Vince in the nose.

Shouts of confusion and protest erupted from the other guards as John ripped the pistol from the man's hand, taking him hostage.

Men in the lobby bathroom stalls, pulling on ski masks and jamming magazines into automatic rifles.

"We're going!" John announced, motioning to Trista with his head.

Vince touched his bloodied nose, trying to pull away from John. "You wouldn't shoot me," he blustered.

"Really?" John asked, the guards pointing their weapons at him from their places around the room. "Have you ever killed anyone, Vince? I did, once. It's the kind of thing that keeps you up at night. Which is why I won't kill you"—he jammed the pistol into the back of Vince's arm—"but I will blow your elbow away if I have to!"

"Let him go," one of the guards barked.

"Trista." John turned to her. "Get out of here and run." He ignored the guards as he spoke over their demands. "Don't go anywhere near where the assassination is supposed to be." He wrangled the squirming Vince. "Run!"

She stood, moved past them, toward the door, opened it.

John shoved Vince and followed Trista out of the door.

Devin sat perfectly still, watching Angelo across the aisle.

Their eyes locked. The bus shook, hitting some kind of imperfection in the street. Their gaze didn't break.

"You're here to stop me," Devin stated, still tense and prepared.

Angelo's eyes, dark and intense, seemed to look right through Devin. In a fraction of a second his eyes darted down, and when they came back up, the intensity was gone. "No." Angelo took a quick look at the few people in nearby seats, apparently trying to determine if they were being listened to. He whispered, "I'm not well." He articulated the statement with more lucidity than Devin thought possible.

"I know," Devin agreed.

"There's too much going on in my head," he whispered, looking as if he might cry. "The human mind isn't supposed to endure this much information from conflicting sources. It's confusing and distressing."

Devin listened patiently, then spoke. "What do you need, Angelo?"

Angelo wiped his face with the back of his black coat, dark hair shifting. "I'm not well," he repeated, "but I do have the ability to reason. And I can see that my attempting to stop you won't prevent you from trying. Or the others, for that fact."

Devin leaned closer. "Why are you here, Angelo?"

"I am a reasonable person," Angelo said again, his lucidity starting to slip, "and I hope that you are too."

"OK," Devin accepted. "What do you have to say to me?"

"The reckoning," Angelo stated with sudden stability.

Devin frowned. "What?"

"When the Firstborn are removed, the reckoning will come, and the Firstborn will be destroyed. And then," he sighed, "the truly bad things will happen."

"What things?" Devin asked, watching Angelo slip toward confusion again. "Angelo, what things?"

"It's in the prophecy of Alessandro D'Angelo."

"What prophecy?" Devin demanded.

"It's hidden," Angelo muttered.

"Where? Where is it hidden?"

Angelo's head hung for a moment, stringy hair covering his face, then looked up, eyes tortured. "I'm still a man," he said, face pained. "I know you can't let them kill innocent people. But if you interfere—even if you fail—you'll doom the Firstborn and countless others."

"How?"

Angelo shook his head. "I don't know how. I just know that when I see the future I see your interference—and then I see what they did to me. I see"—Angelo winced as he said the word—"*pain.*"

"Who?" Devin asked. "Who caused you pain?"

Angelo shook his head. "I honestly don't know."

The bus stopped.

"This is your stop," Angelo conceded, eyes darting toward the hydraulic doors as they opened automatically.

Devin stayed sitting. "You're really going to let me go?"

Angelo looked back at him. "I won't stop you. I know better than to try. But," he added, "you'll have to live with the consequences of whatever choice you make. You can trust that

I'm not completely out of my mind, and let a man be executed and others hurt, or you trust your conscience and intervene."

Devin blinked, not certain what Angelo was doing.

"Go!" Angelo blustered, standing, pointing toward the door. "Hurry! There's isn't time!"

Shock hit Devin like a breaking wave. Had Angelo suddenly lost faith in his own ability to see outside of the confines of time? Or had he suddenly gained some strange confidence in Devin?

"Get out of here!" Angelo growled, something flashing in his eyes that had only seemed to be there in muted tones up to this point. Something irrational, flawed, self-destructive, and alone—humanity.

The doors started to close.

"Wait!" Devin shouted toward the driver. "This is my stop!" The doors cracked open again, and he moved toward them, left the bus—

—and ran.

One of the guards who had chased after John and Trista walked back into the hotel room.

"Where is Temple?" Vince asked, bleeding into his hand as he clutched his nose. Temple had slugged him right in the nose and hit him harder than he'd first realized.

"We didn't see. We're going to have to track them down before—"

Vince's phone rang in his jacket, and he removed it with his free hand, trying not to bleed on himself. He checked the caller ID—*Clay Goldstein*. Vince flipped the phone open. "Mr. Goldstein?"

"Let it go, Vincent," Clay said with the casual ease that characterized him.

"What?"

"John and Trista; let 'em go. This is something they think they've got to do."

Vince stepped into the hotel bathroom, spitting a glob of blood into the sink. "I'm Overseer," Vince protested.

"You're only Overseer because I say so."

"I'm not your puppet," Vince growled, washing blood down the drain.

"The agreement was that you did what I said and I'd support you as Overseer. It was supposed to give me distance and keep me safe—not give you license to harass our people and let senators die on national television."

"I'm still Overseer," Vince argued, pulling tissues from a box.

Clay spoke firmly. "I made the calls, Vince. I'll have your job by this afternoon—and if you want any place of authority in the restructuring, then you'll do what I say."

Vince closed his eyes. "Fine. I'll call them off."

Trista ran down the stairs as fast as her legs could carry her. John caught up and rushed past her to slam through a door. He held it open for her as they ducked down another hallway, through another door, then exploded into the sunlight.

They were at the back of the hotel, near a loading dock. "Where now?" Trista asked, looking around.

John turned to her, a look of shock on his face. "No," he said, "I don't want you anywhere near this."

"What?" she asked, mind racing.

John took the gun he'd grabbed from Vince and put it in her hand. "Take this. Stay safe."

"John," she argued, "I'm coming with you."

He grabbed her by the upper arms, holding tight. "Listen to me, Trista! Angelo warned me!"

"About what?" she asked, knowing that every single moment they wasted was another moment closer to massacre.

"He told me that the Thresher wants you dead. And I can't let that happen, Trista!"

"What?" she stammered, his strong hands holding her arms tight, bright eyes looking deep into hers. The whole world seemed to be spinning.

"I know I've said it all before, but this may be my last time to say it ever again." He nearly shook her as he spoke. "I have to do this, Trista. I have to go, and you have to stay safe."

"I'm not afraid," she said, shaking her head, sorting through the dizzying spiral of thoughts.

"If anything ever happened to you," John said, eyes red, "I'd go crazy. I'd go completely crazy. I can't let that happen. I'll die before I let anything happen to you!" He stopped and looked into her eyes with his own soulful gaze. "I love you, Trista. I love you more than I've ever loved anyone in my entire—"

She kissed him before he could finish. Long. Passionate. As if it were the last time she ever would. As if it were the only time she ever had. John tried to step away, but she held on to him. He returned to her, embracing her with strong arms—then tore himself away.

John backed away from her, slowly at first, eyes still locked. Then he turned and ran.

Trista felt something tear at her heart. She had always aspired to control her heart, to be the master of her feelings. But there had always been one thing that took every weakness in her and turned her into a slave to her heart. She hated him for it. And yet…

Trista watched as John disappeared around the corner of the hotel.

"I love you too, John," she whispered.

The journalists set up outside of the hotel just at the front doors, filling the sidewalk with tripods, cameras, and bustling people. Television and print journalists alike formed around the area, making a pocket for the senator when he arrived through the glass doors ahead of them. There was a podium with a dozen or so microphones set up in the middle of it all for the senator to make his statements.

A cameraman wiped the sweat from his forehead and watched as the senator's security approached, asking to see the contents of their bags. It was ridiculous, he thought. He'd never seen this kind of security for a senator before.

"Three minutes," an aide announced, letting them know that the press conference would begin shortly.

Security might be tight, the cameraman thought, but at least it made sure they were all safe.

John Temple ran toward the street, staring out at the cars—then saw the cargo van with tinted windows.

There.

He could feel it. Dalton Waters was in that van.

John ran, rushing as fast as his body could carry him, watching the vehicle roll along at thirty miles per hour. Just fast enough to see the vehicle going out of sight.

The van came to an intersection filled with cars and stopped at the red light. John pushed himself, feet coming down in a steady patter of lightning-quick steps.

Just ahead.

He dodged between a set of cars and came up beside the van—this was it. He could feel it. The guns, the masks, the men, the plan.

John grabbed the side door handle, opened it, climbed into the backseat, slamming the door shut. The two men sat in the front, a black bag between them.

"What the—?" the driver shouted, shocked and confused.

Dalton, wearing a sport coat over a bulletproof vest and a pulled-back balaclava, turned to see. "John?"

"You can't do this!" John stated with firm resolve.

"Who is this?" the driver demanded, turning to Dalton.

Dalton ignored the question, swiveling in his seat. "What are you doing?"

The light turned green, and traffic began to move. The driver looked confused for a moment before driving forward.

"I know what's going on," John said, "and I'm not going to allow it."

"Get this guy out of the van!" the driver shouted, before releasing a string of panicked profanity.

A small yellow walkie-talkie in Dalton's hand crackled. "All teams in position. Are we a go?"

"You're compromised," John said to Dalton, still focusing on him. "The plan is compromised. Tell them to abort!"

Dalton lifted the walkie to his mouth. "All teams"—he focused on John as he spoke—"we are a g—!"

John lunged forward, reaching for the walkie-talkie, trying to rip it from Dalton's hands. Dalton bashed the radio into the side of John's head and pulled a gun, shoving the pistol toward John's face.

John stared down the muzzle and froze.

Senator Warren Foster walked out of the glass doors of the hotel and stepped up to the podium, cameras clicking in a loud volley of sound. There was chatter from everyone in the crowd, all trying to get their questions answered.

He gestured to everyone to be quiet. "Thank you for coming today," he said with the smile he'd been practicing, the one that his people told him made him a potential candidate for the presidency someday. "If you're all patient, I'd like to get to all of your questions this morning."

A flurry of hands raised.

"Yes, you," he said, pointing to a reporter, signaling that he would accept their questions—and the conference began.

Devin thundered down the sidewalks. The hotel was ahead. A tall building with bright lights for signs and floodlights illuminating its sheer walls. Green glass and gold etchings covered everything, art deco across every visible surface.

He could see it. Feel it. The future was arriving at a breakneck speed—driving his burning legs to catch up with the very force and time. Against the very momentum of inevitability.

His vision seemed to blur as he pushed himself forward—the impact of each footfall reverberating up his legs and through his body.

Closer and closer.

Devin shoved through the doors of the hotel and stopped. He was at the wrong end of the building.

To his immediate right were the stairs to the overhead monorail train. Ahead and to the right was the casino. Directly ahead—down a promenade lined with shops, stores, restaurants, and bars, expensive polished surfaces and trinkets of outrageous price—was the lobby. That's where the press conference was taking place.

Brightly lit with an incredibly high ceiling, marble floors, and gaudy architecture lined by colored lights and flat-panel television advertising the sights and the shows. Like a museum of ludicrously expensive designer baubles.

Devin took a step forward toward the sporadic patches of people.

"Get out of the van!" Dalton ordered.

John stood his ground, staring into the gaping void of the gun barrel. "No!"

"Just shoot him!" the panicky driver shouted. "We're almost there. There's no time. Shoot him now!"

Dalton pulled the black balaclava over his face, hiding his identity but still revealing conflicted eyes. "John, I'm only going to ask one more time, and then I really will shoot you—*please*, get out of the van!"

John looked at the speeding traffic around them, wondering if he was expected to jump and take his chances.

"We'll pull over for you!" Dalton pleaded.

"This is it," the driver said, removing a rifle with a wooden stock and a set of drum magazines beneath it to each side. "Take the rifle. Shoot this guy and take the rifle!"

Dalton let his eyes move quickly to the rifle for a moment.

John capitalized—swatting at the pistol in his face, pinning it against the driver's seat. Dalton turned back to John, punching with his left, sending John sprawling back into the bench seat.

He shook off the blow, and when he looked up, Dalton had dropped the pistol and grabbed the rifle from the driver.

John tried to attack, but Dalton was out of his seat—the rifle butt slamming into John's chest. His lungs felt like they were shattering. Dalton stepped forward, pushed the rifle laterally into John, pinning him down, the drum magazines driving into his shoulders.

"I told you to get out!" Dalton shouted, angry.

"Less than a block!" the driver announced. "Take care of him and get ready!"

John took a fist as he tried to struggle free. The world swam—the world outside blurred in motion.

"I'm not"—Dalton choked, exerting himself in trying to subdue the viciously fighting John—"in position!"

The driver's voice grew even more intense. "Get the window open!"

"I'm not in position!" Dalton stammered again, taking a knee to the stomach.

"This is it!" the driver shouted. "Do it now!"

John felt Dalton pull away and grabbed at the rifle, trying to stop him. The wooden stock of the rifle hit John in the side of the head like a club. John hit the floor of the van hard. He looked back and saw Dalton—pointing the rifle toward the unopened window:

At the sidewalk.

At the press conference.

At people...

John cocked his leg and kicked Dalton in the side as hard as humanly possible.

Dalton fired the rifle.

Fully automatic. Blasting out with the van window. Spitting broken glass and casings and muzzle flash and smoke. Deafeningly loud.

John pulled to his feet and threw himself at Dalton.

The glass door behind the senator exploded. "Gun!" one of the security guards shouted, and Senator Warren Foster threw himself down behind his podium, hearing someone scream as a reporter went down. Panic overtook him. Someone was shooting at him. Someone was really doing it. Someone was really trying to kill him.

Rough hands grabbed him, pulling him away—a security guard. The world spun. Everything was happening so fast, there was no time to get his bearings—he had to do what he was told: follow his security and get to someplace safe.

They pulled him back through the front doors into the spacious lobby. Four guards—two holding him tight, two with pistols drawn.

"Get him to security!" one of the guards shouted, waving

the bystanders away as they scurried from the lobby or stood, staring in confusion.

"Go!" one of the gun-wielding guards shouted, pointing toward the security station fifty yards away. He shouted again, "Go!" but was cut off by the blasting noise of a shotgun.

Devin ran forward full steam, watching the first of the senator's guards go down as two men with shotguns burst from a bathroom near the front desk. They wore brown coveralls, black masks, and Kevlar vests.

A security guard shot at the two men—aiming instinctively at the central body mass. The bullet hit one of the attackers in the vest, and he stumbled back. A shotgun blast and the guard went down—Foster's security pulling the senator toward the guard station as quickly as possible.

Devin reached for the FN Five-seveN and raised it, aiming down the promenade. The assaulting shotgun crew seemed distracted for a moment, trying to control the crowd. What little security was reacting seemed confused.

A bathroom door opening to the right—a man with an M14.

Falling back toward a hotel bar, Devin felt it seconds before it happened. The door opened—another assassin, dressed like the other two, only with an M14 automatic rifle. Devin fired blindly with the FN handgun as he took cover around the corner, just inside a hotel bar.

There were shouts of panic and worry from inside the bar as the occupants scattered. Return fire came from the new gunner, shooting wildly into the establishment. Glass containers and mirrors were obliterated under the onslaught of charging bullets, wreaking havoc on the bar.

Devin thought as quickly as possible, trying to sort through it all despite the shattering world. The point of the crew outside had been to get security to pull the senator inside. These gun crews were here to surround the senator once he was pulled inside and to kill him—and Devin had stepped into it.

Three gunmen, he counted so far. But John had said there would be eight.

The incoming fire lulled for an eerie moment of quiet, and Devin leaned from cover, firing and missing with a string of five rounds that popped effortlessly from the sleek pistol. He ducked back before the return fire started. Wherever the rest of the other gunners were, he had to act fast before they showed up.

His heart thundered.

He'd made it in time, but everyone might still die.

John took a heel to the chest as Dalton came down on him. Fighting him into submission, Dalton brought down the rifle butt again.

John could feel himself losing control of the situation as the driver cranked the wheel madly, trying to get away from the scene. He was tossed inside the van as it took a turn too sharply. Dalton lost his balance with the swerve, landing in the bench seat.

John stood—steadying himself against the door—the whole van shaking side to side.

Dalton was up, rifle dropped somewhere. He grabbed John by the hair with two hands. The van swerved again, and John felt Dalton use the momentum, ramming John's head into the hard glass of a window.

His vision blurred, filled with bright lights from the impact.

John spun, attacking with an elbow, connecting with Dalton's skull.

The driver shouted something about traffic as he made another sporadic move, the van hopping up onto the curb. John lost balance and hit the floor.

Sirens in the distance.

"Get the rifle!" the driver shouted.

John was on his side. He turned his head and saw the rifle Dalton had used, tumbling across the floor of the van, beneath the seat. He reached for the rifle and took a heel to the shoulder. Dalton must have seen it too, his feet moving around the seats, heading toward the back of the van where the rifle lay.

John pushed himself up and leapt, headfirst, over the seats, reaching for Dalton as he grabbed the rifle. They hit the seat in a flailing mess, wrestling for control of the weapon, the barrel waving toward the front of the van.

Then something went wrong, and the M14 went off in a wildly swinging burst of gunfire.

It was like a ripple that moved from the back of the van to the front—holes blowing through the seats, front dash, and windshield, spitting out clouds of stuffing, sparks, and glass.

The driver was hit, and what was left of the windshield was washed in a spatter of blood.

The van went out of control, tipping to the side. Glass burst from what few windows were still unbroken, framing shrieked, and the world went spinning.

Chapter 20

Devin pulled out of cover, pistol lifted.

There were gunshots and shouting. Suppressing fire ripped in the direction of the hotel's front doors, the gunmen shouting at the bystanders to stay down and get out of the way. People were flooding toward the exits in droves, largely ignored by the gunmen. It was still an assassination, not a massacre—there was only one person they were looking for.

Devin couldn't see any of them just yet. He stepped around a pillar that stood against the wall.

The gunman with the M14 turned to Devin and lifted the rifle. Devin leapt behind the nearby pillar, the blunt thunder of the fully automatic weapon barking down the promenade, brass casings bouncing across the marble floor. The shooting stopped, and the gunman yelled at a nearby bystander.

Stepping out, Devin took aim and fired a quick succession of rounds. He missed the gunman's head and bounced a bullet off Kevlar, hitting the shoulder. The gunman let go with the impacted arm and held the rifle with one hand, firing wildly as he tried to wrestle the weight of the weapon under control with just one arm.

The pillar—gold and green, covered in scrollwork—pocked as one of the stray rounds hit it. Devin slammed his shoulder into the wall, pulling behind cover again.

He couldn't see the senator. Or the other gunmen. Or the security guards. Maybe it was too late already. Maybe they'd already killed the senator and completed the assassination.

The M14 continued its heavy fire, brass jingling—

—then stopped.

Devin paused, listening.

The sound of the drum magazine being dropped from the weapon.

Devin broke cover, advancing fast. The gunman looked up. He was trying to jam a magazine into the rifle—ten feet away.

One shot to the head.

The gunman dropped.

Ahead—a hundred yards?—the two-man shotgun crew was firing wildly out the shattered glass doors. They didn't seem to see Devin as he approached. One of the shotguns went dry, and the gunman reached into a bag for shells, loading. The other grabbed a yellow walkie-talkie. "Team two, team three! Where are you?"

He rushed down the hall, dead security everywhere. It looked like Devin was the only resistance that remained. He moved past crouching bystanders, looking for the senator. Then he saw him—covered in blood, pressed against the wall next to one of his dead security team.

"Mr. Senator!" Devin shouted, grabbing him by the arm, pulling him up. "I have to get you out of here!"

"Who . . . ?" the senator stammered.

The senator didn't finish. The shotgun crew at the doors had realized what was going on. They turned and fired. Buckshot pattered around them, too far away to hit with anything resembling precision.

"Come on!" Devin shouted, dragging the senator back toward the entrance he had come in—then stopped.

Another set of gunmen, armed with M14s, had arrived, approaching from the same direction Devin had come originally, cutting off their escape. Brown coveralls, Kevlar vests, black masks—two of them. Devin shoved the senator behind him, blasting at the assassins with an unexpectedly rapid series of shots.

The gunmen went for cover, startled by the fact that someone was shooting back.

Three more rounds went their direction before they fired back blindly.

Devin's mind raced. The shotgun crew was charging from behind, dead security to the right, the new crew arriving ahead of them, and the casino to his left. He grabbed the stunned senator again, dragging him to the left, down the steps, into the casino—toward the forest of slot machines and poker tables.

Trista drove the rental car down the Vegas streets, the small handgun sitting on the passenger's seat. The sounds of sirens were all around. Things had begun, and they were bad. She told herself that the police had everything under control and that John was right about her needing to get as far away as possible. But she could feel the future.

John—shot in the chest.

Bleeding.

Dying.

She couldn't leave.

Not yet. Not if she could still change the future.

John Temple blinked, body hurting all over. He looked around at the interior of the wrecked van. Seat belts dangled against the light that shone through the cracked and broken windows. The van had lost control when the driver was shot, hitting its side as it tipped over the curb and sliding across the sidewalk.

John lay for a moment longer. He hurt too much to move. Nothing was broken as far as he could tell, but who knew what else might have happened. Internal bleeding, concussion. Just because he couldn't spot anything on the outside of his body that alarmed him didn't mean he was OK.

Something nearby moved. John looked. It was Dalton Waters, reaching for the rifle he'd dropped as he tried to crawl out of the badly damaged van. John groaned as he tried to follow after.

Dalton reached for the black bag that had been inside the van. Grabbing it, he stood. The van rocked with the shift in weight.

"Dalton." John choked. It hurt to speak.

Dalton gave him a glance through the black mask, then turned back to the front of the van and kicked at the fractured windshield. The laminated safety glass popped out in a sheet, crumpling to the ground. Dalton stepped out, disappearing into the bloom of warm light.

John ignored the pain, pushing himself up, staggering forward. He crawled past the driver's seat, where the body of the driver hung suspended, locked in place by the seat belt. Blood dripped down a dangling arm and head. John caught his gag reflex before he was able to vomit and held it in.

He stepped into the golden sunlight, looking around.

Where was he?

Some kind of sidewalk filled with kiosks and tourists who stared at their newfound entertainment. He was at the foot of one of the hotel and casino complexes. Off the Strip? Probably. He didn't recognize the place.

"Are you OK?" a guy in his twenties asked. "Do you need an ambulance?"

"Don't worry," a woman shouted, phone to her ear. "I'm calling 9-1-1!"

Police sirens had already begun, getting close fast.

John scanned for Dalton. "I'm looking for—"

"Hey!" somebody shouted. "What are you doing?"

They were looking at Dalton, who knelt over his black bag, locking a new drum into the M14 rifle. A man stepped toward him, and Dalton swung with the butt of the rifle, forcing the bystander back. He shouldered the hefty black bag, firing a deafening string of bullets into the air.

People scattered.

The first police car appeared up the street, lights swirling.

"Out of the way!" Dalton shouted with anger, pulling the rifle to his shoulder, aiming toward the police car.

John plowed forward—half a dozen rounds too late—a trail of bullet holes tracing their way from the police car's grill all the way up to the flashing light that exploded. The car screeched to a stop—the driver wounded.

John rammed with his shoulder, sending the remainder of the shots uselessly wide.

There was a blur of motion, and John felt himself stumble, thrown off and sent sprawling, hitting the sidewalk with his chest. A gun barrel jammed into his back.

"Get up!" Dalton ordered. He pulled John to his feet, holding him by an arm, the muzzle of the rifle tipped into John's back.

He was being pulled backward—toward a restaurant.

John suddenly realized what was going on.

He was a hostage.

Devin pulled the senator behind a slot machine.

The senator stammered, "Who—?"

A harsh "Hush" was all the senator got as a reply. Devin peeked around their obnoxiously chiming cover—as much hiding as anything. The exit was a hundred yards away at best. Maybe if they ran…

A gunman with one of the vintage M14s stepped into view, blocking the far exit.

Devin cursed his luck and looked back in the direction he had—

Thunder shook the air as a rifle hacked out a violent burst. A slot machine took the blow, blasting lights and glass to bits.

He pulled back behind cover, blind-firing with the pistol, popping trios of bullets.

He crouched as the return fire began, the senator crouching beside him, shaking in fear.

"Are you—?" the senator started.

"Shut up!" Devin ordered, impatient with the shell-shocked official. "Do everything I say, or we're both dead!"

"Do you see him?" one of the gunmen shouted, trying to coordinate with the others in the room.

Devin grabbed the senator by a lapel and pulled him as fast as he could, head down, to the end of the row of slot machines. He looked quickly, eyes peeking over the cover. The majority, if not all of the gunmen were in the casino now, all exits covered.

They were surrounded—and they were being hunted.

Dalton Waters shouted as he pulled his hostage through the restaurant. The place was darkly lit with yellowish lightbulbs at infrequent intervals. The place appeared as if it either hadn't opened for the morning or was just opening now. There were no customers, only wait staff that scattered at Dalton's command.

"Dalton..." John tried to say, still off balance from being grabbed.

How had John gotten involved in all of this? Dalton wondered. He'd always hoped that the interior team wouldn't be necessary—that he'd be able to hit the senator from the van in the drive-by. But John had ruined that hope. Maybe everything. At least one of his people was already dead, and it was John's fault. And now he was in danger of getting cornered, and that was John's fault too.

A trio of police officers approached the glass doors at the front of the restaurant. Dalton lowered the M14 with one hand, firing wildly, blasting glass. The police—too afraid to risk their lives—backed away. And they'd stay away, Dalton thought, because unlike him, they were afraid to die.

"Out of the way!" Dalton shouted at a hostess, and she did what she was told as he pulled his hostage into the kitchen.

Devin listened to the sounds of feet moving along the casino carpet as the gunmen called instructions to one another. He motioned to the senator to stay and went prone, leaning around the corner of their position.

A moment to orient himself. A moment to brace his shooting arm. A moment to look.

In the dull metal side of a brass-colored slot machine he saw the warped image of an assassin moving perpendicularly to his left. Another moment as Devin held his breath.

A set of legs in brown coveralls stepped across his view ten feet away. The assassin was looking the wrong direction. Devin reacted fast, firing a burst from the handgun. Several rounds missed, but one hit a leg, sending the gunman to the floor, howling. The M14 in the man's hands raised, and Devin pulled behind cover as the return volley exploded in their direction.

He grabbed the senator, pulling him across the floor in the prone position. The senator tried to stand, but Devin yanked him back. "Keep your head down!" he hissed.

A maelstrom of fire ripped their position above them. Scraps of glass and plastic rained down on them as bullets and buckshot blasted at the cover around and overhead.

Suddenly the shooting stopped.

Devin pulled the senator, bringing him to a stop around another set of machines. Everything was quiet except for the electronic jingle of the machines, advertising their presence.

"Anybody see them?" one of the gunmen asked, breaking the silence.

Footsteps moved slowly and steadily at a distance.

"They aren't here anymore."

"He got my leg!" the wounded one groaned from where Devin had left him. "Be careful—he's got a gun."

"The senator?"

"No! I think he's security. Black guy. Shoot him for me."

Police, Devin thought. Where were the police in all of this? Security was all dead or immobilized, and that left the police—who were either useless or chasing after that van that had made the drive-by.

The footsteps got closer. On the other side of the slot machine rows? Either way, they were too close.

The senator must have heard it, shuddering as he tried to control his breathing.

Footsteps pressed softly into the carpet a short distance away, and the slot machines sang their jolly songs. Just inches away, the senator let out a frightened sound.

Devin looked around and saw a spilled scotch glass lying sideways on the floor. It must have been dumped by a casino guest in the mass exodus. He grabbed the glass, feeling its weight in his hand, palming the wide cylindrical object. Devin steadied his grip, trying not to let his hands slip on the condensation. A moment to listen, then he threw it as hard as he could down the row. The glass shattered against the metal frame of a slot machine.

"There!"

A gunman with a shotgun rushed in the direction of the breaking glass. Devin was already aiming when the man realized he'd been duped.

Blam-blam-blam!

Devin's pistol went dry, and the approaching gunman fell behind cover.

"What happened?" another of the gunman called out.

"I took one to the vest," the assassin choked out with surprise. "But I'm bleeding!"

Devin dropped the empty magazine from the handgun and fished in his jacket for another. He'd forgotten that the FN Five-seveN was designed to penetrate body armor. A claim that some considered exaggerated but had apparently worked well enough at close range to cause some damage.

There was some groaning from around the corner as Devin shoved a new magazine into his gun. The shotgun peeked around the corner without aiming and fired.

A seat flipped, thrown by the hearty blast. Devin shot back at the gun hand before it disappeared back around the corner.

"Keep back," another gunman shouted. "Work around them, and hurry."

"Oh no!" The senator moaned. Devin grabbed him and pulled him around another corner toward the card tables and out of sight.

John felt the impact as Dalton threw him into a stainless steel table, a pile of freshly grated cheese shifting as he hit. They were in the restaurant kitchen. The staff ran for the exits, compelled by the sounds of gunfire. Dalton peeked around the corner, into the dining area, then back at John.

"Am I your hostage?" John asked.

Dalton grunted, shoving a stack of pots and pans off a countertop, throwing his black bag on top. "I don't know."

"Are you trying to escape?"

Dalton reached into the bag, pulling out a yellow walkie-talkie. "Not now, John!" He turned the device on, adjusting the radio frequencies.

John shook his head, eyeing Dalton's gun. "You were really going to kill a senator, weren't you?"

Dalton grumbled. "We may have already."

"But it's wrong," John said, shaking his head. "Don't you see that?"

He didn't answer John, dialing in to the channel he was seeking. "This is lead; is anybody there?" he asked.

A crackle of static. "The target is cornered, but we're having trouble getting him pinned down."

Dalton seemed to panic for a second, glancing at John. "Can you get the target? Do you need help?"

"I don't know. We're trying, but he's got somebody with him that seems to know what they're doing."

Dalton groaned, slammed his fist on a stainless steel tabletop, and spoke into the radio again. "I'm on my way!" Without saying any more Dalton turned toward the back of the kitchen and moved toward the door.

"Wait!" John called after, suddenly being ignored. "You're not actually thinking of—"

Dalton was already out the back door. Gunshots followed in a fully automatic tear. John burst through the door, following, and saw Dalton in the sweltering alley between the restaurant and a parking complex. Dalton was more than a hundred yards away, firing his rifle at a police car that was trying to block his escape.

John chased after.

Was Dalton really going to try to run back to the hotel? Maybe it wasn't that far. Or maybe he didn't care.

Either way—he was only proving himself to be more dangerous.

Devin looked around at the card tables, wooden, tapering upward. A center display with a car, presumably available for winning, was in the middle of the room, surrounded by three art deco pillars. Devin peeked over the top of the table he was using as cover and saw two of the gunmen looking the wrong direction.

"OK," he whispered to the senator. The man's eyes were huge with panic, but he was obviously trying to pull himself together. "I know you're scared," Devin said. "I understand that, but we have to make a run for it. Do you understand?"

The senator looked Devin in the eyes, nodding.

"OK. Here we—"

"Got 'em!" a gunman shouted triumphantly from the left.

Devin fired a fast volley, driving the enemy back, then dropped to his stomach, pulling the senator with him.

At least one of the gunmen jumped up onto a card table, firing at a downward angle. Felt-top tables shredded with the impact of bullets—card shoes exploding, sending playing cards fluttering through the air like snow. It was a hell made of raining lead and a deluge of debris.

Surrounded. Cut off. Scared. Devin felt like curling into a ball and dying. "This way!" he hissed sharply at the senator, unwilling to succumb to fears. They weren't going to be able to survive this much longer.

The gun chatter stopped.

"Look out!" one of the gunmen yelled to the others. "Behind you!"

"Stop!" someone shouted. "LVPD!"

The police had arrived.

The gunfire resumed, but there weren't any bullets headed toward Devin and the senator this time. They had turned toward the police.

Looking behind him, Devin saw that the casino exited back into the leg of the hotel promenade twenty yards away. They weren't out of this yet. "Come on!" Devin ordered, pulling the senator with him. He moved as fast as he could with the frightened senator, every step a challenge. Almost—

"There!" a gunman shouted. A bullet burst off a nearby wall as they ran into the promenade.

There was a moment of quiet as Devin looked around and then saw the stairs leading up to the monorail. "This way!"

One of the gunmen stepped out of the casino, and Devin fired, forcing the gunman back around the corner. He squeezed off rounds until the gun went dry, making sure the senator had gotten to the stairs before turning to follow. A few quick seconds and Devin was on the stairs, the sounds of heavy footfalls chasing behind him, gaining fast.

Devin reached the top of the stairs.

He saw the monorail station. Doors open. A waiting car.

Chimes warning that the doors were closing.

The senator braced against the wall to the left of him.

A fifty-yard dash to the car. Only seconds.

Footfalls approaching fast.

Devin grabbed the senator by the sleeve and charged at the monorail.

Dalton Waters ran, moving as fast as his heavy bag and cumbersome rifle would let him. The black balaclava on his face was starting to snag and make him sweat. He was burning up in his suit, and the Kevlar vest was only making things worse. The Nevada sun was blasting down from above, turning the entire city into an oven. Sweat covered every part of his body.

The police didn't seem to be following him. They were probably still so wrapped up in forming perimeters around the attack location and the van's crash site that they didn't have any more units to dispatch.

The hotel was only a little farther ahead. Across the street and—

"Lead?" His radio crackled, almost inaudible against the sounds of rushing air and rustling fabric. "Are you there?"

He stopped and keyed the radio. "Yeah?"

"The senator made it to the monorail, headed north. Can you make it to the next station in time?"

Dalton looked up, seeing the monorail start moving his direction. "On my way."

He ran toward the rear entrance, fishing a handgun out of the black bag before ditching it, tossing the M14 rifle at the same time. He pulled the balaclava off his head, tossing it aside—cool air rushed against his sweaty face. It would be easier to get around in the hotel without all the gear.

A few seconds later he was at the rear entrance, and then he was inside.

The monorail car traveled over the Las Vegas scenery, moving to the next hotel on the Strip.

Devin jammed the last magazine into the FN Five-seveN and sat on the floor of the empty monorail car. He was breathing so hard he thought his lungs might burst. His face burned, and his hands were shaking from the exertion and stress. The car was moving slower than Devin would have expected; maybe there was some sort of technical problem slowing the monorail down.

"Who..." The senator wheezed, sitting next to Devin, trying to catch his breath. "Who are you?"

Devin offered a hand, and the senator shook it.

"I'm just a concerned citizen."

The senator tipped his head back, resting it against the wall of the monorail car. "What's your name?"

"Devin," he said with a moment of hesitation, always reluctant to spread his name around in the wake of destruction. "Devin Bathurst."

"I'm Senator Warren Foster. I—"

"I know," Devin said with a nod.

"How did you make it to me?"

He shrugged. "Wrong place at the wrong time."

"And you just happened to have a gun on you?"

Devin was quiet for a moment. "Long story."

The monorail began to slow, and they stood.

"Well," the senator said with a sigh, "thank you for...."

Devin didn't hear the last part. Looking through the glass,

he saw Trista Brightling standing at the station. He frowned. What was she doing here?

The doors eased open. Devin waited for the senator and escorted him off of the monorail car.

Trista approached fast. "Devin!"

Dalton had already made it around the corner into the monorail station when John caught up with him. He stopped, digesting the scene as a whole: Devin, stepping off the train, the senator with him. Standing between John and the tableau was Dalton, pistol in hand, lifting it.

Suddenly, from the corner of his eye, John saw something else—

"Trista!" he shouted, realizing that she was stepping in the way of Dalton's shot two feet in front of him—preparing to take the bullet. "Trista, no!" he shouted, nearly hoarse.

Trista saw him. Their eyes met. He could see it—she wasn't going to move.

John slammed into Dalton's back, knocking him forward, stumbling into Trista. Dalton recovered fast, grabbing the stumbling Trista by the hair, jerking her upward. She reached for something—a gun. A violent motion, and the handgun tumbled from her fingers, hitting the floor.

"Trista!" John screamed again, nearly in tears.

Dalton pulled Trista in front of him, using her as a shield, swinging his pistol directly at—

"John!" Trista screamed, the muzzle of the pistol pointed right at him.

BLAM!

Trista stumbled backward to the ground, her support falling free.

Dalton hit the floor—a shot to the forehead, Devin's Five-seveN smoking.

Trista pulled herself to her knees and saw John come running at her. He dropped down beside her and cradled her in his arms. She stared at him. His eyes, overcome with concern, looked her over, hands touching her face.

"Are you OK?" he asked.

Trista nodded, gripping his arms. "I'm fine."

The world around her was filled with chaos and destruction, but John Temple—reckless and free—was here. Now. Present.

People moved around them in a tumult of confusion, but John's hand cradled her cheek—and she was fine.

Chapter 21

Hannah stood in the sanctuary of the dusty, tinder-wood church. The older woman sat on the steps leading up to the pulpit. The woman was short, maybe five-two, midsixties, short gray hair, a yellow T-shirt, and blue jeans. The others, including Dominik, stood around them, speaking emphatically with the woman in what must have been Ukrainian. The woman's name was Misha; Hannah had been able to work that out from the conversation.

Misha looked at Hannah. "Who are you?" she asked, seeming more offended than anything, accent thick.

Hannah didn't say anything.

"You come here," Misha continued, annoyed, "you wave gun around and trespass. Who are you?"

"What you're doing is wrong," Hannah said.

Misha frowned. "What?"

"What you're doing is evil, and I can't let you do this."

Misha looked at the others, confused and offended, then back to Hannah. "I am businesswoman. I do what makes money, and this makes money."

"It's still wrong."

"Says rich girl," Misha sneered. "You have everything. You have money. You have never had to live poor."

Hannah shook her head. "There are other ways to make money."

"Says you, rich girl."

"I'm not rich," Hannah said, trying not to argue with dangerous captors.

"You don't starve to death. You aren't left to die when the capitalists take over your country," Misha said. "We have to find a way to live. To survive. To make money and not starve to death in a world where we do not have as much of a portion as others."

"So you kidnap girls?" Hannah said, angry.

"Not always," Misha disagreed, as if Hannah had no clue what she was talking about. "We offer girls from Ukraine jobs in the United States. A chance to come to a new place—to be in the West. They want it; we give it to them. And," Misha said, spreading her palms, "we make money. Enough money that we can stop being poor and be rich like Americans."

"Do you tell these girls what they are going to be doing?" Hannah asked skeptically.

"No!" Misha laughed as it were a ridiculous thing to ask. "We offer them jobs. Good jobs. Waitress, secretary, nanny—these kind of things. We tell them that they can come to America to do these things and send money back home to their families."

"And they accept?"

Misha nodded vigorously. "Many."

"But they aren't working as waitresses and nannies," Hannah said with a frown.

"No," Misha laughed again, "there is no money for us in that. We sell them to pimps and strip clubs. Things that people like to pay for. Things that make money."

Hannah felt her stomach twist into knots, nausea nearly overpowering her. "And they don't run away?"

"How?" Misha shrugged. "They come here and we take away their passport. They have nowhere to run or go. They are illegal aliens and prostitutes. They know better than to try to run."

"Don't *any* of them try to run away?" Hannah asked, anger, pain, and disgust filling her body as she thought it all through.

"That is stupid question. Where would they go?" Misha asked. "They do not know their way around. We get most girls through family; they know it is not smart to go back. They know we will hurt their families if they run away."

The whole thing washed over Hannah in a hideous deluge of futility. "They must fight back, though."

"No," Misha said, again seeming confused. "Our girls are very beautiful but very weak."

"And the ones that aren't?"

Misha considered for a moment. "We make sure we take certain kind of girl—but the ones who try to be strong must be taught."

Hannah shuddered, not certain if she wanted to ask or know. "How? How are they *taught*?"

Misha waved a hand. "Like a horse. You must break them. If you are going to keep a girl, you must break also."

"How?" Hannah asked, fury rising in her.

Misha smirked as if Hannah were the most naive creature she had ever seen. "They have to be raped. Often. If they are trouble, they have to be hit and scared. They have to know who is boss and what they are good for."

Hannah shook her head. "You've got to be kidding me."

"Why?" Misha shrugged. "These girls serve twenty, thirty men a night—they need to be ready for it."

"You're sick," Hannah growled, feeling depraved just thinking about it all.

"But we're here," Misha said without remorse. "We make money, and we keep doing what we do as long as people pay. Maybe it is human pain." Misha shrugged. "But the pay is good, so we won't stop."

Police swarmed the scene, cordoning off everything they could. The monorail station had been completely shut off from the public. John, Devin, and Trista had been asked by the police to stay until they could give a statement.

John watched, waiting for the inevitable moment when the police would want to speak to them, wondering what he would say to them about who he was and why he was there. Across the station the senator sat on a bench, talking to his people.

Trista came up on John's right side, standing next to him.

She didn't say anything; she simply took his hand and held it. He smiled to himself.

Devin stepped up on the other side, not noticing the two of them holding hands. "Have you ever had to talk to the police about this kind of thing before?"

John shook his head. "Not in a long time."

Across the station one of the senator's people—tall, bald, and thin, wearing a pinstripe suit—was talking emphatically, motioning for what appeared to be the most senior police officer to come to him. The bald man flashed credentials of some kind, pointing at John and the others, continuing his conversation with the policeman. They reached some sort of agreement, nodding to one another. The bald man began walking their way.

"Who do you suppose that is?" Devin asked.

"I have no clue," John replied, shaking his head.

"Me either," Trista added.

The man stopped a few feet from them and smiled. "Hello," he said courteously, "my name is Mr. Crest. I would like to speak to you in private."

John looked at Devin, wondering if going with this man was the right thing to do. Devin nodded.

"Lead the way."

They followed Mr. Crest through the hotel to an empty back room where he motioned them to sit across from him at a long table.

The room was small, with bare white walls and no windows. Fluorescent lights filled the room with their usual washed-out glow. Mr. Crest sat, adjusted his thick glasses, and smiled at them. "Can I get you anything?"

They each declined in their own awkward way.

"Are we in some kind of trouble?" John asked, saying what he assumed the other two were thinking.

"No," Mr. Crest said, continuing his political smile, "not at all." He opened his wallet, removing an ID card. "As I said, my name is Mr. Crest, and I work with the OGA."

John looked at Devin. "OGA?"

"Other Government Agency," Devin said with a nod, accepting the ID card for preview before sliding it down past John to Trista.

"What does that mean?" John asked, heart beating faster than he expected.

Devin looked directly at Mr. Crest. "You're CIA."

Crest shrugged. "Why would you say that?"

"Because," Devin began, clasping his fingers on the tabletop, "I was in military intelligence. OGA is almost always a codename for the CIA."

"Or the NSA," Crest added, "or a dozen other agencies that want to remain anonymous but still need to be called something."

"But probably CIA," Devin asserted.

Crest smiled. "Don't be so quick to make that statement, Mr. Bathurst. OGA can be a designation for any governmental organization, including the FDA or the Department of Transportation."

"I doubt you're Department of Transportation," Devin said humorlessly.

"And you're right," Crest conceded. "But I'm not CIA, either."

"I guess that leaves FDA," John interjected with a chuckle. Nobody else laughed. "Sorry, stupid joke."

"No." Crest reached for his briefcase, standing as he opened it. "I'm not with the Food and Drug Administration either." He opened a file, glanced at the contents, then closed it and set the briefcase aside. "I am with an undisclosed agency that is very interested in what you have to offer."

"Have to offer?" Trista asked.

Crest clasped his hands on top of the closed folder and

looked them over. "Yes," he said with a nod. "Because of your affiliation."

"Affiliation with whom?" she asked.

"The affiliation you all have," Crest said in all seriousness. "Because you are members of the Firstborn."

"Uh..." John tried to think of something to say without lying outright.

"We don't know what you're talking about," Devin stated without hesitation.

"Yes," Crest said without blinking, "you do know what I'm talking about, Mr. Bathurst. And the OGA is very interested in having you come to work for your country."

Devin was silent for a moment before speaking. "What do you think you know?"

Crest cleared his throat. "The United States government worked with the Firstborn in an official capacity for the first time during the Second World War. The organization that I work for—the OGA—has been keeping files on the Firstborn for more than sixty years."

"Sixty years?" Devin mused, looking at the other two, who said nothing. "So what makes you think that any of us belong to this 'Firstborn'?"

"One of our people," Crest said slowly and carefully, "saw a possible future in which an attempt would be made on Senator Foster's life."

"Saw a possible future?" Devin asked.

"Yes," Crest said candidly. "A member of the Domani, as they are called. Those who see the future. This person saw something else too."

Devin attempted to remain calm. "And what would that be?"

"The involvement of members of the Firstborn." Crest smiled. "People with courage and resolve. The kinds of people we look for at the OGA."

Devin gave accepting nods. "And who was this Domani you got your information from?"

"Professor Saul Mancuso." Crest asked, "Ring any bells?"

A shocked laugh was all Devin could manage for a moment. "Saul? Dr. Saul Mancuso is working for *you*?"

"Yes." Crest nodded, appearing confused. "There was an incident about a year ago that caught the attention of the Bureau of Alcohol, Tobacco, Firearms and Explosives. He had an extremely illegal cache of weapons on his property. He cut a deal with us to get out of serious prison time." Crest flipped through his file for a moment, puzzled. "Why? Do you know him?"

"Know him?" John Temple laughed. "We were at his compound when everything went down."

Devin shot an angry look at John before turning back to Crest. "So Dr. Mancuso saw the assassination attempt coming?"

"Yes," Crest acknowledged with a nod.

"You knew that someone was going to try to kill the senator," John said, "and you let him come here anyway?"

"Insisted," Crest corrected. "We used the senator as a lightning rod to draw out potential assets."

"Us," Devin said with a nod. "This was all a recruiting op," he mused.

"Yes," Crest agreed. "For us the only purpose of any of this was to flush you out, give you a chance to prove yourselves, and then make the offer."

"And if we refuse?" John asked.

"There's the door," Crest said, looking to the exit. "You're free to go. No one will stop you. But"—he looked directly at Devin and opened his file folder—"if you're ready to hear my offer, then I invite you to stay."

John stood. "I'm out," he said definitively.

"Are you sure?" Crest asked.

"You used a human life as bait," John said with a grunt,

Trista standing up next to him. "I don't want to have anything to do with you." John turned toward the door. Looking back he asked, "Are you coming, Devin?"

Devin remained seated, maintaining eye contact with Crest. "I think I'm going to hear the man out."

The door opened, and Hannah was shoved into the dim basement. The door slammed shut behind her and latched, locking.

The basement smelled like mold and mildew and body odor. The place was a filthy mess. It was strangely cool—a perverse relief from the upstairs, where the Arizona heat baked the interior of the church like a furnace.

The faces at the other end of the room watched her, trying to determine who she was and if she could be trusted. Hannah approached slowly. "Hello," she said softly, trying not to make any sudden moves, lowering to her knees and sitting on the edge of one of the yellowed mattresses that had been thrown across the floor in a hodgepodge. "My name is Hannah Rice," she said, as if she was talking to a frightened animal that might run at a moment's notice. Hannah scanned the frightened faces. She guessed that fewer than half of them were over the age of sixteen, and at least two of them were young boys—maybe twelve each.

She could feel their shared past. Their collective feeling of dirtiness and shame. Feelings of hopelessness and pain. "I'm sorry," she said, feeling a heavy tear plummet across her face. "I'm sorry for everything you've had to go through."

"Are you a new trainer?" a Hispanic girl in her twenties asked.

"Trainer?" Hannah asked.

"The pretty women," an African American girl in her teens said. "They come and teach us what to say and do. They recruit new girls. Are you one of them?"

"No," Hannah said, shaking, feeling another tear form. "I came here to help three girls."

"Who?" one of them asked.

Hannah smiled, recognizing the face. "You, Kimberly," she said with a choked smile, hot streams of tears tumbling from each eye.

"Me?" the girl said. Blonde hair and green eyes, a dirty face and dirty clothes. The hint of bruises on her face. Sixteen years old—a woman and a child all at the same time.

"Yes," Hannah said, feeling her smile strain under the flood of tears, recognizing the faces of the other two girls. "And you, Tori, and you, Nikki." She looked them all over. "I'm here to help you all." Hannah considered her own captivity. "If I can."

They all stared at her. Lost and scared.

She didn't know what to say to them, and they certainly weren't used to her yet. Hannah stood and walked to the other side of the room, sitting with her back against the wall. How had she gotten herself into this? How was she going to get them all back out?

She closed her eyes and breathed slowly, trying to clear her mind.

"Hannah?" a young voice asked. She opened her eyes and looked up. The girl named Kimberly was standing over her. "Can I talk to you?"

"Yeah," Hannah said, making room for Kimberly to sit next to her. The girl ignored the invitation and sat down in front of Hannah, two feet of space between them. Hannah tried to ignore the distance and smiled as best she could. "What do you want to talk about, Kimberly?"

The girl was reluctant for a moment, then spoke. "How did you know to look for us here? They said that no one would come looking for us."

"They were wrong," Hannah said firmly.

Kimberly looked at the basement door. "I hate this place," she said.

"I know," Hannah nodded. "This must be horrible for you."

"It's worse for a lot of the other girls," Kimberly shrugged. "Olga was in an orphanage. They couldn't keep her after she turned eighteen, so they set her up with a work program."

"But it turned out to be this?"

Kimberly nodded. "One of the others has a husband and a son back in Russia. They gave her pictures of both of them and said they'd kill them if she caused any trouble."

Hannah tried to think of something to say that would cheer Kimberly up, something that might remind her of something other than this hideous dungeon of a place. "I spoke to your mother," she said with a smile, "and I knew I had to find you."

Kimberly shook her head. "She must be so mad at me for sneaking out. I just wanted to get out and meet people." She wiped a very wet tear from her face. "I can't believe how stupid I was. My parents must be so angry."

"No," Hannah said, reaching for Kimberly. "Your mother is just very—"

The girl recoiled before Hannah could touch her.

Hannah paused, taking a moment to look into the girl's intense eyes. "Kimberly," she asked, "did they hurt you?"

"You want to know if they raped me?" Kimberly asked flatly, accepting the factuality of her situation.

Hannah lost her air as she watched the girl speak so casually about something so terrible. "Yes," Hannah said with a nod.

"No," Kimberly said, "they left Tori and Nikki and me alone. They said that we were going to be sent to another country—and that they would do it there." Kimberly looked at a door at the other end of the basement. "But they take the other girls into that room. The new girls scream and cry, but the ones who have been here longer know there's no point." Kimberly was quiet for another moment. "It scares me to think about what it's going to be like when it happens to me."

"No," Hannah said, looking Kimberly in the eye, "it's not

going to happen to you. I'm not going to let it happen to you. I won't let anything bad happen to you."

Devin watched as Crest took a piece of paper from the file in front of him. "I had a chance to pull this up before I brought you in here." Crest looked over the sheet. "Have you by any chance been in the area of Ohio in the past few days?"

"It's possible," Devin replied, dodging the question.

"Well, it appears that a partial fingerprint was lifted from a Ka-Bar combat knife embedded in a man's chest."

"And?" Devin remained cool.

"That partial matches your fingerprint, which is on record from your days with the armed forces. The place where the body was found was covered in your fingerprints, despite the fact it appears someone tried to wipe them away."

"I see," Devin said acceptingly, trying not to say or do anything rash.

"And then there was a double homicide in the suburbs of Las Vegas last night. A known criminal by the name of Anthony Scarza and his associate George 'Scud' Pryor."

Devin continued his nonchalance. "So?"

"Again," Crest continued, "your fingerprints were found."

"You said Scarza was a criminal," Devin replied. "I'm certain there were other prints in the house. Prints of people with criminal records."

Crest shrugged. "I can't speak to that. But your fingerprints were there, as well as on a murder weapon in Ohio. That makes you a suspect in an investigation that could seriously damage your career."

"Perhaps."

"Speaking of your career," Crest continued, eyeing another document. "It appears that your employer, Domani Financial—who curiously shares the same name as the forward-seeing order of the Firstborn to which you also belong—is being investigated by the Securities and Exchange Commission and the Internal Revenue Service." Crest leaned back, pushing the file away from him. "So it looks like you're going to need a new job, Mr. Bathurst," he said coyly. "One that can make you friends. The kind that can make charges like murder and obstruction of justice"—he gave a dismissive gesture—"go away."

John stood in the hall with Trista, watching her face in profile. They had stepped out of the meeting with Crest but had been told to stay in the hall and not go too far. Two security guards stood across the hall from them, giving them their space.

It had been a strange and emotional day so far. The kind that brought a person's perspective and priorities into an unusually sharp focus. The kind of thing that made a person think about who they wanted to spend the rest of their life with…

"Trista?" John said. She looked at him with dazzling eyes.

"Yes?" she asked.

"I wanted to talk to you about something."

Her cell phone rang. "Just a second," she raised a finger, checking the caller ID. She frowned. "It's Clay Goldstein." She turned to John. "I should take this."

He nodded. "Yeah," he said with an accepting smile, "you probably should."

"I'll just be a second," she said, opening the phone. Trista said hello and turned away, delving into conversation with Clay Goldstein.

John stood alone for a moment, looking the other direction, and saw someone else.

"Angelo?" he said, confused.

He stood alone and still in the hall, ten feet from John. "Mr. Temple," Angelo replied with a nod.

John approached Angelo, watching the security guard follow

at a distance. "What are you doing here?" he asked.

"She's a remarkable woman," Angelo said, glancing past John toward Trista.

John turned, watching her talk on the phone, and smiled. "Yeah. She really is." John looked back. "I love her."

"Sadly," Angelo said, "she thinks she loves you too."

"What?" John stammered. "Really? Why is that sad?"

"Because it's her willingness to cross lines," Angelo said, "her willingness to accept others who are not like her, including people like you. That's what makes her dangerous. That's why the Thresher wants her dead."

"What are you saying?" John asked.

"I'm saying that you're endangering her by letting her cross that line."

John was incredulous. "What?"

Angelo nodded, continuing. "She turned down the man in Belize because she's still in love with you. She came back to see if she still felt the same way."

John stood there for a moment, letting it all sink in—the thought that she reciprocated feelings for him. "I'm willing to cross those lines too. Why doesn't the Thresher want me?"

"Because you're weak."

"Weak?" John asked.

"Yes," Angelo said with a nod. "You don't even have the strength to walk away from her to protect her."

"I'm going to get her hurt," John said, remembering the way she had nearly died in the monorail station. "Aren't I?"

"Yes," Angelo agreed, "and if you love her you'll do everything in your power to put distance between yourself and her—because if you don't, you'll get her killed."

John could feel his heart sink. Angelo believed what he was saying, and John couldn't help but see it too. The crazy wanderer was right.

"But," Angelo continued, "none of that is going to matter once the reckoning comes."

"The what?"

"The end of the Firstborn," Angelo said without hesitation.

"The end? Do you mean destruction?"

"Yes," Angelo said, "and the deaths and suffering of countless others."

"How do we stop it?" John asked, grabbing Angelo's arm.

Angelo looked at the hand on his arm, scowling dangerously. "Would you listen to me if I gave you an answer?"

"Of course," John insisted.

"Even though you refused to listen to me before?"

"How do I stop it?" John asked again, more intensely than his good sense told him to approach such an unstable person.

"It's too late," Angelo said, regretfully.

"Why?" John asked, grasping for some explanation that might make enough sense to refute. "Why is it too late?"

"Because of what is happening *right now*," Angelo said morosely.

"What's happening?" John demanded.

"Hannah Rice," Angelo said.

John could suddenly feel it.

The dark basement. Near the Mexican border in Arizona. The feeling of futility and loss. The girls—so many girls. All of them trapped in a hellish existence.

Hannah was in trouble. Desperate trouble.

John turned from Angelo, rushing toward the room Crest had taken them into, shoving the door open. Devin and Crest were still sitting where they had been when the door flew open. They turned their attention to John.

"Devin," John said, looking at his friend, "it's Hannah. She's in trouble. We have to help her, but she's near the Mexican border." John looked at his watch. "Which means that we have to leave *right now*."

Devin stood, turning toward the door. "You'll have to excuse me, Mr. Crest," Devin said courteously, walking toward John, "but this is something I have to deal with."

"What if I could help?" Crest offered, standing.

Devin stopped less than a foot from John. "Help how?" Devin asked without looking back.

Crest took a piece of paper out of a folder. "In my hands I hold an offer from the OGA. Sign it as a show of good faith, and I'll make sure you have transportation and backup that will get you to your friend in time. I'll hold on to the contract. If you feel good about things after working with my people on this, I'll file the paperwork. If not, then I'll tear up the contract."

Devin remained still, thinking for a moment, before looking at John.

John felt something terrible in his stomach—something about Crest, but there was no way to say it or articulate it for Devin.

"I made Hannah a promise," Devin said, looking John in the eye, as if he could tell what John was thinking. Then Devin turned and moved toward the table, took a pen from his pocket, and signed the document.

"OK." Crest nodded. "Follow me." Crest moved past Devin and John, leading them down the hallway. "The Las Vegas airport is a five-minute drive from here," Crest explained, moving briskly. "The plane will take you to Yuma, Arizona. They have an airport there. The flight will take only about forty-five minutes. I'll set up transportation with my Department of Defense contact out of Yuma army base."

They were halfway down the hall when John heard someone call his name. He turned back and saw Trista standing there, approaching fast. "John, wait!"

"Trista," he said with a bittersweet smile, remembering what

Angelo had said to him just minutes before.

"I just got off the phone with Clay Goldstein," she said with the hint of a smile. "He's officially the new Overseer, and he's restructuring the business aspect."

"OK," John said with a nod. "He'll certainly do a better job of that than I did."

"He's offered me a job," she said, waiting for John's reaction.

"Good," he said with a nod. "You should take it."

She looked down for a moment then back to John. "What do you plan on doing?"

"Right now?" he said. "We're going to help Hannah—but then I'm setting out to figure out how to stop this reckoning that Angelo is talking about."

She nodded, listening intently. "Do you need help with—"

"No," John said, cutting her off, stepping close. "You have to get as far away from me as you can," he ordered. "Every moment you're near me you're in danger."

She blinked. Confused. Shocked. Angry. All of it coming at her faster than she seemed to be able to process it.

"Mr. Temple," Crest said from the end of the hall, waiting with Devin, "are you coming?"

John nodded, then looked back at Trista. "You have to promise me you'll be safe—and that you'll stay as far away from me as you can!"

He turned to walk away, and she grabbed his hand. "John!"

He turned back. "Yes?"

Trista threw her arms around him. "I love you, John."

"I love you too, Trista," he whispered. "And that's why I have to go."

Then he pulled away from her, looked at her for what might be the last time, and followed after Devin and Crest.

Less than fifteen minutes later they were in the air.

Chapter 22

Misha sat in the sanctuary pew of the decrepit church. Her nephew, Dominik, sat next to her. She looked at the disgusting dragon he had tattooed on his arm. It didn't mean anything, as far as she knew. It wasn't the kind of blurry powder blue that his other tattoos were. But those were things he'd gotten in prison in Russia. Melted shoe rubber and urine were used to make those, like the one he had on his chest that represented the crime family he'd worked with, or the one on his back—a church with five steeples, one for each year he'd spent in prison. No, the dragon was an American tattoo, with vibrant color and sharp detail. It didn't have any of the meaning that Russian prison tattoos were supposed to have—it was simply a depiction of his carnivorous soul.

"She was in New Jersey," Dominik said, shaking his head. "And then I saw her again at one of the storehouses we have in Ohio. It's like she's following me."

"Is she police?" Misha asked.

"Don't think so," Dominik postulated. "Seems too young."

Misha nodded, thinking it over. "What should we do with her?"

He shrugged. "We could kill her."

"Ourselves?"

"If we have to," Dominik said. "Or we just keep her here and sell her with the rest of the girls. Make some money."

"Will she be a problem?" Misha asked. "She doesn't seem scared. It might make her hard to control."

Dominik was quiet for a moment, obviously thinking. "I think I can break her will."

"And if you can't?"

He shrugged. "Then we kill her. But there's no point in doing that if we can make some money off of her. The worst that happens is I waste some time with her."

Misha thought for a moment. Dominik did have a point. "She is pretty," Misha agreed. "Not as beautiful as Ukraine girls, but still very pretty." She looked at her watch. "We need to take the girls across the border to hand them over to the buyers. Could you stay here and watch things while we're gone?"

"Sure," Dominik said. "That could give me some time with the trespasser. I'll have her broken in no time."

Hannah sat silently on the floor, Kimberly two feet to the side. They hadn't spoken for what seemed like an hour, sitting silently in the dungeonlike basement.

The floorboards overhead creaked. Someone was walking toward the back of the church. A door opened. Footsteps on the stairs. They were coming down into the basement.

Hannah turned to Kimberly, eyes wide. Trying to think of something to say or do. She stood, pulling Kimberly to her feet, standing in front of her.

The door opened. Misha and Dominik looked over the room to see if anything was out of the ordinary.

Misha spoke. "Kimberly, Tori, Nikki"—she motioned for them to come—"it's time to leave."

Hannah looked over at where the others were huddled, wondering if the girls would obey. A moment, then the girl named Tori stood, followed by Nikki.

"Wait," Hannah said to the girls, motioning for them to sit again. "Don't get up. Don't do what they say."

Misha looked past Hannah. "Now!" she demanded. "Or Dominik will beat you. Understand?"

Tori turned her attention to Hannah, watched her face for a moment, then walked the rest of the way across the basement to where Misha stood. Nikki followed.

"Put out your arm," Misha instructed, and Tori obeyed, receiving a quick injection in the arm. "Now you, Nikki." She also obeyed. "Good," Misha said with a maternal tone, running her hand across the top of Nikki's head. "This will make you sleep during the drive. OK? Now go upstairs and Zoia will take you to the truck before you fall asleep."

The girls obeyed, going quietly up the stairs.

Misha looked at Hannah. "Now you, Kimberly."

Hannah adjusted her stance, placing herself more directly between Misha and Kimberly. "No," she declared, "you can't have her."

Misha looked back at Dominik, motioning him toward Hannah.

He stepped forward and grabbed Hannah, pulling her away.

Hannah fought. Tried to struggle, but her hand slipped and she felt Kimberly pulled from her as she screamed, watching the girl receive her injection. Dominik grabbed her tightly from behind.

"Her too!" Dominik ordered.

Misha looked down at the syringe. "I don't know if there is enough to completely—"

"Do it!" Dominik growled, trying not to lose control of the squirming Hannah.

Misha approached, grabbing a section of exposed arm. There was a pinch. Then a burning under her skin.

Dominik threw Hannah down, and she hit one of the mattresses.

"I'll wait until the stuff starts to kick in," Dominik said to Misha, motioning her toward the stairs. "You take them to the van and get going. Tell me how it goes when you get back."

Misha nodded, leading Kimberly toward the stairs. Dominik followed.

Then the basement door shut.

Hannah stood, rushing toward the door, grabbing at the knob. The locked door wouldn't open. The knob wouldn't turn. She was trapped.

The world shifted a fraction of a degree. The drugs were already kicking in. She remembered what Misha said about there not being enough. Maybe it wouldn't affect her at all. Maybe she would be just fine and nothing would—

Her knees buckled, feeling disconnected from her body. Everything seemed to slip three feet away. Hannah dropped to her knees on the mattress, looking at the others. "We're going to have to get out of here," she said, gray filling her peripheral vision.

"We can't," a woman with a Russian accent said. "If we ever tried to run away, they would beat us and—"

"Listen to me!" Hannah stammered, feeling herself weaken. "You can't be afraid. You have to keep fighting..."

Her arms felt like they were made of rubber, giving way under the weight of whatever drug it was that they had pumped into her.

The basement door opened somewhere behind her. A footstep, heavy and resolute. Steps coming toward her, one after another—slow and deliberate, each step echoing like thunder.

A meaty hand touched her shoulder, rolling her over onto her back.

Dominik stared down at her.

His scowling face. Dark eyes.

He pulled her to her feet, dragging her toward the door at the other end of the room. The room that Kimberly had pointed to. The room of screaming and suffering. Dominik let go of Hannah and she dropped to her knees. He opened the door, stepping into the darkness. He hit a switch. Fluorescent lights flickered on, clicking as they warmed up. He walked to the center of the room and the filthy bed there.

Hannah didn't wait. She pushed herself up, stumbling toward

the stairs. One step in front of another, a foot catching every few steps. The light at the top of the stairs. A burst of speed, ramming across the threshold with a total lack of grace, turning the corner toward the church door, opening it. Sunlight flared in her eyes, and the world went awash in white. A moment to adjust, then she saw it—the truck, like the one in Illinois, three quarters of a mile away.

They were getting away, and she had to—

Someone grabbed her from behind, throwing her back into the church sanctuary. She hit the floor and looked up at Dominik, who lumbered toward her.

"What do you think you're doing?" he asked angrily.

Hannah scooted away from him, pushing far and as fast away as she could. Without effort he caught up with her in seconds, picking her up and throwing her onto a pew.

"Now," he said, getting close, putting his weight into her, breath foul, "I'm going to break you."

Dominik grabbed her wrists and pinned them back, moving in close. Inches away, he licked her face—

Somewhere through the drugs she could feel herself react.

Hannah moved fast, biting his neck. Her teeth clamped down on the soft flesh, and Dominik howled. He tried to pull away, and she bit harder, feeling the skin break.

Neck bleeding, Dominik gave her a rough shove back and pulled away. He moved to strike, and she pulled up her arms, taking the blow. He shouted in furious anger and tried again.

Hannah shoved back, ramming her knee between his legs. He froze for a second to steady himself.

It was her chance.

Hannah pulled her legs free and delivered her most vicious kick, smashing her heel into Dominik's face.

He flew backward, face and neck bleeding, and toppled from the pew into the aisle.

Hannah leapt up, pumping to the next pew back, running toward the aisle—rushing for the door.

Dominik recovered too fast, chasing after her. Footfalls reverberated through the floor. He grabbed her by the hair and shoulder and swung her into the back of a decrepit pew. The seat plunged forward, knocking over the next two in the row. Dust flew into the aisle in a thin cloud.

She stood, steadying herself. The world was still undulating. A moment of shifting.

Dominik grabbed her. Hannah didn't wait—she threw an elbow into his face as hard as humanly possible. He swung blindly, and Hannah pulled away, moving toward the front of the sanctuary.

Hannah looked for a weapon, something she could use to hit him with.

Dominik opened his eyes. Looked at Hannah with fury, and charged. She tried to get out of the way in time, but he tackled her, their bodies slamming into the pulpit, knocking it down. The old wood broke. Hannah stood, trying to get away, but he grabbed her and threw her toward a railing that separated the choir from the congregation.

She hit the wood, and it collapsed, sending bits of railing smashing free.

Dominik stood for a moment, hand on his forehead, steadying himself as he groaned in pain.

Hannah looked at the smashed wood all around her and saw a wooden post from the railing. She grabbed the post like a club and stood, swinging.

The blow hit Dominik on the side of the head with a sound like a croquet ball being hit with a mallet. He took the second blow with his forearm, blocked the swing, and grabbed at Hannah, throwing her toward the wall.

Her shoulder hit a stained-glass window, half covered in

cardboard duct-taped in place. The remaining glass broke and tumbled to the floor.

Dominik came in fast, punching her in the stomach. Hannah gasped for air, and he threw her down. He shoved her to her back, her shoulder blades hitting the floor. Lifting his knee, pushing it into her chest, he pinned her down with all his weight.

Hannah tried to fight free, tried to break loose from someone so much bigger.

She could feel his past.

He reached for his belt.

All the girls.

She wished she had a gun. A way to defend herself.

The faces and the screaming.

The belt came loose, and he threw it aside.

All the money.

Something sharp prodded at the back of Hannah's knee—a chunk of the stained glass.

The feeling of power.

Dominik leaned in, nearly purring. Face close.

Hannah reached down, grabbing the piece of glass.

Dominik saw that she was doing something and reached for her arms. Hannah fought with all her strength, breaking free. He reached for her arm—

She acted without thinking. It was the self-defense training that had taught Hannah to strike for someplace soft. The shard of heavy glass slammed into Dominik's throat, and his eyes went wide.

He pulled away as fast as he could, scrabbling for the shard. His eyes bulged in shock, fixated on her. Blood bubbled around the protruding shard. He foamed red at the mouth as he coughed splatters of crimson that gurgled from his lips. Dominik's body convulsed and shook, slamming himself against the wall as he choked and gagged. Pained sounds came from his blood-filled mouth as he groped at the makeshift blade. He winced, pulling slowly at the jagged shard. The blue glass turned red in a matter of seconds. Dominik squealed like a pig as he tugged the glass free—slowly, slowly, slowly. The shard came loose with a ghastly slurping sound.

But it was too late for him. The dragon was slain.

A woman named Olga sat in the basement of the church, listening to the sounds of struggle and screaming upstairs.

Then it suddenly stopped.

She held her breath. Footsteps moved toward the basement door, the way they always did. Steps moving downward, announcing someone's arrival.

Dominik?

No, the steps were too soft. It was someone else.

The door opened, and the girl named Hannah stood there, covered in blood. Olga panicked—had the girl been stabbed or beaten until she bled? No. It was someone else's blood.

Hannah stood in the threshold for a moment, silent, as if she didn't know what to say or do. Olga, along with the others in the basement, stared back.

Hannah motioned for them to follow. "Come on," she said, beckoning them to come to the door.

Olga froze. She knew the punishment for trying to escape. She knew the cost of trying to get away, and this wasn't worth it.

"Come on," Hannah said again.

Olga remained still. There was no such thing as freedom. She wondered these days if there was even an outside world anymore.

The girl named Hannah approached. "Follow me," she said sweetly, looking right at Olga. "I'll show you the way."

Olga hesitated. Hannah's hand reached toward her. "You're free," she said with a smile. Olga waited, trying to see if it was some kind of a trick or a cruel joke, wondering if freedom was really such a good thing.

"You're free," Hannah said again.

For a split second Olga let herself believe it might actually be true. She took Hannah's hand, and the girl helped her to her feet.

"Come on," Hannah said, turning to the others, beckoning them to join her, moving toward the stairs.

Olga followed, walking up the stairs behind Hannah, waiting for the moment when she would wake up. When she would know it had all been a dream. When Dominik would arrive and stop them and beat them…and worse.

None of those moments came.

Olga arrived at the top of the steps and turned toward the sanctuary. The place was a disaster.

Somewhere behind her someone opened the church doors. Turning around she could see the others, moving out of the doors.

Olga took a step forward. Then another. Could it be true? Was it really happening?

As she stepped out into the sunlight, she saw the others standing around her, all looking up at the sky and out into the landscape.

No walls. No bars. No chains.

They were free.

Misha sat in the passenger's seat as they drove the truck along the hot Arizona highway. She hated the heat, and no matter how much she turned up the air conditioning, she couldn't seem to cool off. She had lived in Eastern Europe for four decades before the fall of communism and the rise of the criminals that now ruled her old world. It was cold in those parts of the world, and she doubted she would ever get used to the heat here. Misha fanned herself and looked out the windshield at a road sign.

They were less than ten minutes from the Mexican border. Then they'd sell these brats and she'd go home where it was cool.

Just a little longer, she told herself.

Where are you going?" one of the women asked as Hannah moved toward the car. They stood outside of the old wooden church, sun beating down.

"I have to get the others," she replied, opening the car door.

"Are you coming back?" another asked.

"Yes," she said in earnest, "but I have to go."

Finding the keys in the ignition, Hannah started her car and turned it toward the road. Slowly she drove past the freed captives before she hit the gas.

"This way!" Crest motioned, and Devin followed.

They exited the plane at the Yuma airport, getting out on the landing strip. A set of Black Hawk helicopters was fifty yards away, rotors chugging.

"These choppers are from the Yuma military base," Crest shouted over the sounds of jet engines and helicopter blades. "The pilots and choppers are property of the United States Army. They are not allowed to cross the U.S. and Mexico border, and the military personnel are not allowed to engage in hostilities on domestic soil without a presidential order—which I wasn't able to get at such short notice."

"Meaning?" John asked, coming alongside.

"Meaning that they can get you where you need to go, but once you're there it's up to you. They can't back you up. Which means you're on your own if things go bad."

"Understood," Devin said, keeping pace.

"I had them put Kevlar vests and firearms on the choppers

for you." Crest stopped and turned to John. "Do you know where they are?"

John nodded. "I think so."

Devin raised an eyebrow, not sure he liked the uncertainty.

"OK," Crest said with a nod, reaching out to shake their hands. "Good luck."

The car screamed down the desert highway.

Hannah rubbed her eyes. There hadn't been enough drugs in her system to knock her out, or even really disable her for long, but she could still feel the effects. Her judgment was impaired, and her depth perception wasn't good. She didn't care. If the police caught her, they could have her license for all she cared.

But she wasn't stopping now.

She was already too far behind. Too far away. She had to catch up.

She wasn't going to lose these girls. Not now. Not after traveling across the entire continent to find them. Not after all the pain and anguish that came from it all. Not after all those people had died.

Hannah saw a sign for the highway and the border crossing. That was the way they had gone. She could feel it. She knew it in the pit of her twisting stomach. This was the way to go.

She pulled the car onto the highway and shifted gears, pressing down on the gas. They were driving a truck. A slow one. And they were hauling illegal cargo. Unlike Hannah they cared if they were pulled over and caught.

She laid into the accelerator, watching the needle climb and the world outside blur. The engine howled violently. The world. The moment. The pursuit—fractured into a rapid fire of chaotic colors:

Golden sun—crisscrossing the ground.

Brown dust—hanging in the air.

Black asphalt—blurring beneath her.

Red needle—climbing up the speedometer.

Like flying. Weightless. Every distant object flashing into immediacy.

The vehicle moved faster and faster, breaking eighty miles per hour. Then ninety. The needle crossed the one hundred line.

There was no stopping now.

"Sorry about the delay," Crest said into his cell phone, standing on the desert landing strip—one of his superiors from the OGA on the other end. "Bathurst has been with me since he signed the papers."

"Good," his superior replied. "I'm glad you were able to convince him. He'll be a valuable asset to the Firstborn program."

"Agreed," Crest said with a smile.

"Do you think he suspects that we were the ones who provided the white supremacy group with the weapons and intelligence for the assassination?"

Crest looked around to see if anyone might be watching or listening. The landing strip in the Arizona sands was deserted. "Judging from his demeanor? I doubt it highly. But that's the problem with working with these so-called Firstborn. We've always got the tiger by the tail when we do something like this."

"We'll still need to take care of the senator if we want to protect our work."

"Agreed," Crest said with a nod. "We'll have to think of something. But we knew that was a possibility when Professor Mancuso told us about the likelihood of Firstborn involvement."

"Yes, he did. And I would say that gaining Bathurst as an asset is still far more valuable."

"True," Crest concurred. "Which brings me to the next item of business."

"Yes?"

"It turns out the stories were true. There is an organized Firstborn movement."

"That is interesting."

"It gets better," Crest continued. "Their central office in Manhattan is being audited and investigated by the IRS and SEC. It's exactly the kind of leverage we need." Crest smiled to himself. "It's Christmas for us."

High above the ground the drooping orange sun cast strange shadows across the desert wastes.

"Do you see anything?" Devin asked over his headset.

John looked down at the Arizona desert, watching it race by beneath them in its golden hour. The chopper blades pounded at the air. He shook his head. "No," he replied into the headset, hearing his own voice in his ear.

John focused, reaching out to the source of all his knowledge. "Come on, God," he whispered into the headset.

The copilot glanced over at John, confused.

John closed his eyes, feeling the chopper carrying them along through the sky, flying at incredible speed. Muttering a prayer, he let himself go into the sensation of vertigo.

His eyes opened, and he looked down. Miles away, on the highway, he saw a car tearing across the pavement at top speed. "That's her. That's Hannah."

Misha sighed. They were maybe four miles from the border.

"Huh," the driver said to himself, looking in the rearview mirror. "Somebody's in a hurry."

Misha frowned, leaning forward enough to see out the rearview mirror, and saw what he was talking about—a car, silver and midsized, was racing toward them, fast. Something clicked in her mind. She recognized the car.

"That's the car that the girl came in," she said.

"Is that Dominik? Maybe he needs something."

Misha squinted, trying to make out who the driver was.

It wasn't Dominik.

The car moved so fast she thought it might shake apart.

Hannah saw the truck come into view ahead of her, maintaining her breakneck speed, ripping past the barren countryside.

Something flashed in the rearview mirror. Police lights. She'd been spotted. But it didn't matter. Speeding tickets and prison didn't matter. There was only the threat of losing the girls.

The size of the truck grew exponentially in the front windshield as she began to catch up. There were only a few choices now. Her first instinct was to ram the truck and run them off the road—but who knew how the girls were situated. Maybe they were buckled in, but probably not. Running the truck off the road might hurt or even kill the girls. She wasn't taking that risk.

That didn't leave much in the way of options.

She was gaining fast, pulling up alongside the truck. Hannah looked up at the driver, and he made eye contact with her—he recognized her.

The truck swerved, smashing into her from the side.

"What do you think you're doing?" Misha shouted. "There's a policeman back there! They'll pull us over too!"

"They won't pull us over when she's the one driving so fast," the driver argued.

"They may stop us at the border if they see strange damage," Misha countered.

The driver groaned as he watched the pursuing car fall back a short way. "Then what do we do?"

"Just get to the border," Misha ordered. "We'll figure things out once we've crossed!"

John watched as the chopper swooped, getting closer to the ground faster than he'd expected.

"The silver car," Devin said to the pilot, directing the man where to go, "and the truck it's following. We need to get down there and stop them!"

"We may not be able to do that," the pilot said. "If we do anything to endanger citizens, law enforcement, or military property, we will be in violation of our orders."

"Just get close," Devin ordered.

John watched as Hannah's silver car accelerated, trying to pass the truck, only to get hit from the side again. He gasped, holding his breath. If whoever was driving that truck wasn't careful, they were going to crash, and the girls were inside there. He could feel it.

The ground below ripped past, highway lines sleeting by.

Hannah's car backed off for a second, the police car behind her coming up fast. John could feel people start to panic. It was only a matter of moments before one of them—any of them—did something stupid and got somebody killed.

"Pull over to the side of the road and…"

Hannah ignored the policeman's words as he blared them over his speakers. If he wanted to stop her, he would have to make sure they closed the border—but there was still the chance they would only stop her and the truck would get through. And she couldn't risk that.

Hannah accelerated again, pulling up close to the truck. It swerved again, blocking her from passing. Far in the distance two other police cars were joining the chase. Where had they come from? What were they doing patrolling a moonscape like this area? Her eyes dropped from the rearview mirror, and she saw the sign. The border was only a mile away. The police must have had something to do with border patrol. At this speed that was less than a minute to stop the truck.

Fewer than sixty seconds.

A helicopter buzzed overhead. She must have been causing more of a stir than she had realized.

"Pull over to the side of the road, and stop your engine!" the police car ordered again.

Less than half a mile.

Hannah jammed her foot into the accelerator and pulled to the right of the truck. The vehicle swerved again, and she dropped off the side of the road, hitting the rocky dirt. Dust exploded up around her in a cloud.

The truck hit the rumble strip and stopped its swerve—ill equipped to deal with the soft shoulder that would suck it off the road.

Hannah lay into the gas, fighting to keep the car up to speed despite the drag of the dirt, the vehicle threatening to slide out of control. A gut-wrenching moment, and she was past the truck, blasting by. She adjusted the car and pulled back onto the road.

The tires hit the pavement, and the car began to fishtail. Swinging dangerously into the oncoming traffic—a pickup truck's horn blasting.

It was like driving on ice. She'd done it before in the Colorado winters. The key was to not panic. To keep a still mind.

Everything seemed to slow as the vehicle straightened out, racing forward. Somewhere in another world she hit the brakes, and the car peeled out—the back end swung to the left. Tires screamed against highway. Thick clouds of white leapt upward as the rubber of the tires flash-boiled on the pavement, laying black streaks and throwing up the stench of scorched petroleum.

The car jerked perpendicular to the road, directly in front of the truck rushing toward her passenger side. They tried to slow, horn screaming, brakes locked, rubber shrieking.

The passenger's side exploded as the truck hit her.

"*No!*" John shouted across the headset, words clipping and crackling. The truck plowed into Hannah's car, twenty yards from the border crossing.

"Bring us down," Devin ordered, quieter than John, but equally intense, and the chopper began to lower.

The only sound was the hissing of the burst radiator. The only smell was the nauseating combination of burnt rubber and the sweetness of leaking antifreeze.

The only sensation was that of pain and disorientation.

Misha recovered slowly. Her eyes lifted painfully, looking up at the smashed windshield. The girl had succeeded in stopping them. But they were close to the border—close enough to get across on foot.

Flashing lights in the mirror caught Misha's attention. The police would search the truck. They would find the girls, and they would all go to prison. She was struck with a second wind. The instinct to survive. Misha reached for the glove box and opened it fast, digging out the pistol. She didn't know what it was called, but she knew how to use it, and she would if she had to.

She shoved the passenger door open and climbed down onto the pavement, moving toward the back of the truck. The police car had stopped close, but the officer was too busy talking on his radio—probably getting some kind of backup. The other two cars were coming in fast behind the first, slowing to a stop behind it.

Misha opened the back door to the truck; the others who were in the back with the girls looked up.

"What happened?" one of them asked.

Misha didn't answer, grabbing at the first girl she saw—Kimberly. The heavily sedated girl stumbled as Misha pulled her from the truck. "Up," she ordered, dragging the girl toward the front of the truck where the crash had been.

Misha knew that if she was going to have to cross the Mexican border, she was going to need to bring something with her that would make some money. One of the girls would be enough. That would bring her enough money to make it back to the United States and continue business.

A helicopter was touching down; nearby, men were getting out. Misha ignored it. She looked down from the helicopter and saw the crushed passenger side of the silver sedan, the girl named Hannah stumbling out.

"Stop!" Hannah shouted.

Misha didn't stop. Border patrol guards came rushing from their stations toward the wreck, ignoring Misha and the girl. Only a little further and she would cross out of United States jurisdiction.

"Stop!" Hannah shouted again, stepping in front of Misha.

"Out of my way," Misha ordered.

"Stop her!" Hannah shouted, pointing, trying to block the way. Misha panicked, seeing all the faces suddenly turning toward her—and she lifted the handgun and pointed it at Hannah.

"Put it down!" someone shouted from behind.

Misha turned fast and looked.

Two men—one black, one white—wearing bulletproof vests and holding guns.

She shot at them, and they opened fire.

The barrel of a handgun flashed at the level of her eyes just before her sight was smashed into darkness.

Epilogue

THE YUMA AIRPORT was all but empty.

Hannah stood in the concourse with Kimberly, waiting quietly. She had rescued Kimberly and the other girls the day before. And today, as the sun was setting, she was sending the last of the girls on her way.

"You still haven't told me how you found me," Kimberly said, looking up at Hannah.

"Well," Hannah said, "would you believe me if I told you that God called me to find you?"

Kimberly watched Hannah for several seconds. "I guess that's the only thing that makes sense." She was quiet for a moment. "Like the one sheep out of a hundred."

"That's right," Hannah agreed. "The shepherd left the ninety-nine to find the one." Hannah turned back toward the windows showing the runway, a jet slowing to a stop and taxiing toward them. "That must be it," Hannah said, looking down at Kimberly. "Are you ready?"

The girl looked hesitant. "I'm sort of scared. Does that make sense?"

Hannah watched the people exit the plane, walking toward the airport doors. She spotted the person she was looking for. "Yeah," she said with a nod. "I can see how you would be scared. But I don't think you have to be."

"Kimberly!" a woman shouted from the door.

The girl's mother and father rushed toward them. Kimberly left Hannah's side and ran to her parents.

Her parents held her as she cried.

Maybe not like the lost sheep, Hannah thought. Maybe more like the prodigal son, who squandered his inheritance on wild living, only to be welcomed back by his father with love and acceptance. Like the bride of Christ—freedom lost and bought again.

Maybe that was an overstatement, but Hannah didn't care. All she knew was that Kimberly was in her parents' arms. And she was free.

"Have you decided what you're going to do now?" John Temple asked, coming up alongside her.

"I don't know," Hannah said, brushing a tear away. "Maybe I'll go back to school. Make another attempt at having a normal life." She turned to John. "And you?"

"I'm going to find Angelo," he said, leading her toward the airport door. "He seems to know a lot about this 'reckoning' that's coming. He seemed to know how to stop it."

"Where is he?" She followed John into the setting sunlight.

"I don't know." John shook his head. "I think he's still in the Nevada desert somewhere." He smirked. "Now that I'm here, I think I'll take some time to reconnect with God and fight the devil in the wilderness, like ancient monks used to do."

Hannah nodded. "You'll have to let me know how that goes." She stopped for a moment. "What about Trista?"

John looked away. "Some things aren't meant to be."

"And you and Trista aren't meant to be?"

John shrugged. "I guess we'll find out in due time."

They walked across the parking lot to where Devin Bathurst stood.

"So, what's your decision?" John asked Devin. "Are you going to accept the offer from the OGA?"

Devin nodded. "I've signed the papers."

"What's this?" Hannah asked. "What's the OGA?"

Devin filled her in, and she nodded. "It's strange. Clay Goldstein talked about power—said how some people find it in religion, some in politics, some in business. Looks like that's what's happening here."

"What do you mean?" John asked.

"Well, it's just that the Firstborn are restructuring into a business." She turned to John. "You're embracing your religious duty in the wilderness." She turned to Devin. "And you're going to work for the government." She thought for a moment. "I guess everything is changing."

"I guess everything is," John agreed.

Devin was quiet for a moment, then spoke. "Well, then I guess there's just one thing left to do."

Angelo walked along the desert highway, watching the sun set, trying to thumb a ride.

He could feel them—John, Devin, and Hannah—together. Praying together. The three of them kneeling in the Arizona desert. But their reason wasn't money, power, or the demand for a religious experience.

Angelo felt something change—something about the coming reckoning.

There was something about these three—coming together in humility for no reason other than love and mutual respect.

He smiled.

He felt something he hadn't felt in a long time—about the past, the present, and the future. About life. About the world. There was a word for it. Something distant and special.

Then he remembered the word.

Hope.

The word was *hope*—and for the first time in as long as he could remember, he was filled with it.

Acknowledgments

General

Jamin Walters – *For doing so much to help promote these books*
Scotty Gallagher – *Thematic development*
Ryan Olsen – *Technical Advisor*
Mark Fauth – *Technical Advisor*
Scott Miller – *Fire-Sciences and EMT Advisor*
Lee Vary – *Breaking writer's block*
Russel Garret – *Various and profound contributions*
JL – *For introducing me to the pressing issue of human trafficking*

Proofreaders

Very special thanks to those who took the time to look over this book and give feedback:

Scott Coffey
Kirstin Roberts
Wil Davis
Shannon Davis
Cathleen Walters

Editorial

Lori Vanden Bosch – *Amazing Content Editor*
Dinah Wallace – *Phenomenal Line Editor*
Bob Liparulo – *Friend and support*
Jeff Gerke – *Friend and mentor*
Debbie Marrie – *The person who makes everything happen*
Chip MacGregor – *Marketing Advisor*
James L. Rubart – *Marketing Teacher*
Frank Redman – *Because we writers all desperately need honest feedback*
Eric Wilson – *A scholar and a gentleman. A writer's writer. Thank you.*

Sue Allen – *For giving the fine talent you brought to the Left Behind series to a small book like this.*

And the countless others who made this book possible.